PANGEA ONLINE 2

Magic and Mayhem

S.L. ROWLAND

ALSO BY S.L. ROWLAND

Tales of Aedrea

Cursed Cocktails

Sword & Thistle

Pangea Online

Pangea Online: Death and Axes

Pangea Online 2: Magic and Mayhem

Pangea Online 3: Vials and Tribulations

Sentenced to Troll

Sentenced to Troll

Sentenced to Troll 2

Sentenced to Troll 3

Sentenced to Troll 4

Sentenced to Troll 5

Path to Villainy: An NPC Kobold's Tale

Collected Editions

Pangea Online: The Complete Trilogy

Sentenced to Troll Compendium: Books 1-3

CHAPTER ONE

"Boom! Headshot!"

The rifle kicks back against my shoulder and the whir of plasma beams echoes down the cavernous metal tunnel, but for a moment, I savor the sweet victory of a no-scope sniper kill.

The lizard-man in full battle armor falls to the floor in front of me and a few seconds later, his body dissipates into the ether. I don't trash-talk, it's not my style, but it feels good to stand over his dead body and do a little dance for half a second. I can still hear him cursing in the time it takes for him to fully dematerialize and wait for his respawn.

He can savor my delicious dance moves while he plans his revenge.

His plasma rifle lies on the floor, free for the taking. I pick it up and check the stats.

*Item: **Plasma Rifle**. 70% charge. Hold charge for two seconds for a power blast.*

It has a better charge than the sniper rifle I'm

currently using, so I switch them out, leaving my weapon behind for anyone who comes upon it.

A timer counts down at the top of my vision. Three minutes, forty-seven seconds remaining. My team, Team Purple, is down by eight kills to Team Green.

Weapon fire brings me back to the situation at hand. The map in the bottom corner of my vision shows three green dots approaching from the next corner. I turn to run the other way, but two more approach from my rear.

I'm trapped. With enemies on both sides, there is no way I can shoot my way out of this. Five against one, it's just not possible.

They're close enough now that I can hear their chat. In a team deathmatch in Spaceworld, players can talk to each other when they are close enough, even if they aren't on the same team.

"Let's get this little twerp," a deep voice booms.

"Yeah, it's time to show him who's boss," says a more high-pitched female.

I've had a bit of a target on my back ever since winning the Pangea Online Developer's Tournament. Overnight fame does that, though. I entered the tournament to win the money for my best friend's sick mother. A lot of people were sympathetic to my cause. A lot of the hardcore gamers weren't.

Both groups come to a stop on each side of the tunnel. The barrel of a rifle pokes around the corner up ahead.

If I'm going to die, I might as well take a couple of these bastards with me and give those following my livestream a show.

I switch through my weapons and find my last two sticky grenades.

"Guys," I say, knowing they can hear me. "You don't have to do this. We can all still be friends."

I activate the grenades and attach them to my body.

"I bet you'd like that, wouldn't you? Get him, team!" the deep voice yells.

The first three turn the corner and I stand there, my hands in the air. They don't even hesitate to mow me down. Plasma beams fill the corridor, hitting me from both sides. All the while, cruel laughter dances in the air around me. My vision goes red and then instantly, I'm no longer in the tunnel, but watching the match from a bird's eye view as my opponents huddle around my lifeless corpse, bringing their crotches up and down across my body.

Joke's on you, fellas. An explosion sends all five bodies crashing against the walls.

A small badge flashes across my vision.

Multi-kill! X5

The camera changes again and I'm looking through the point of view of one of my teammates. We're only down by four kills now.

"Well done, Esil. I'll take five kills for one death any day. Now, come on, team. Let's turn this around," says Talia. Her voice is crisp, authoritative. I've played a few matches with her and she seems like a natural leader. She's charismatic, friendly, and always pushing her teammates to play better without tearing them down. That's part of the reason I agreed to join her team for a few games.

"Thanks. They've really got it out for me. Maybe we can exploit that and use it to our advantage."

"Good idea, but first, we need a sacrifice."

"Put me in, coach," says Buzz. Buzz is my best friend and part of the reason I'm even here at all. If he hadn't helped me out during the tournament, I never would have had a chance.

"You sure?" I ask.

"Yeah, why not. I love taunting these turdbags."

I check through my weapons while Talia gives Buzz the plan. I respawned with the same kit I selected at the beginning of the match. I could have changed it while I was waiting to respawn, but I like the set up. I have my plasma sniper rifle, a pistol, one concussion grenade, and two sticky grenades that stick to the first surface they come into contact with.

In a deathmatch, a character's stats and items don't matter, only the kit they select for each game. There is no magic and everyone is on the same playing field. Only skill matters.

I'm an okay shooter with an assault rifle. Not good and not bad, though sometimes my aim goes wide from the recoil. With a sniper rifle, though, I have laser focus.

"So, what's the plan?" I ask.

"We're all going to go and hide in the elevator shaft at the end of the hall," Talia starts. "We're sending Buzz out into the open. He's going to shoot off a few rounds and draw them in. Once they surround him, he's going to pretend he's talking to you and mention something about the elevator shaft. When they come to kill you, we'll all be there."

Before I can even say anything, Buzz is running down the hallway, shooting his rifle at the ceiling.

I follow Talia and the others, seven of us in total, towards the elevator shaft. We crouch as we walk, giving off no indication of our whereabouts on the map. Shooting a weapon reveals a player's location for five seconds. Running and jumping reveals it for one second.

Voices come across our chat as we walk.

"What the hell is this clown doing?" It's the same woman from before.

They must be on the level above ours.

"Easy picki—" But the chat cuts off as they chase after Buzz.

"Come and get me, you sweaty ball sacks!" Buzz yells into the chat. They might not hear him yet, but they will soon. He laughs maniacally, and I can hear the whir of his rifle through the chat.

Pretty soon, several dots show up on the map, circling Buzz in every direction. Then, I hear the click of his rifle. It has overheated.

"They're coming in on me," he says. "Get ready." There is a small pause before he speaks again. "Guys, please. Don't kill me and I'll tell you where he is." Another pause. "Okay, just don't kill me. Promise?" Silence. "He's hiding in the elevator shaft." Buzz's mic goes silent.

We all take our position against the back of the elevator. The dots of our enemies all head in our direction. Once they are in the tunnel, they disappear. It feels like minutes pass as we wait for them to approach, none of us speaking. Thirty seconds ticks down on the match clock. We're still down four kills. Our opponents could wait this out and win, but I'm counting on their desire to embarrass me on their streams to give us a shot at winning.

"We know you're in there, Esil." It's the same guy I no-scoped. "Why don't you just come out so we can get this over with?"

My eyes are fixated on the elevator door. Twenty seconds tick down until game over. I don't wait for them to open it. My fist smashes against the open button and a loud hiss fills the air as the shaft opens.

I pull the trigger before the door fully opens, firing my pistol without aiming at whatever stands on the other side. By the time the doors spread wide apart, several of our opponents are on the ground. Light and sound battle for supremacy for the next few moments. Everyone is yelling and cursing on both sides. I take fire to my shoulder and my vision goes bright red as my health bar falls rapidly. Dropping to the floor, I quickly switch items and toss my grenades in rapid succession. My health bar hovers at five percent and the doors close in front of me.

To my right, Talia leans against the wall, her hand on the close button. A loud explosion rocks from the outside of the elevator as the timer hits zero.

Double Kill!

Team Purple: 45
Team Green: 44
You win!

My teammates cheer as we are transported to a lobby. In the lobby, our kits disappear and we all wear our normal clothes. Several of our teammates form a dance party in a circle, each taking their turn in the spotlight.

Buzz wears his black tunic, dented battle helm, and heavy metal shield emblazoned with the outline of a wolf. He spends most of his time in the Norse fantasy worlds and looks the part. Talia's armor is not that different from the military armor we wore in the last match, except hers is solid white. She spends most of her time adventuring through spaceworlds and battling aliens across different planets.

I still wear my green tunic and wolf belt that I bought my first day in the game. I've thought about upgrading, but they hold so much sentimental value that I haven't been able to put them down.

"You down for one more?" asks Talia. "We've got a good thing going."

"I wish I could, but I need to get back to head-quarters."

"Still working on the hush-hush experiment you can't tell us about?" asks Buzz as he wraps his arm around my shoulder.

"Still am."

After I won the Developer's Tournament, Benjamin, the President of Pangea Online, offered me a job as the alpha tester for their new full-immersion programming. If everything is ready to go, today will be my first test run.

I wish I could stay and play with my friends, but I'm also excited for this new opportunity. If full-immersion works out, then there would be no difference between the experience in Pangea and the real world. It could change the world as we know it. Plus, Aleesia will be there. She convinced Benjamin to let her work on the team as part of an internship for her schooling. I haven't seen much of her in-game recently, so I know she's been hard at work.

After saying my good-byes, I take the portal to my in-game home. Fenrir, my legendary wolf mount, lies sprawled out on the floor. I run my fingers through his soft black fur and scratch him behind the ears. Taking a seat on the couch, I drift away for a moment.

I've come so far from the boy I was several months ago. I moved out of The Boxes and into a nice apartment in Pangea Headquarters, eating fruits and vegetables that I didn't even know existed. Sometimes it's hard, knowing that Buzz and Grayson are still living in The Boxes, unable to breathe fresh air or eat food that isn't processed. If I ever have the chance, I'll try my best to get them out.

A ding interrupts my thoughts and I notice I have a new notification. It's from Aleesia.

Esil,

Today's the big day. Meet us in the lab in an hour. I know I haven't been able to tell you much, but I'm so excited to finally show you!

CHAPTER TWO

Sunlight momentarily blinds me as I take off my headset. My apartment, located at the Pangea Headquarters campus, has big bay windows that allow me to look out into the world like I have never experienced before. The company moved me out of Civic City because Benjamin said that once the alpha testing actually begins, I'll need to be close because they could need me at any time, day or night, if there is something to test.

It doesn't bother me one bit. My new apartment is nicer than the one I had in Civic City, and there is no comparison between it and the box I used to live in with its cramped corners, stale air, and complete loneliness. I set the headset on the table and walk over to the window to crack it open. I can actually open the windows here and let in the fresh air!

After stripping out of my haptic suit and dressing in normal clothes, I make the trek from my apartment to the lab. A few workers nod at me as I pass. A man trims the leaves on a small bush with red berries that I could have never imagined existed a few months ago. In The Boxes, everything was gray and drab with no plant life to speak of. Even though I've been here a few weeks, I still haven't gotten used to the beauty of it all. Several drones zoom through the air, weaving between the trees and birds, delivering packages to the workers inside the head-quarters.

The headquarters of Pangea Online Entertainment is immaculate. The mirrored surfaces of all the buildings reflect blue skies and green trees. Things those living in The Boxes have never had the luxury of seeing.

I take my time through the entrance and down the long marble hallways until I come to a stop at the labora-tory. The scanner outside reads my handprint and then the hiss of air announces my arrival as the door slides open.

Aleesia and Benjamin stand on the bottom floor, engaged in conversation. Several technicians scurry about, checking settings and making notes on their digital pads.

"Welcome, Esil," says Benjamin, noticing me as I lean against the railing up above. "Today is the big day. Are you excited?" he asks, teeth flashing in a smile. His blond hair is neatly parted to the side. He wears a dark gray suit with a red pocket square. I've never seen the man in anything other than a suit.

"I can't wait."

Aleesia climbs the stairs and wraps me in a hug. Her hair brushes against my face and the smell of lavender washes over me. I love the way she smells.

"Just wait. This is going to blow your mind!" Her eyes are wide and full of excitement. She kisses me on the cheek and runs off again. I don't know how big of a part she can have in all of this since she is still a student, but she's been here almost every day since she started the job. Still, she is in a position many of her classmates would kill for. I guess that's a perk of having a father who is a developer.

A large tube filled with a blueish liquid sits in the middle of the room. Several cables and a mask dangle from above it. That's what I'll be getting into for my full-immersion gameplay. I'm a little nervous about drowning if something happens while I'm in game, but in addition to all the technicians and scientists who are here to make sure the game works correctly, there is a doctor.

"Alright, come on over here, Esil, and we'll give you the rundown of today's events." Benjamin waves me down to the giant tube.

When he starts talking, a man in a white lab coat starts taking notes.

"Today, we're trying something that has never been done. Something that has the power to change the way we view the world. This may be the beginning of creating a world that is better than our own. Where anyone, anywhere can be anything they want." I watch him closely. Is the speech rehearsed or is he just that good?

"For a long time now, Pangea Online has been the best at online entertainment. The time has come for us to not only be the best, but be better. What you're about to experience is unlike anything the world has ever seen. In your haptic suit, no matter how real the world looked and felt, it was never completely immersive. Sure, you could feel the weight of an axe in your hand, the touch of the fur on your wolf, and see the most minute details in every blade of grass, but you could never smell the way Fenrir's paws smell like earth, or taste the smooth, cinnamon burn of Fire Whiskey. You could never feel the wind gently blowing against your skin after you crossed a stream or truly experience what these things could add to the world around you. Today, you will."

Okay, I'm officially hooked.

"And you plan to offer this over all of Pangea?" I ask. That's no small order.

"In time. As you know, Pangea Online is huge. There are hundreds of gameworlds for users to explore. It will take a while to bring all of them up to the standards of what we hope to achieve. First, we have to perfect the technology. That's why we have you here. It's easy to talk about the lofty ambitions. It's quite another thing entirely to bring them to fruition. Your father knew how hard it was to bring an idea into the world. That's a passion I still cherish. We're starting small. One world. Brand new, not available anywhere else in Pangea. We've input several quests throughout it, but the programming inside is meant to evolve. It changes as you change. In time, when we introduce more players, it will change again with them. We're hoping to create a constantly evolving world, so immersive, in both reality and gameplay, that users will never want to leave. And maybe one day, they won't have to." A smirk dances at the corners of his mouth. I'm not sure if he meant it that way, but that last sentence sounded ominous.

"What do you mean by that?"

"All in due time. Get ready to strap in."

The technician leads me up a ladder to a platform behind the giant tube.

"My name's Marty. I was a big fan of you in the tournament," he says as he fiddles with several buttons that I assume control the tube. His glasses continuously fall down his nose as he works and he keeps having to adjust them. Freckles cover his face, taking prominence over his alabaster skin.

"Thanks." I stare at the machine before me. So many switches and buttons. I'm officially an experiment.

"I'm sorry, but I'm going to need you to strip down."

"What? Like, naked?" Nobody told me I was going to be showing my goods. I mean, Aleesia and I haven't eve—

"Come on, Esil," Aleesia's voice booms from an intercom. "It's for science. Besides, the water's warm."

I can hear the laughter in her voice. How long has she known about this?

I strip down, using my hands to cover myself, while Marty tells me some of the details of what is about to happen.

Across the room, Aleesia and several others work diligently behind a pane of glass.

"The liquid you're about to submerge into is filled with millions of tiny nanoreceptors. Your body will move as you move inside the game and the density of the liquid will change to correlate with that experience. Tougher tasks make it harder. Easier tasks will do the opposite. The receptors will report feedback on everything you do while you're in the game. The mask gives you air, but the liquid does most of the work. These two receptors here—," He points at the two dangly wires that hang next to the mask. "—attach to your temple. That is how we get you in the game."

He attaches a harness around my chest and shoulders. It also has dozens of receptors designed to give feedback on my vital organs.

"What am I supposed to do once I'm in game?" I ask as he attaches the two receptors to my head.

"Today, just walk around. Try out the game, see what if

feels like. Do a little exploring. We're giving you thirty minutes to start, then you'll come out and report back to us what you think, where we can improve, things like that. Let's make sure everything feels right before we leave you in longer."

That doesn't sound so hard.

"How do I log out when time is up?"

"We'll pull you out this first time, but in the future, you should be able to focus on leaving, kind of like when you teleport in other worlds inside Pangea, and it will log you out automatically."

"And can you contact me while I'm in game?"

Marty pulls the mask over my face and checks that the fit is tight.

"We can send you messages, but you can't contact us. And just like in other gameworlds, you have to be in-game to communicate with other players directly. Enjoy your time in The Broken Lands."

Broken Lands, huh? It has a nice ring to it.

Once everything is secure, the harness lowers me into the tube. The liquid is warmer than I expected and almost jelly-like in consistency. I'll definitely need a shower once I get out. I open my eyes once I'm underwater and everything is a blur. I'm briefly aware that I'm still naked before everything goes black.

CHAPTER THREE

I open my eyes, disoriented. Wooden beams run across the roof overhead. Something buzzes next to me. When I turn to see what it is, a strong whiff of manure hits me in the face and my stomach churns for a second. Flies buzz back and forth through the air.

My back itches when I sit up. I must be in a stable. Hay sticks to my backside and I brush it off.

Holy cow! The hay made me itch. I can actually smell the manure. This is amazing!

It's hard to explain the difference, but it feels like an invisible veil has been lifted. I know I'm in the game, but damn, does it feel real.

The gentle neigh of a horse in the next stall catches my attention. My vision is completely clear. There are no icons or maps, even when I focus for them to appear. It's almost lifelike. Hell, it is lifelike.

I rub the hay off my back and realize I'm not wearing any clothes, aside from a pair of underwear.

Well, this will be interesting.

"Hey, get out of there!" A woman rushes into the stable, brow furrowed. Her hair is a straggly mess and she waves a frying pan animatedly in my direction. "I've told you vagrants before, our stable is not a substitute for the inn! Now get out!"

I stand up in all my naked glory. The chill of the morning air nips at my uncovered skin as I try to decide on my next move. Before I get that far in my thoughts, the woman lets loose the frying pan and it hits me in the shoulder. I expect my vision to go red, but instead, a sharp pain shoots through my shoulder and across my chest.

"Ouch! That really hurt," I say.

"Yeah, and there's more where that came from if you don't get the hell out right now!"

I pick up the frying pan and use it to cover my nethers as I run past the woman before she has a chance to deliver on her promise. My shoulder still throbs as I run by, and the skin is flushed and puffy. The pain feels so real. I'm not sure how much players will enjoy full-immersion if it hurts like this. I can't begin to imagine what being stabbed would feel like.

Running past the woman, I escape into the yard. Corn-fields abound in every direction as I pass the small wooden house and rush down the dirt driveway to the road. The outline of a small town looms several miles in the distance.

A cawing crow squawks at me from a nearby field. He sits on the shoulder of a scarecrow, unafraid of the straw man. A thought dawns on me.

The papery husks of corn scratch against me while I walk through the field. When I arrive at the scarecrow, the crow caws again and then flutters into the sky. I unlace the tunic from the scarecrow and put it on. It's a little large, and stiff from who knows how many days in the sun, but at least I have clothes now. His pants are a little baggy, but they work as well.

Once I'm dressed, a bar briefly flashes in the corner of my vision and I see my experience go up. It disappears just as quickly and when I try to focus on it again, nothing. Whatever stats are happening, it's going on behind the scenes.

I'll have to tell Benjamin to work on that. It'll be infuriating for players to not be able to access their stats and achievements in-game. I'm sure they are going for the most realistic version possible, but people still want to be able to know what they are working toward and how to gauge their progress.

With my new clothes, I set off toward town. After a while, my feet begin to ache and I am once again painfully aware of the realism. Tiny rocks stab at my feet with each step. I'll need to find shoes somehow, but I don't have any money.

The rhythmic trot of a horse announces a carriage approaching from behind. I step to the side to allow the carriage to pass, but it slows down and a man wearing a wide brimmed hat stands to greet me.

"Howdy. Need a ride into town?" the man asks. He has shaggy hair that falls to his shoulders. His face is weathered and worn, probably from years in the sun. Dark gray eyes stare out at me.

"That would be great! My feet are killing me."

"Hop in the back and I'll give you a lift. Try not to squish the vegetables."

I climb in the back of the wagon loaded with carrots, beets, onions, and a dozen other vegetables.

"Name's Carter," he says as he snaps the reins and the horse starts trotting again.

"I'm Esil. Nice to meet you. Where are we headed?"

The wagon bumps along and I feel every rock and hole we pass over.

"I'm heading to the market in Carolton to sell off some of my produce. How about you?"

"Nowhere in particular. I was hoping to buy some shoes, but I don't have any money."

"Times have been tough recently, that's for sure. There's a lot of dark things going on across the land. Say, if you help me out with some work, I'll buy you a pair of shoes. What do you say?"

"Sounds like we've got a deal."

We journey along in silence for a while before the wagon comes to an abrupt halt.

A group of men wearing black cloaks block the road. Five in total. They stand tall, holding pitchforks.

"Dammit," moans Carter.

"What's going on?" I ask. He obviously knows something because he seems more resigned than panicked.

"Bandits. They're gonna take a cut of my produce before they allow us into the city. They're usually only out at dusk, taking the money we've earned, which is why I tried to get an early start, but I guess people caught on and now they're changing their ways."

A fire ignites inside of me. If there is one thing I hate, it's bullies. "We can't let them do that. You worked hard for this and they can't just take it away from you."

"Two of us against five of them. We don't have a shot."

I don't expect much from Carter, he is just a farmer after all. But I can't sit by and watch him get robbed right in front of me. They said the world evolves based on the choices we make, so maybe I can inspire the common people not to sit by while thieves and bandits take what doesn't belong to them.

But how can we possibly get past them?

"I've got an idea."

Carter looks at me, eyes wide.

"How fast can this wagon go?"

"Pretty fast, but it'll be a bumpy ride." The five men still stand in the middle of the road twenty yards ahead.

"Let's run them over. How can they expect to stop a speeding wagon with only pitchforks?" I hold the frying pan in my hand and give it a twirl. "Besides, I've got this."

A smile dances at the edge of his mouth, but I can still see the concern in his eyes.

"Come on. If you stop, they'll always take from you. Put up a fight and you might never see them again."

He slowly nods and then pulls the reins in his hands, mumbling something under his breath.

With a crack of the whip, the wagon jerks into motion, gaining speed down the bumpy dirt road. The cloaked men look at each other for a moment, unsure of what is happening. I grip my weapon, ready for whatever happens next.

We're seconds from crashing into them when they jump to the side. A bandit attempts to lodge his pitchfork in the wheel, but it snaps like a twig, sending splinters flying. I bring my frying pan down hard on his head and the man falls to the ground. A rush of adrenaline courses through me when I see them in our dust. I turn to congratulate Carter, but he is hunched over in the seat, blood dripping from his shoulder.

"Oh no, what happened?" I ask.

Carter grimaces and pulls on the reins, slowing the wagon to a more moderate pace. I climb into the front and take a look at his wound. Three large punctures flow freely, spilling blood down his arm.

"The bastards got me as we passed." For a split-second, I see a health bar over his head at about fifty percent. Just as fast, it disappears. I need to get him into the city and see if we can find some type of medical help.

I move Carter to the side and take the reins. I speed up the wagon and soon the outskirts of the town come into view. Carter continues to bleed, forming a small puddle in the seat around him. His face has lost all color, leaving him gaunt and white.

Two guards stand outside the town gate. They aren't resplendent by any means. Their armor is dented and tarnished in places, unlike the guards in the Mortican Mountains with their shimmering plate polished so well I could see my own reflection. No, these guards are far from their home castle. The low men on the totem pole. They scowl at me as we come to a stop at the gate.

"What happened to him?" one of the guards asks, not a hint of compassion in his voice.

"We were attacked by bandits but managed to escape."

The guard glances at the other and raises a brow.

"Managed to escape, you say? Why didn't you just pay them and be on your way?"

"And give up what he worked so hard for? Listen, we need to get inside and get my friend some medical attention. Will you let us pass or not?"

"You plan on selling those vegetables?" the guard asks, looking in the back of the wagon.

"Of course."

"Then it's two copper to get into the city. That's the cost of selling."

This doesn't seem right. And I have a strong feeling these guards are in league with the bandits we just passed.

I'm about to argue when Carter reaches into his pocket and pulls out the two coppers.

The guards move aside and the gate opens.

People hustle back and forth inside the town. I search for anything that looks like a healer, but all I see is the market, a blacksmith, and row upon row of houses.

A young woman passes by, carrying a basket of herbs. Her dark hair is braided down her back and she wears a blue tunic.

"Excuse me, miss. Do you know where I can find a doctor?"

She looks up, startled.

"Doctor?" she asks, evidently not knowing the word.

"Uhm, a healer?"

Recognition dawns on her face.

"Ah, yes. Our healer is on the other side of town. There is a white mark on the building. You will know it when you see it."

As we make our way through the heart of the town, I can't help but notice how downtrodden everyone looks. No one makes eye contact and they all keep a healthy distance from one another. Something is definitely going on in this town.

I recognize the healer's building as soon as we come across it. It's a small cottage, painted black, with the outline of a white hand on the door. A few rats scurry underneath as I pull the wagon to a halt and tie up the horse. An aura of darkness surrounds the building. I don't like the look of it, but the woman said this is where we would find the healer, and Carter doesn't have much time.

He barely acknowledges me as I lift him from the wagon and carry him towards the entrance. At the door, a smell more rotten and sour than I have ever experienced overtakes me, stopping me in my tracks.

The door is locked, and it takes a few moments for anyone to come after I knock. I'm surprised when a beautiful woman in a white dress opens the door and invites us inside.

"My friend was attacked. He needs help."

She nods and motions for me to step inside.

Skulls and shrunken heads hang from the ceiling. A snake coils in a jar sitting on an ivory table. Several potions and frothing liquids bubble and brew as she leads me into a room in the back. The woman seems out of place with everything here. What have we just entered?

She points at an empty table, instructing me to place Carter there, but says nothing.

His eyes flutter as I lay him down as gently as I can.

"Can you save him?" I ask.

A blank stare is the only reply I receive. She steps over to Carter's body and places her hand on his injured shoulder. Her lips begin to move, silent at first, and then more audibly. She chants in a language I cannot understand. As she chants, her white dress darkens at the edges. Small tendrils work their way up through the fabric, changing it to gray and then black, until finally it is as dark as a starless night. Not only that, her beautiful face is now wrinkled and full of warts.

She continues chanting. The black tendrils that worked their way through her dress now move down her arm. I'm too shocked to move.

They reach out from her arm, injecting themselves into the wounds on Carter's shoulder, and he jerks violently. His eyes shoot open, wide and white.

I rush to help him, but something stops me in my tracks.

The next thing I know, my vision goes black.

CHAPTER FOUR

The warm gel smothers me. I stretch out my hands, reaching for Carter, but everything is a blur. I want to rush forward and stop the old witch from hurting him, but I can't. The harness pulls me out of the tube and up onto the deck.

"What the hell!" I scream as soon as the mask is removed. "She was killing him and you pulled me out right then? Why?"

"Easy there, Esil. It's just a game." Marty tries to calm me, but it felt so real. "We told you only thirty minutes. Besides, things never should have gotten that far. You were supposed to walk around and explore, not attempt to start a riot."

"A riot? I was just protecting an innocent traveler. Besides, it's not like I had any kind of direction. There were no prompts or missions. I basically had to find my own way."

Marty hands me a robe to cover myself with. Everything about the experience felt incredibly realistic and it feels like part of me is still there.

"Pretty great, huh?" asks Benjamin. He looks up at me from the floor below as I climb down. "Don't worry about Carter. He's an NPC, he'll be just fine. Now, tell me everything. What was it like?"

"It felt as real as standing right here," I say. Maybe that's why I felt such a strong desire to help Carter. "I think you'd do better to make the prompts and stats more visible. I saw flickers of them but could never focus on anything and see what it actually meant." I talk to Benjamin for a while as he asks questions about the user experience, the characters, and quests.

"I think you've already set the world moving in a different direction than it was this morning," he says, a devilish grin on his face. "The witch was never supposed to appear day one."

There is a small table towards the back wall. I take a seat and pull my robe tight. "What did she do exactly? To Carter."

"I guess you'll find out tomorrow when you log back in. Now let's get you cleaned up. There is a shower down there on the right. After that, check in with the doctor and he'll run a few tests."

"Tomorrow? I have to wait an entire day before I can find out what happened to my friend? Why do I have to wait? Put me back in now."

"Friend? You've known him for less than an hour. I'm sorry, Esil, but you'll have to wait. We're not exactly sure how this type of immersion effects the body, so we're taking it slow so we can monitor you and make sure everything is okay."

I get it, but dammit, I need to know what happened.

The steaming water washes over me as I sit in the shower. I close my eyes, remembering the dark tendrils that crept into Carter's body. After the transformation the witch went through, it couldn't be good. And what did Benjamin mean by the world is already moving in a different direction?

Aleesia wraps me in a hug when I return.

"That was so cool, the way you took charge and changed the game. I can't wait to see what happens next."

"What do you mean 'took charge'?"

"The initial quest was just for you to explore the city, but you changed it. Now who knows what will happen? There could be political or magical ramifications based solely on what you did. The way the AI works is that it changes based on the player base. Every choice you make effects the world, and today, you made some big choices. We put in the initial coding and commands, now the AI does the rest. We just monitor it."

"So are you saying the game is still going on while I'm not there?"

"Exactly." A wide smile stretches from ear to ear. "It's just like the rest of Pangea. Time keeps moving, but instead of the NPCs waiting around for users to interact with them, they carry on their lives as if they were real people."

All the more reason to go back and check on Carter.

"What now?" I ask.

"You wait until tomorrow to log back in. I have some details to take care of for now, but maybe we can meet up later this evening?"

"Sounds good." She gives me a kiss on the cheek and then disappears.

There is not much for me to do for the moment, so after checking in with the doctor, I go back to my apartment and log into Pangea.

Fenrir waits for me in my home portal. It's been a while since I last took him into a gameworld. I should take him out and let him stretch his legs.

"Want to go exploring, boy?"

His ears perk up and his giant tail wags, smashing into the couch and inching it across the floor.

Welcome to Obsidia, Land of a Thousand Volcanoes.

Fenrir and I spawn on the side of a cliff. Far in the distance, mountainous volcanoes smoke and glow against the gray sky.

Something falls on my head, turning my vision bright red, and I look up to see a monkey tossing coconuts in my direction. It hugs the tree with long, spindly arms, its brown fur blowing in the mountain breeze. Between throws, the monkey howls, its eyes wild with fury. What the hell did I do to him?

Monkey. Level 32. *It's all fun and games until someone throws poop.*

Another coconut flies in my direction. This time, I lean to the left and the coconut whizzes by my ear. I can hear it clacking against the rocks as it tumbles down the cliff. I've spent so much time playing in non-RPG worlds over the last few weeks that I haven't sorted my inventory or checked my stats in days.

The monkey loads up another coconut and I search through my inventory for the best way to fight the annoying creature. I have my axe, a spear, my staff. Oh, and Grappler.

Item: The Grappler. Ray Gun. +7 Strength. Ability: Grapple, fires a grappling hook and attaches to the first object it hits. 30 second cooldown.

I equip Grappler and use its special ability, firing the grappling hook at the monkey. It lodges around the monkey's shoulder and when I retract it, it jerks the monkey screaming and flailing in my direction. The monkey collides with my body, causing it to drop the coconut.

The monkey bares its teeth, intent on ripping out my flesh, but I grab it by the shoulder and toss the raging furball over my head and off the cliff. Its howling screams echo on the wind before suddenly stopping at the same time my XP bar goes up.

With the monkey out of the way, I have a chance to canvass the area. A small path leads higher into the mountainside. We appear to be on one of the few habitable mountains filled with animals and vegetation. Several volcanoes spew lava into the sky and many more smoke ominously. If we climb the summit, I'll have a better idea of where we should go next.

I urge Fenrir forward and his powerful paws grip into the earth. We pass palm trees and flowers the size of my body. Everything is tropical. Several monkeys howl from deep within the trees. Birds chirp and insects buzz as we continue to climb and soon arrive at the top of the mountain.

From this height, the world unfolds in every direction. This must be the tallest peak in all of Obsidia, because nothing blocks my view. For miles and miles, volcanoes and mountains stretch across the horizon.

A gorilla sits behind a small hut talking with a human and a dwarf. A panama hat falls low over his eyes. The human wears a blue button-up shirt and khaki shorts with hiking boots. The beardless dwarf wears nothing but a loincloth. With dark olive skin, he is the most hairless dwarf I have ever seen.

"Crikey," says the man, pointing at Fenrir. "That's a big wolf."

"What is this place?" I ask.

The gorilla comes forward, his muscles rippling with each step. His knuckles brush the ground as he walks.

"I run the traveler's stop for this mountain. Name's Flufu."

"Flufu?" I ask. He does not look like a Flufu.

"Yes." His eyes cut at me. "Got a problem with that?" His giant fist clenches and then opens. I'd hate to be on the receiving end of a punch from him.

"Nope, not at all. Um, so what does the traveler's stop offer?"

He relaxes a little, though his eyes still radiate suspicion.

"I sell items explorers might need. Potions, food, weapons, maps. Things like that."

"And bananas," says the dwarf.

"Benji here loves bananas." He points to the dwarf.

"Really? I've never seen a dwarf eat anything other than meat and ale."

The dwarf's eyes cut at me.

"I am not a dwarf. I am a Menehune," he says curtly before turning around and walking back to his seat.

"I'm sorry, did I do something to offend him?" I have no idea what it could have been, but the little guy is pissed. He practically has steam spilling out of his ears.

Flufu smirks at me. "You called him a dwarf. He's a Menehune. An ancient race of the Hawaiian peoples."

"How was I supposed to know that? He looks like a beardless dwarf."

"You fantasy guys," says the gorilla. "No culture. What brings you here anyway?"

"I wanted to let my wolf stretch his legs. Maybe find a quest. It's been a while since I've taken one."

"Well, you're in luck," says the human. "There's a board over there where people post all kinds of quests they need help with."

He leads me over to a large wooden board. Several handwritten notes are posted. I look through them, seeing if anything interests me.

Quest: Searching for phoenix feathers. Many are located in the heart of a dormant volcano. Bring five to the white temple on Monteluna Mountain to claim your reward.

Quest: The Night Walkers are taking over the island. Come to the Shadow Island after dark to rid the town of the ghosts of slain warriors.

Quest: Looking for a partner to help clear a hidden dungeon. More details available upon request.

There are a few more, but the hidden dungeon catches my eye.

"How do I find out who is offering the quest?" I ask.

"That's what I'm here for," says Flufu.

"Okay, well, who is looking to clear the hidden dungeon?"

He tilts his massive head back and laughs, deep and boisterously.

"What's so funny?"

"You're going to need to go make amends with Benji."

The Menehune sits at the table sulking to himself. Do I even want to clear a dungeon with him? He doesn't have a weapon, nor does he look like a remotely good fighter.

I think about turning around and finding another quest, but Fenrir nudges me in the shoulder with his snout, as if telling me to get moving. I guess I should at least give it a chance.

"Fine." I shrug.

I take a seat next to Benji, and Fenrir sits at my feet.

"Sorry about earlier. That was insensitive of me. I've never heard of the Menehune people before."

He sits silent for a moment before responding.

"It's okay. You were ignorant. Children cannot be judged for their ignorance, however, if it happens again, that is stupidity. And stupidity threatens the entire world."

What the hell just happened? This guy just went from goofball to ancient sage in about two seconds.

"Um, so, you're looking to clear a dungeon?" I ask.

"Indeed. It is no small task. There will be many dangers, which is why I do not wish to go alone."

"Can I help?"

He stands up and looks me over. Then he moves into my personal space and grabs me by the arm. He lifts my arm, inspects it, and places it back down. He does the same with my left. Then he grabs my ears, chin, and nose, all in the same fashion. What he is looking for, I have no idea.

"You can come," he says. Evidently happy with whatever he was looking for.

With that, he stands up and takes off down the mountain.

"You better follow him if you want to clear that dungeon," laughs Flufu from beside his hut.

I hurry to catch up. Benji is already well down the mountain. He moves fast to be so small.

When I catch up to him, he turns and smiles. It's oddly comforting and creepy at the same time.

"Do you have any weapons?" I ask.

"Indeed."

"And magic? Do you know any spells?"

"Indeed."

That gives me nothing to go off of.

"Do you plan on sharing anything with me at any point about what we are getting into?"

"All in due time."

"What does that mean?" I rub my hands through my hair. I feel like I've made a big mistake helping him with the quest.

"To find your way into the mountain, you must first become one with the mountain."

He grabs me by the arm and the next thing I know, we're surrounded by black smoke.

CHAPTER FIVE

When the smoke clears, we're inside a dark cave. A few fires burn along the floor, igniting a narrow path that stretches out before us. I can feel Fenrir's presence in my inventory, but I can't call him to my side. Mounts must not be allowed here.

"Where are we?" I ask Benji.

"The heart of the mountain. Listen closely and you can hear its heartbeat."

I focus on the sounds around me, but all I hear is the crackle of the fire. What is he playing at?

"I don't hear it."

Benji's eyes bore into me, unamused. Maybe he was being serious.

"Close your eyes." I do as he instructs. "Now listen."

With my eyes closed, I try to expand my hearing. The crackle of the fire becomes more intense and I can begin to pinpoint individual fires and follow them along the cavern.

And then I hear it. Slow at first, a dull beating begins to echo around me. I search for its source, but I can't pinpoint it. It feels like it's coming from the very walls. The more I focus, the louder it becomes, until the beat pounds around me like a thousand drums.

A gentle hand grips me on the shoulder and I open my eyes.

"The heart of the mountain beats within us all. We have a perilous journey ahead, and the mountain does not relinquish easily what it holds, but if we respect the mountain, it may give us what we need."

"And what is that exactly?" Does Benji ever speak in anything that isn't a riddle?

"The Pearl of Monteluna. It is a rare and magical item. Help me retrieve it and you will be rewarded."

Congratulations! You have been offered the quest 'Retrieve the Pearl of Monteluna.' Reward: Increased alliance with the Menehune and 50% of spoils. Do you accept? Y/N

I accept the quest and Benji moves forward down the cavern. The beating of the mountain subsides, but I can still hear it faintly if I listen.

"Wait," I call out to Benji. "Before we go, let me check through my stats and items." It's been a while since I've been on a quest and I don't want get into a fight unprepared.

He nods at me and stops, leaning against the cavern wall and cleaning his fingernails with his teeth.

I bring up my stat page.

Level 25:
   Strength - 14
   Agility - 4
   Vitality - 5
   Intellect - 6

Dexterity - 5
Stamina - 0

I must have leveled up at some point over the past few weeks, because I have a stat point to allocate. I add it to Vitality, increasing my health a small amount. Even after the developers fixed the bug that made all miners extremely strong, I am still a formidable opponent based on my strength alone. I can't battle outside of my level like I used to, but I've learned enough over the past few months to give most players a run for their money.

My dwarven boots offer me great Stamina regeneration, never allowing me to completely run out, so I've never put a single point into Stamina. I equip my elvish spear, as it is still my best weapon for now. As much as I love my battleaxe, I think it's important to make sure I have the best gear possible. As of right now, my gear consists of the following items:

Item: Dwarven Boots of Stamina. Soulbound. Cannot be traded or discarded. *These ancient Dwarven Boots recharge 2% Stamina every five seconds.*

Item: Elvish Battle Spear. +12 attack. +15% armor penetration.

Item: Vampiric Ring. Grants 2% lifesteal per attack.

Item: Forgotten Chainmail. +12 armor.

Item: Benevolent Shield of Healing. +10% health. Unique ability: Double-edged shield. The next attack will be blocked and heal both attacker and defender for 5% health. Cooldown: 5 minutes.

Item: Ring of Power. +15 attack. Unique ability: Double Ring of Power's attack bonus for 30 seconds.

After the bonus is up, Ring of Power offers no bonus for 60 seconds.

I also have Staff of the Water Ancients, which I can switch out if I need to cast magic.

Item: Staff of the Water Ancients. +20% magic damage on elemental attacks.

I have a few health and mana potions, but no other buffs at the moment. It would have been smart to stop by Flufu's hut before we left to pick up any items we need, but with Benji already leaving me in his dust, there just wasn't time.

With all of my items equipped, I feel ready to take on whatever comes next.

"I'm ready."

Benji nods and sets off down the path.

The path into the mountain is narrow, barely wide enough for Benji and I to walk side by side. We follow it for a while. Nothing but the crackling of fire greets us. I check my map, but as it is unexplored territory, the only visible parts are where we have passed.

Finally, the tunnel empties into a cavernous room where stalactites and stalagmites cast eerie shadows in every direction, making the walls feel alive. In the far back of the cavern, a pool glistens and gently sloshes against the mountainous rocks.

"A spring?" I ask.

"Indeed. Springs are the blood of the mountain, bringing life to the surrounding areas."

Something splashes in the depths of the pool and then one of the fires goes out, casting part of the cavern in darkness.

"Ah, yes," says Benji. "So it begins."

"What's happening?" I ask, taking a defensive position with my spear pointed outward.

"The mountain is ready to test us."

In the dim light, a long purple tentacle reaches out from the water. Then another. And another. What comes out next is the thing nightmares are made of. Eight long tentacles hold up an octopus body with the head of a shark. It's razor-sharp teeth gleam in the firelight.

Sharktopus. Level 35. *Hugs and kisses. XOXO.*

The giant monster extends its tentacles, pulling itself to its full height and towering over both of us.

Beside me, Benji begins making gestures in the air, drawing symbols and leaving trails of glowing filament as if writing in the air itself. An aura surrounds his body and when the sharktopus approaches, Benji pulls his hands back against his chest, cupping them. A tiny ball of light swirls between his palms. The longer he holds it, the bigger the ball grows. The sharktopus is nearly on us when Benji pushes the ball of light from his chest and it shoots out like a cannon, hitting the monster square in its shark face.

The blast knocks the creature back several feet, taking out a tenth of its health.

"Wow, that was awesome! What was that?"

Benji smirks. "Ancient battle magic. Now, fight!" Benji springs forward like a ninja, hitting the ground with a roll and disappearing into the cavern.

Carefully, I approach the creature. The blast from Benji has made it more cautious and it surveys my every move.

I cast Resilience on myself, increasing my attack speed by twenty percent. With the increased attack speed, I lunge at the monster, stabbing swiftly. My spear rips into one of its legs before it jerks away. Dark blood stains the end of my spear.

Another blast of light slams into the monster's body, knocking it off balance. I move in to strike again, but a flailing tentacle collides with my ribs, knocking me into a stalagmite and breaking it in half. My vision flashes red and I lose twenty percent health.

The sharktopus is down to two-thirds health now. It seems we have a good shot of defeating it if we can keep at a distance. I cast Mud Pits and several splotches of mud appear on the ground, slowing any enemy movement inside them. The monster's tentacles stick, leaving a trail of mud that stretches with each step.

I move in with my spear, hoping to land a few attacks while the monster is slowed, but it sees me coming and shoots black liquid out of the shark's mouth. It covers my face and I can't see anything.

Alert! You have been blinded by ink.

My vision is complete blackness. In a panic, I back away from the sound of battle. The sound of Benji and the monster fighting roars in front of me, so I attempt to retreat in the other direction.

"Watch out!" Benji yells, but it's too late. Tentacles wrap around me just as my vision returns and squeeze tight. They lift me high into the air and then thrust me against the floor, reddening my vision and dropping me below half health.

The monster releases me and springs forward like a spider at Benji. He makes a symbol with his hand and an orb of protective light surrounds him. The sharktopus wraps its tentacles around the orb, but it can't break through the barrier. Benji stands inside, his face set in concentration as he attempts to hold the spell.

I switch to my staff and cast Haunted Earth. Roots spring forth from the ground, wrapping around several of the sharktopus's tentacles. Then, I cast Waterfall and after a two-second wait, water pours from the sky, barraging the monster. It has surprisingly little effect, perhaps because it is a sea creature.

The monster slams the orb protecting Benji against a nearby stalagmite repeatedly until tiny cracks begin to form on its surface.

I need to do something before it cracks. But what?

I switch to Grappler and fire off a few laser beams at the monster. This gets its attention, because it drops Benji and rushes in my direction. The way its legs move is a grotesque motion of bends only a boneless creature could have. All the while, its hundreds of teeth gnash against each other.

A large group of stalactites hang from the ceiling nearby. I fire the grappling hook and it wraps around the largest one. I retract it just as the monster extends its tentacles towards me, leaving it swiping at air. The gun pulls me with such force that I boomerang around the stalactites, back in my original direction towards the sharktopus still in pursuit.

Thinking quickly, I equip my spear in my other hand and collide with the monster at full force. The spear hits the sharktopus in the mouth, shattering teeth and lodging in the beast's throat before it collapses to the ground in a puddle of ink and blood.

Critical hit!

You have slain Sharktopus.

"Well done!" says Benji. He flashes me a big, toothy grin. "That's a way to use your surroundings."

We check the body for loot, splitting the gold and items.

Item: Shark's tooth.

Item: Vial of Ink.

There is a loud rumble, causing several stalactites to fall from the ceiling and shatter on the ground. Near the back of the cavern, a crack forms in the wall and after a few seconds of rumbling and grating rock, it widens until it is the size of a door. It looks like we get to move on to the next level.

Once we pass through the newly-formed entrance, the mountain shakes and the door closes again behind us. Win or go home, it seems.

What waits ahead is one the most beautiful and terrifying things I have ever seen. Dozens of jellyfish float through the air, blocking our path. Electricity zips and zaps from their long, flowing neon tentacles, igniting the dark cavern like some seedy underground city. The fires from the earlier stage are gone and the only light emanates from the glow of the jellyfish. I find myself entranced in their hypnotic glow and something calls to me in their depths.

I take a step forward and a large bolt zaps me from the nearest jellyfish. It stuns me momentarily and depletes my health by a fifth. How are we supposed to get past them? There are no stalagmites hanging from the ceiling for me to fire Grappler at. Only smooth surfaces and dozens of electric mines waiting to electrocute us any time we get near.

Benji just smiles.

"Something funny?" I ask.

"Indeed. I was born for this," he laughs.

He gestures with his hands, carving out a spell against

the air, and a gust of wind rockets him into the sky and over the first wave of jellyfish. He lands on the head of one of them and bounces. When he hits the jellyfish, its light dims. Miraculously, he is not shocked, but instead, the jellyfish slowly descends to the floor and comes to rest. He bounces from one jelly to the other, until he comes to a stop far in the distance. I only know where he is by the small dot on my map.

"It's easy!" he yells. "Stay on top of them and they can't hurt you."

Easy for you to say. You're three feet tall!

The field of jellyfish looms before me as I try to determine how in the hell I'm supposed to get on top of them. They are too high for me to jump to and their stingers drag too low for me to go underneath.

If only there was a way for me to launch myself in the air.

That's it! I'll use my spear to vault me on top of them. I take a health potion and once my health is full, I equip my spear and stand back as far as I can to get a running start.

Marking the spot in my mind where I want to aim my spear for the best leverage, I take off as fast as I can run. The light from the jellyfish is both welcoming and terrifying as they flicker and glide through the cavern. One wrong move and I'm toast.

I jab the spear into the ground and press hard, using my strength to catapult me into the air. I expect to fly high, but instead, I torpedo onto the hood of the closest jellyfish, losing all sense of balance. The hood bounces me like a trampoline and I flail into the air, straight into the tentacles of another jellyfish.

Electricity runs through my body, immobilizing me, and my health ticks down with each zap.

It was a good run, Benji, but it looks like you're on your own.

Red flashes across my vision in violent waves until it suddenly stops and a strong hand tosses me to the ground.

The large, animated eyes of Benji look down at me as he roars with laughter.

"Ah ha ha!" he bellows. "You really are something else."

I take my remaining potions and my health slowly ticks up.

"Well, excuse me for not having a special spell to shoot me into the air," I snap.

"Would you like to?" he asks.

"Like to what?"

He moves his hands through the air and a cloud forms beneath him before suddenly rocketing him into the air. He lands beside me with a soft thud.

"Learn the spell? I can teach you." A wide smile creeps across his face.

Seriously? He could have taught me a spell at the beginning and saved me a lot of humiliation.

"Why the hell wouldn't you teach me to start with?"

"I wanted to watch your brain work," he laughs. "It was a good effort, but poor execution. Come here."

I do as he says and he places a small hand on my arm, sending a rush of energy through my body.

Congratulations! You have learned Cloud Burst. Cost: 50 mana. A cloud of energy forms beneath your body and rockets you into the air. 5 second cooldown.

"That's awesome, Benji! Thanks!" The five-second cooldown isn't too bad either. It'll come in handy in a fight for sure.

"Now what do you say we get a move on?" Benji turns

and shoots himself atop the jellyfish again, not waiting for my response.

He bounces across the electric field, dimming the rainbow of lights as he goes.

When I focus on my new ability, I feel a rush of energy form beneath me. Almost like it could lift me into the air if I let it. My hands have already memorized the motions of the spell and I carve it into the air in front of me. The longer I focus, the more the power builds. I release the spell and a cloud forms underneath, propelling me into the air with such force that I slam against the ceiling, losing a fifth of my health.

Benji laughs raucously from across the cavern. I'm glad he is getting a good laugh out of my embarrassment.

A few more attempts and I finally have a good feel for how far holding the spell will shoot me. It's time to put it into action.

The energy builds around my feet and with a burst, the clouds launch me atop the sea of jellyfish. I land on the hood of one and it bounces me further, the light beneath my feet dimming as it does. It's a strange sensation as I travel from one jellyfish to the other, never fully stopping. I'm not even sure I could stop if I tried. My only option is to keep my balance and join Benji on the other side or die.

Once I get the hang of it, the bounces come more naturally. I can anticipate where I will land and the direction the bounce will send me. The dimmed jellies offer less of a bounce than the others, so I try to avoid them and pass across the sea as quickly as possible.

Benji waits for me on the other side and offers me a round of applause when I stumble to the ground, mentally drained but in one piece.

"Well done. Now we face our final test."

A lone chest sits on a pedestal at the end of the cavern. The neon tentacles of the jellyfish reflect off its gleaming surface.

"The pearl is in there?" I ask.

Benji shakes his head.

"No, the way to the pearl lies within."

Another riddle. I wish he would just tell me what he knows. We approach the chest with trepidation. For once, even Benji is not smiling. It's making me nervous for whatever could be inside.

The latch to the chest is not locked. The deep brown wood has light streaks that run through it, like the stripes of a tiger. The gold that surrounds the edges contains dents and scratches from where it was crafted by hand. Benji runs his fingers across it, taking in its beauty.

"This was crafted by my people, by the Menehune." he says with pride. "Are you ready, my friend?"

I nod, mentally preparing myself for whatever may come next.

He flips the lid and the sound of dozens of wings fills the air.

CHAPTER SIX

Hundreds of birds fly through the cavern around us. The air above is so dense with the flutter of wings that they block my view of the ceiling. And still, birds continue to spill out of the chest.

The birds chirp and squawk in a violent discord. Everything is pure pandemonium.

Benji backs against the wall, a terrified look on his face. Is there something I am missing? Because I don't feel terrified at all. They are just birds.

When the last bird flies out of the chest, it closes with a snap and a lock appears through the latch where before there was none.

A snowy owl swoops down at Benji and for a moment, I forget about the quest. Visions of Merlin, my horned owl, flash through my mind. The adventures we went on, merging with his body in order to see the world from hundreds of feet off the ground, and then his death as he was ripped apart by a gargoyle while helping me through the final stage of the Developer's Tournament. I never would have won the tournament without his help. Without so many people's help.

Benji casts a spell to my right, bringing me back to reality, and I turn to see him sitting inside of his protective orb while the owl pecks at it in an angry attack. Another owl joins in, and then another until there are a half dozen pecking furiously. Surprisingly, I seem to go unnoticed.

"What the hell is going on?" I ask.

Benji doesn't look at me, his eyes focused on the owls, but he answers, "Owls are ancient enemies of the Menehune. In the olden times, giant owls would attack us and take our people off into the mountains to devour us."

Of all the birds overhead, only the owls are attacking. The rest, in a rainbow of colors, big and small, flutter about in a watercolor of chaos.

"What are we supposed to do now?" I ask, but I feel I know the answer. There wouldn't be a lock on the chest unless we were supposed to find a key to open it. My guess is that it is attached to one of the birds above us.

"We have to open the chest," he says, proving me right.

"And how exactly do you plan on doing that from inside your shield?"

Benji cuts his eyes at me.

"I don't plan on leaving my safe zone. You see how these owls look at me. They want me for dinner. The irony is that a Menehune is the only one who can equip the pearl, but the owls are only prejudiced against the Menehune. That's why I needed your help. Find a way to open the chest and I will be in your debt."

I scan the maelstrom overhead, looking for anything that resembles a key. Tiny sparrows dive and swoop. Birds of prey screech, their dangerous talons ready for attack. The long beak of a pelican protrudes as its giant wings flap, forcing smaller birds out of the way. Dozens of trop-ical birds flutter haphazardly, increasing the chaos. Nothing looks metal. Nothing looks like a key.

The more I watch them, the more nervous I become. So many talons and sharp beaks could rip me apart if they had the notion. Even if I do find the key, how do I get it without pissing off the entire lot?

Benji says something, but the birds are making so much noise now that I can't make out what he is saying. We should have set up a party chat before heading into the mountain. If I'm going to find the key, I'm going to have to do it on my own.

Focusing on the chaos overhead, I search for anything out of the ordinary. Not that dozens of birds of different species flying together in a cave with no entrance is ordinary.

They swoop and dive, and I begin to see patterns in the way they move. What initially looks like disorder becomes an elegant dance. There is a formula to the way each species moves. The sparrows dive in quick, shallow spurts. The falcons and hawks glide with grace. The tiny hummingbirds zip to and fro, never slowing for a moment.

Once I see the pattern of the movement, I am able to isolate the particular bird groups' flight patterns from the others. They suddenly all become visible and the rest of the birds are but a blur in the background. I switch my focus from bird to bird, searching for a key, for anything out of the ordinary.

And then I see it.

A blue hummingbird with a silver key dangling from its neck. The key blends perfectly with the silver coloring of its underbelly, but occasionally, when the bird darts, it catches the light from the jellyfish in a way that only metal can.

I keep my eyes locked on the tiny bird as it weaves in and out of the chaos like lightning made flesh.

Now that I know where the key is, how do I catch it? They are too high for me to reach and it is impossible for me to use Grappler on something so small. I doubt I would be able to attack it without angering the birds that surround it, so it seems my only option is to go up there and catch it with my hands.

I focus on the spell that Benji taught me. My hands move automatically, carving the spell into the air while my eyes stay focused on the key. Energy rushes through my body and I wait for the right moment to release. When I do, a cloud of energy propels me into the air. Birds scatter from my advance in a cacophony of flutters and squawks. A startled seagull attacks me, reddening my vision and proving that if I disturb them too much, they will turn on me just like the owls did on Benji. I reach out for the tiny hummingbird as it flies by, but he eludes me and I fall back to the cave floor emptyhanded.

This is going to be trickier than I thought. I've lost sight of the key, so I take a moment to check on Benji. He is still safe behind his forcefield, though tiny claw marks have scuffed the edges. He looks over to me and gives me a thumbs-up. I guess he isn't too worried about his shield breaking.

With my attention once again on the birds overhead, I begin my process of narrowing down the flight patterns until I am able to spot a hummingbird amongst the madness. It doesn't take quite as long and soon, I am watching the silver key zoom through the air once again. This time, I have another plan.

I cast Resilience on myself, increasing my attack speed, and then follow up with Cloud Burst. When I rocket into the air this time, my reaction time is much quicker and I catch the tail feather of the hummingbird. It feels like I have him, but the feather shakes loose and he disappears into the crowd.

If only there was a way to thin the herd.

Another idea crosses my mind, but if it fails, then we'll be back at square one, and the idea of fighting the shark-topus and crossing the jellyfish sea doesn't sound the least bit appealing.

In order for this to work, I need to be fast. Faster than the speeding dive of a falcon.

Once I've located the key, I take a deep breath and mentally prepare myself for what comes next.

First, I cast Resilience on myself. I need quick reflexes and what I'm about to do will take less than the fifteen second limit on the spell. Then I cast Waterfall. After a two-second delay, a torrent of water pours from the ceiling, drenching nearly half of the birds and sending them to the stone floor soaking wet. I have a few seconds before they will be dry enough to fly again.

I search the remaining birds and find the key. Once the key is in sight, I use Cloud Burst and rocket in the direction of the hummingbird. With most of the birds on the floor below, there is less confusion and debris and I am able to snag the tiny bird around the body with a quick movement. Falling to the floor, I remove the key from the bird's neck and release him back into the air.

The soaking wet birds are beginning to regain their senses and I can see they are mad as hell. I have no intention of letting them attack me before I make it to the chest. I cast Mud Pits on the floor, slowing their rise, and run towards the glittering chest. The key slides in perfectly and I turn it to the right. With a click, the lock falls open and I lift the lid.

A gust of wind fills the cavern and the next thing I know, the birds are being sucked into the chest in a swirling vortex. Several try to fight the pull of its magic, but they are no match. One by one, they all disappear back inside.

The lid closes with a thud and rattles briefly before reopening. This time, a bright white glow emanates from whatever is inside and an angelic hum fills the cavern.

Congratulations! You have completed the quest "Retrieve the Pearl of Monteluna." Reward: Increased alliance with the Menehune.

Footsteps slosh in the wet cavern behind me and a firm hand grips me on the shoulder.

"You did it, Esil. Take a look inside."

I do as Benji instructs. The light from inside the chest is blinding at first, but then it slowly fades until I can make out the outline of a pearl the size of my fist. Its milky white essence is flawless, a true wonder.

"Isn't she beautiful?" he asks.

I can't deny it. There is something special about the stone that sits before me. It has an almost calming quality to it.

"What does it do?" I ask.

Benji reaches into the chest and removes the pearl. As soon as he touches it, a soft glow, almost holy, radiates from his skin.

"It gives me the power to heal."

That's cool and all, but I've seen people heal before. Aleesia has a healing spell. This was a lot of work for a simple healing stone.

He must sense my suspicion, because his eyes cut at me, almost in anger.

"Look, you got your pearl, no need to be angry." But it's too late. Whatever I did has sent Benji over the edge.

He carves a spell into the air and pulls his arms back to his chest, forming a ball of energy. It grows rapidly, and he unleashes it in my direction. The fiery ball soars towards me and I attempt to dodge out of the way, but it hits me in the ribs, draining my health and tossing me back towards the jellyfish. I bounce into one of them and the shock from its tentacles immobilizes me. My vision is dark red and my health drains even more, down to fifty percent. I'm unable to move as Benji slowly walks over to me, for once hulking over my paralyzed body.

This is why you don't do quests with strangers. Because they will use you, abuse you, and then probably laugh about it later.

"Fine, then, you little dwarf, get it over with."

A comical grin flashes across Benji's face as he leans over me, his hands glowing white. Anger flares inside of me for being so stupid. For trusting someone I barely knew.

Benji places his hands on my chest and suddenly, my vision returns to normal. My health bar shoots up and I'm able to move freely.

It all makes sense now.

"You, asshole!" I shout. "You could have at least told me you were wanting to show your new ability so I didn't think you had betrayed me."

Benji roars with laughter. "You should have seen the look on your face. Priceless!" He clutches his stomach, his large eyes brimming with tears. Once he regains his composure, he speaks again. "The cooldown is very long, but once every ten minutes, I can fully heal an ally. The Pearl of Monteluna will be the difference between success and failure on many quests from now on."

He pulls the pearl out and holds it like it like a newborn child, like it is the most precious thing he has ever touched. Perhaps it is.

"I owe you a great debt for your help today. If ever you need a healer, reach out to me and I will be there."

After tucking the pearl away again, Benji grabs me by the wrist. There is a loud pop and we are surrounded by black smoke. When the smoke clears, I am back outside the mountain, standing next to Fenrir.

The small Menehune is nowhere to be found.

After such an exciting adventure, I spend the rest of the day in the countryside of the Mortican Mountains, farming the countryside, until Aleesia is free from work. We talk about our days. I tell her about the adventure with Benji and she tells me how excited everyone is to have me back in the game. I'm pretty excited myself, though I am worried about what happened to Carter. I sure hope he is okay.

We race across the plains and I am struck by the beauty of Aleesia's dark elf. Before the Developer's Tournament, she was a high-elf with pale skin, blue eyes, blonde hair and a calming demeanor. But during the last task, she used a powerful spell to help me through the stage. The side-effect of the spell changed her race to a dark elf permanently.

It turned her ivory skin to charcoal, her blue eyes red, and her blonde hair black. Even still, she managed to keep the calmness that drew me to her in the first place. She hasn't streamed much since the tournament. I think working on the full-immersion programming has been more than enough entertainment for her.

I only stream for an hour a day myself, performing the minimal content I agreed to when I signed the contract that allowed me to move out of The Boxes and into a one-bedroom apartment in Civic City so that I could focus on the tournament full-time. There are still several months left on my contract, so I have to stream for so many hours a week until its terms are completed. It's not that bad, honestly. I have developed quite a following and for once, I seem to be getting more love than hate mail.

Not that I need the money from streaming now. After finding out that I was not just an orphan, but the lost son of Howard Allen, famous developer for Pangea Online, Benjamin has worked to make sure that I never need to work again if I don't want to. I have a stake in the company and will be set up for life once all the paperwork goes through over the course of a few months.

I'm heir to more money than I could ever imagine, more money than I could ever use. Maybe once it's mine, I can do some good with it.

Aleesia and I get off our mounts and journey up the side of one of the mountains, battling orcs and goblins. My followers tune in, commenting on my play and begging me to stream more. It's mindless leveling, but it keeps my fans happy for the hour we spend together each night. Once the hour is up, Aleesia and I log out and go back to my apartment, where we share dinner. I make us pasta with vegetables. One of the things I've enjoyed about my new life the most is learning how to cook.

"It's the most amazing thing I have seen," she begins, taking a bite. "Usually, we input our programming and then the game runs its course, making every decision based on the rules we have constructed. This is different, though. The AI, it is actually creating its own set of rules and basing them around what you do. It has created new rules since you left. It's like it read your mind and has tailored the game towards you. I can't even begin to imagine what will happen once more players are added. The possibilities—"

The buzz of the intercom cuts her off. Someone is trying to contact me.

"Yes," I answer. There is only one person who would message me through my apartment's intercom at this hour. Benjamin.

"Great. I'm glad you're there. There has been a new development with the in-game world for the full-immersion unit. We need you down here now."

CHAPTER SEVEN

"What do you mean 'new development'?" Aleesia asks as we walk into the lab.

Benjamin stands next to the full-immersion unit while Marty prepares the equipment. Benjamin's eyes are focused on a tablet, but he looks up when we approach. It looks like I might be going back in. Several other technicians scurry around the room or sit in the control room, monitoring screens.

"The AI has modified our code with some of its own." His eyes glow with excitement. "Nothing out of the ordinary, but it has taken out some of the fail-safes and added in an element of what looks like time compression."

"Time compression? But programmers have been trying to crack that for years. How? And can we manually overwrite the new data?" Aleesia scrunches her face at the news.

"We could, but I'm interested to see how this plays out. We've been testing the formula for time compression for hours now and it all seems to add up. Time in the video game goes by almost three times faster. For every three hours in game, only an hour of Earth time passes. This in itself could change the future of gaming. Hell, the world."

"So what do you need me for?" I ask. This is all fascinating, but it's way over my paygrade. There's no way they would send me in to test out something that a computer created. Would they?

"I want you to log in. You'll be the first person to ever experience time compression. Don't you want to know what that is like?"

It would be cool, but... "Is it safe?"

"We've run the numbers over and over. It all lines up. If we wait, there is no telling what might happen in-game. It's already been six hours since you logged out. That means almost a full day has passed since you set things in motion."

Aleesia takes my hand in hers. "Benjamin, I know we wanted to have Esil log in at least every twenty-four hours, but this is day one. Do you really think his body is ready for so much so soon? We don't even know the effects time compression could have on the mind, not to mention his body." At least someone is concerned about my safety.

"Our doctors are on hand. If anything seems out of the ordinary, we'll pull you right out. Our initial estimates for in-game time were cautious. We wanted to play it safe, but this is too good of an opportunity to miss. It's not everyday that an artificial intelligence starts making its own decisions. Of course, nothing happens without your approval, Esil. Just know that we do have other players in waiting who would do anything to be in your shoes."

The threat isn't lost on me. If I don't go into the game, then I'm out of the alpha testing.

The doctor checks my vitals and then Marty suits me up.

"Good luck," he whispers as I submerge into the warm gel.

I close my eyes and when I reopen them, I'm slouched in the corner of an alley. Has my avatar been here the entire time or does it disappear when I log out? I still wear the same oversized tunic and pants I stole from the scarecrow. A rat squeaks and scurries into a crate nearby. A tiny health bar hovers over its head. The tag disappears after a second and then only returns when I focus on the animal. That must be one of the changes the AI has made. It feels good to have a little familiarity of a gameworld to remind me that this isn't real.

The stench of whatever is inside the crate makes me gag. It smells like a nice combination of rotten eggs and vomit. The joys of full immersion. I take a deep breath, gathering myself while I go over the course of events that happened earlier in the day. Carter was stabbed and I took him to the healer. She transformed into a disgusting hag and began injecting Carter with some black magical liquid. That was the last thing I saw before being pulled from the game.

If Benjamin is right and nearly eighteen hours have passed since I was here, then that means Carter could be anywhere, dead or alive. My best bet is to check at the healer's building where I left him. The black cottage with a white handprint on the door is seared in my mind. If he's not there, at least maybe it will give me a clue as to where to go next. It's my fault he was hurt in the first place. If I hadn't convinced him to challenge those bandits, he never would have been impaled. I owe it to him to find out what's happened.

At the end of the alley, I notice the streets are nearly empty. All is quiet except for a few soldiers who seem to be patrolling. The click of their boots on the cobbled streets echoes through the otherwise silence. The sun is low in the east. It couldn't have risen more than an hour ago by its positioning. I logged in just at the beginning of a new day it seems.

I keep behind the wall, only peeking one eye around the corner, when a prompt flashes across my vision.

Increased Sneaking. *When the cats are away, the mice will play.*

Well, that's cool. I wonder if that was a change Benjamin made or the AI? Either way, it's nice to see when I level up and increase my skills.

Two guards meet in the middle of the courtyard and I strain to listen. They both wear leather armor and carry spears. Dull helmets cover their heads. Whoever they are, they aren't the kingsguard. More than likely, they were commoners who joined the military for steady pay and a bit of adventure.

Increased Eavesdropping. *Someone is a sneaky little rat, aren't we?*

Is the AI taunting me? I listen harder and the muffled voices of the guards become clearer.

"Go ahead and ring the bell. If it was up to me, I'd leave the whole town locked up and toss away the key, but Jacob says the scum are free to move about during the day until we get this mess sorted. A little bit of black magic is enough to burn the whole town to the ground if you ask me. But I guess he doesn't want another Harbor's Edge on his hands. The commonfolk almost went into a revolt when that happened. Not that I wouldn't mind poking a few if it came to that." He laughs, stabbing his spear through the air. The other soldier turns to leave and a few moments later, a loud ring echoes through the streets. It doesn't take long before the sounds of doors and shutters opening and the click of hooves on stone welcomes the town to bustling life.

The only thing missing is conversation or the bickering of barter in the market. Suspicion radiates from everyone who passes, and the only talk comes in the form of hushed whispers. Dozens of townspeople fill the streets and their health bars flash in front of me before disappearing. If I focus on a particular person, it reappears. There are no names or other indicators of who they are.

I lock eyes with a young red-haired man and decide to ask him for answers. He wears a patched-up coat that's frayed and tattered along the edges.

"Excuse me, sir." He hesitates for a moment, his feet shuffling as he looks at something in the distance. When I step in front of him, he resignedly comes to a stop.

"Yes?"

"What's going on here?" I ask. The confused look on his face forces me to elaborate. "I just came into town this morning. What's going on with everyone?"

His eyes widen when he responds. "If I were you, I'd turn right back around this instant. This town is cursed. There are rumors of black magic and a dead man was said to be walking the streets last night. I hear they have him locked away in the town dungeon. If I had the money, I'd be gone myself." He looks me up and down and stares for a moment at my bare feet. "Though judging by the look of you, I'd say you're in the same state as me. Best be keeping to yourself or you might find yourself in the dungeon as well. Townsfolk love to blame outsiders for their problems." He nods and hurries down the street.

Black magic and zombies. This isn't the same world I entered this morning when a farmwoman chased me off her property with a skillet. Bandits were the worst problem then. Things have definitely gotten darker. Did I cause all of this?

I step in line with the crowd, trying my best not to arouse suspicion, and follow my way through town to the black cottage where I left Carter. Along the way, I overhear several conversations. The townspeople are scared. They all speculate on the source of the magic and tell tales of a town called Harbor's Edge that was burnt to the ground several years back over the fear of black magic. They are terrified of it happening to Carolton. The fear is palpable. It's in the very air.

The black cottage appears around the corner and I find a safe spot to hide and observe between a leather shop and blacksmith. The white handprint on the door seems brighter than earlier. Or perhaps the house is that much darker. The building calls to me from across the street. Is Carter still inside or is he the zombie that was captured last night? I sit back and watch for a moment, curious to see if anyone comes or goes. The last thing I want is to be caught by surprise. If what the townspeople say is true, then the healer has to be responsible for the black magic.

I wait in the alley for what feels like half an hour before the door opens. The young girl who directed me to the healer when I first entered town exits carrying a basket. She wears the same dull blue tunic as earlier. Was this all a setup? Did she know what the healer was going to do to Carter? Another prompt flashes across my vision.

Increased Patience. *Sometimes, it's better to be smart than lucky.*

Ha! Talk about being rewarded for doing nothing.

I follow the young woman down the street, careful not to be seen. Along the way, I am prompted twice with increased sneaking notifications. I don't know how they affect my character, but it feels like I'm lighter on my feet by the time she comes to a stop.

Two guards stand sentry over an entrance that leads to an underground tunnel which I assume is the town dungeon. She says something to them and they cross their spears, preventing her passage. She waves her hand, almost imperceptibly, at her waist and just as quickly, they uncross their spears and allow her to pass.

Did she just use magic?

Increased Magical Awareness. *You now have increased intuition when it comes to spotting magical abilities. Your view of the world will never be the same.*

That's interesting. Did I just discover a hidden society? Based on people's reaction to the rumors of black magic, it's a taboo subject. Does that mean that people believe in magic, but not dark magic? Or is it all a mythical subject that people fear but never see? I'm sure I'm about to find out.

Once the woman disappears past the guards, I make my approach.

"Halt!" shouts a guard.

"The dungeon is off limits," says the other.

"I'm with the girl you just let pass," I say, hoping I can ride her coattails into the dungeon, but the two guards look at each other, confused, before taking a defensive stance and pointing both spears in my direction.

"No one has passed into the dungeons and if you don't step back, you'll find yourself on the pointy end of my spear!" The wooden spear with a steel tip dances inches from my face.

They don't remember her passing. She must have wiped their mind somehow.

I back away, hands raised in submission.

"My mistake," I say, and disappear into the crowd before the soldiers have more to say. The last thing I want to do is make a scene.

I wait for what feels like forever for the young woman to exit the dungeon. My magical awareness increases again when I watch her lull the guards into a momentary slumber so she can sneak by. Once she is out of their sight, they shake their heads as if trying to rid something from their mind.

The woman weaves through the crowd with haste and I do my best to keep up. She turns a corner and when I make it there, she is gone. Using the nearby steps for a better view, I scan the streets for her blue tunic to no avail.

Dammit! I lost her. Looks like I'm heading back to the healer's building. No doubt that is where she was going to begin with.

This time, I walk more leisurely, taking in the town. A calico cat sits in the window of a nearby house and mews at me as I walk past. All of the buildings are so close together, with the occasional alleyway that passes through. It reminds of The Boxes in a way, except these people are free to come and go as they please. I'm admiring a pie through the window of a bakery when I suddenly can't move.

Warning! You have been immobilized.

I struggle to move my body, but it's like I'm frozen in place. My eyes still move, but without the ability to turn my head, my vision is scarce.

"Who are you and why were you following me?" a woman's warm voice brushes against my ear.

So much for increased sneaking.

"My name's Esil. I want to know what you did with my

friend," I say it as defiantly as I can. "You led us into a trap. Your healer, she used black magic on him!"

The woman laughs. "Black magic! Ha. You commoners, so quick to label anything you don't understand as evil. Follow me and I'll show you your black magic."

My legs give out and I fall to the ground. My body was not prepared to hold itself up after she removed whatever spell had me frozen. The woman passes by, not checking to see if I am okay. Jumping to my feet, I follow closely, careful not to lose her again. She comes to a stop outside of the black cottage, its white hand burning brighter than ever.

She knocks three times and the door opens. The inside looks the same as before. Dozens of candles sway in the darkness, casting eerie light against vials of long-dead creatures suspended in an amber liquid. And at a table, drinking tea, sits Carter.

He looks up at me and his eyes burn a brilliant orange.

CHAPTER EIGHT

"Esil!" Carter shouts at me, his eyes burning like hot coals. He knocks the table in his haste to see me, spilling tea from his cup and causing a black cat to leap from the floor to a nearby curtain. The cat hisses at me and scurries out of the room. The stench of sulfur and burning herbs assaults my nose.

Aside from Carter's eyes, everything about him looks fine. He's definitely not a zombie. At least as far as I can tell. The health bar over his head is full and green. It actually goes past the limits of a normal health bar and turns yellow. Does he have some kind of buff? His name also appears over his HP. Maybe the system only gives you details once you discover them.

Carter stands in front of me, his eyes like molten lava, and I can't for the life of me look away. He grabs me by the shoulders, firm and strong, his farmer's strength still intact.

"What happened to you?" I ask. It's been almost a full day since we last saw one another.

"Me? What happened to you? You bring me here and

then you disappear for an entire day. Priscilla said you were in the room and then the next minute, you just disappeared."

"Well, I, uh, I can explain that. Who is Priscilla?" I turn to the woman I followed here, but she just shakes her head.

"That would be me," a voice calls from the other room. It's airy and light, full of warmth and caring. It doesn't fit with the macabre surroundings. This room is dark, the only light coming from several candles and lanterns that hang from the ceiling. All of the windows are covered in thick curtains that block out the daylight. "I am Priscilla, master of potions and healer for Carolton. Though some just call me the ancient one." The woman who had transformed into the old hag appears in the doorway. Her health bar glows yellow, just like the end of Carter's. She wears the same white dress I first saw her in and her face has returned to the beautiful young woman that initially greeted me. Gone are the warts, the gray hair, the black tendrils that reached out to Carter like oily vines. Long, blonde hair hangs down her shoulders, shaping a glowing face.

"You are not from here," she continues. "Not from this plane of existence, correct?"

I nod, not knowing what else to say. I'm not even sure what would happen if I told them the truth. That their entire existence is a plaything for another world. In Pangea, the NPCs would laugh it off with a comment about how I've had too much to drink. Here, I'm not so sure. Where everything feels so real and the AI reacts to every choice I make, I don't know what kind of effects that would cause.

"Something called you back when you were here

earlier. It was easy to see if you have my true sight. I have been here since the beginning and I have seen much come and go across the kingdom. But I have yet to see someone who can truly disappear, not only from sight, but from existence. Not until you."

That's all fine and dandy, but I have my own questions. "What did you do to Carter? Why are his eyes glowing like that, and why is there a zombie in the town dungeon?"

"You brought him here to be healed. I saved his life the only way I knew how. Magic. His eyes will continue to glow until the magic that saved his life has left him. Until that time, a little of what resides in me will reside in him. And as far as the zombie goes, that is not my doing." Her eyes fall on the woman I followed here. "Kindra?"

"What? He's not a zombie. Geez." She stares daggers in my direction. "Not that you could convince those idiots out there otherwise. I was practicing my mind magic on one of the stable boys. He tried to fight it off and fell in a heaping pile of horse shit. What was left is that half of his brain was pretty much useless for the next few hours, so he went around stumbling through town looking and smelling like the dead. He's fine now, though."

"How do you know?" I ask.

"I paid him a visit. He has no memories we ever met," she says with a smirk.

Kindra has the abilities to influence the minds of other NPCs. I wonder if her abilities work on real people. If they would work on me. I mean, she did immobilize me, but was that mental or physical? I hope to never find out. That makes me wonder if I am the only one who can see health bars and status updates. I suspect so, otherwise, the townspeople would have known right away that the stable boy wasn't a zombie.

I'm suddenly aware I've been staring at Kindra far too long and look away.

"How are you feeling?" I ask Carter.

He lifts his shirt and shows me the area where the pitchfork impaled him. Three scars line his shoulder, but the wounds look as if they happened ages ago.

"I feel good. Better than good actually. I feel powerful. Not strong, per se, but like there is an energy in me that could do great things if I knew how to direct it. Priscilla offered to teach me, but I turned down the offer. If what she says is true and that this power will slowly fade over time, I don't know if it is something I would cherish or always long for. For me, it's best if I go back to my life as a farmer without knowing the mysteries of the world."

Carter is a wise man, if a little cowardly. If I had the opportunity to learn magic, I would take it in a heartbeat, even if it was only for a little bit of time. It's not every day that you have the opportunity to experience things that are truly great.

"You have more resolve than I do. I think you can never know too much," I say.

"Perhaps, but I find it hard to mourn a life you have never lived. So for me, the veil remains." He sits back with a smile.

"There are always things that are better left unknown," says Priscilla. She enters the room fully and places an arm on Carter's shoulder. "I gave him the option to know more and he chose what is right for him. I imagine it would not be easy to tend a field knowing you once had the power to magically care for it. Or drive a carriage after being able to communicate with animals."

Carter's glowing eyes widen at the last two sentences. This must be new information to him.

"Wait, you mean there is magic for tending crops and communicating with animals? I thought it was all fireballs and healing spells."

Kindra scoffs in the corner.

"My dear," says Priscilla, "there is magic for almost anything. Sure, fire and healing both play a part, but there are also, earth, water, air, and many other elements that have their own magic. Even the mind." She nods at Kindra.

"Does the world know?" I ask.

"What, about magic? Certain circles know more than others, but even the commoners know that it exists, even if they fear it. Long ago, there was the Age of Mages, where magic ruled above all else. This was back before the world was split, leaving us with The Broken Lands. Magic had a role in everything from politics to farming, and there were a great many mages who grew to be very powerful." She takes a seat and motions for me to do the same. "Society flourished. People lived a lot better than they do now. But power often corrupts. Mages grew distrusting of one another and what started as dissent eventually turned into all-out war. Many of the greatest magical minds of all time were wiped out, and then the non-magical who inherited power had their names and feats erased from the history books."

"Wow, that's terrible."

"Terrible?" objects Kindra. "It's a crime against the nature of the universe."

Priscilla continues, "There are still some who practice magic throughout the kingdom, but we do so in secret and to our own ends. Those who use magic fear the common people just as much as the common people fear magic. Well, those of us who are smart do." She looks at Kindra, but Kindra doesn't acknowledge the jab. "The days of widespread magic use are gone, I fear."

"Priscilla, I've heard a lot of talk about black magic today, but Kindra says it doesn't exist. Is this true? Can you help me better understand how magic works in your world?"

She sighs and rubs her fingers over her eyes. In that moment, her age shows, even though her appearance doesn't. It's a movement that has been done a million times in moments of quiet desperation.

"Black magic exists, but not in the way the commoners fear. It is very rare and is usually done in isolation. It is a corruption of one's own soul more than anything else, and more complex than I could begin to explain. What the commoners fear is the unknown. That there is something out there with power they cannot understand and have no answer for. So they ascribe all magic to black magic.

"I'm sure deep down, they know that some of what I do is magic. But I cover up every spell with a useless ingredient I recommend them to take once a day for a week. I don't attempt to bring people back from the dead and I don't normally save those who can't be saved. The exception being your friend here. It is hard to hide the glowing eyes, after all. Most spells don't have that effect. It's only because my essence invaded his body that he is alive."

"Why him then? Why break your own rules for someone you don't know?"

"Hmmm, it's hard to say. When you both entered my doorway, I knew that you needed my help. I had a feeling in my very being that the two of you would have a part to play in the coming days."

If I had to guess, I would bet that the AI influenced her decision. I try to clear my head for a moment. To remember that this is a game just like any other. There will be quests and battles and alliances before it is all said and done. Somehow, it feels like more than that. These people feel like they live and breathe just like me. They have histories and thoughts. Priscilla has a history that goes back before this world was ever created. How is that possible?

"Excuse me, Priscilla," says Carter, rubbing his hands together. "I think I've changed my mind. I want to learn magic while I can."

"Are you sure?" she asks.

"I am. I've always wanted to be the best farmer I can be. I have no desire to battle monsters with magic, but if it allows me to cultivate and grow, then I am intrigued."

"Very well. Follow me." She stands and we follow her.

Priscilla leads us deeper into the cottage, past the room where she saved Carter's life, through a room filled with of a variety of herbs where a miniature ball of light hovers above them, radiating heat. We pass into another room that is completely empty except for a chair and a lantern.

"This is where I come to think and relive days of long ago," she says. "Have a seat."

Carter and I take a seat on the floor. Kindra didn't follow us.

"First, there are a few things you should know about magic. Most mages only specialize in one type of magic. Though they may expand and diverge and combine multiple elements, there is only one true element at the heart of their magic. For me, that is not the case. I don't know how I was blessed with such gifts, but I am able to master more than one element. Over the eons, I have used my gifts to give many, like

Carter, a chance at experiencing magic with their own minds and bodies."

"Does that mean I can use multiple branches of magic as well?" asks Carter.

"It does, but your abilities will be limited to your own experiences. The connection between mind and magic is great and the more in tune you become with your own element, the greater that magic will become. So let us begin. Carter, I want you to close your eyes and think of fire. Imagine burning coals, a fireplace, a small fire that heats your stove for dinner."

Carter closes his eyes. His eyelids glow from his fiery eyes beneath them.

"Can you see it?" she asks.

"I can."

"Now, reach out to the fire in your mind. Take it in your hands. Don't worry, it won't burn you. Take the fire and hold it. Feel the energy within you, push that energy towards the fire."

A low groan escapes Carter's lips. Suddenly, a spark ignites in the air above his outstretched palms. It crackles a few times before exploding into a small flame.

"Oh!" he exclaims, realizing that he's holding a flame in his hands. "I did this? I did this!"

The fire disappears as quickly as it came.

"Remember that feeling. You can apply it to anything."

For the next hour, Carter conjures fire from his mind, makes water jump from one cup to another, and cuts himself just so he can make the skin heal and regrow. These would be party tricks in most games, but here, it feels like such an achievement. Here, magic isn't unlocked by picking up a spell-book, it is created in the mind. The stronger the mind, the stronger the spell.

Once Carter has mastered the basics of magic, Priscilla takes us back into the room filled with herbs. The glowing ball of light draws my attention. It's amazing how it simply hovers in the air like a miniature sun. When I reach out to touch it, the hotter it becomes until I feel a slight burn on my skin from its heat.

"I think this is where you will be truly glad of your choice," she tells Carter. "Your progress is only limited by your imagination."

Carter strolls between the plants, running his fingers along their leaves. He treats them with reverence. For him, plants have been his livelihood. It makes sense he would feel connected to them. He stops in front of a tiny, dark green plant. Its leaves are prickly with a waxy coating. He lifts the clay pot and examines its contents.

"I've never seen this plant before," he says.

"Devil's Breath," says Priscilla. "Its leaves are extremely poisonous when eaten, but it makes the most beautiful flowers when it blooms. The flowers have special properties used in several potions."

"Wait, I thought you said your potions were fake," I chime in.

She laughs. "Only if they are a ruse to cover my magic. I make real potions, and I also sell herbs and spices for potion-making on the side. It has become a hobby of mine."

I turn back to Carter, who stares intently at the plant before him. I focus on the plant and a translucent scroll pops up in my vision.

Devil's Breath. Plant. *Poisonous leaves frighten many from using this magical herb, but the rare flower it produces is a key ingredient in many euphoria potions.*

Congratulations! You have learned the skill

Analyze. *Any time you focus on an item within your skill level, information about it will appear in your field of view.*

That's super cool. It feels like the AI is already changing the layout of prompts based on what I prefer.

Using my new analyze skill, I search the room, learning about various plants.

Mock Rose. Plant. *The leaves of this deadly plant curl into the shape of a rose. The red underside of the leaves lures many hapless insects to their death.*

Drowsy Parsley. Plant. *A cousin of the traditional herb, drowsy parsley must be handled with care. A touch is all it takes to send one to slumber.*

Carter closes his eyes and the Devil's Breath begins to shake. Its prickly leaves twinge and unfold, growing in size. A tiny bud blossoms from the center and unravels, displaying a sky-blue flower in the shape of a cone.

A smile sweeps across Carter's face.

He picks up another plant and I focus on it to reveal its name.

Crawling Woundwort. Plant. *This plant is capable of removing itself from the earth and replanting in a different location. Its medicinal properties aid in the treatment of wounds.*

Carter pulls the plant from its planter and holds it by the stem. It is long and thin with tiny purple flowers that protrude from the side. Two long leaves stick out like arms and the roots move back and forth like dozens of tiny legs dangling in the air. Carter places the woundwort on the ground and it begins running around the room.

It hides behind a planter, poking its flowered head around the side to watch us.

"It's like a whole world I never knew about," he says. "There is so much more than carrots and potatoes."

"The world is a magical place for those who open their eyes," says Priscilla.

"Do these plants exist everywhere, right beneath our noses?" asks Carter.

"They do, though it takes magical intuition to be able to recognize them for what they are. Most people see what they want to see, and the magical properties are hidden from them."

I notice Carter focusing on a vine that winds up the wall. He closes his eyes for a moment and the vine begins to unclasp from the wall, winding through the air like a snake. It strikes and stops inches from his face. He winks at me, one bright orange eye disappearing, and then the vine strikes fast at my hand, wrapping its tendrils around my arm.

"I—I feel the power of this vine. It could break through your skin, maybe more if I wanted it to." He takes a deep breath. "How can I ever go back?" he asks, and the vine releases me.

This is way too real. An NPC contemplating how his life will be affected by knowing about the use of magic. I wouldn't be surprised if this new AI had the ability to give its characters depression, anxiety, anger even. Not just simulated versions, but the real thing.

Maybe I can help, but first, I need to know more about the history of this world.

"Priscilla, how did the early mages get their power?"

She smiles as if she knows what I'm thinking.

"Some were born with the gift. Some acquired it."

"For those who acquired it, how did they do it?" If I can find out how magic is bestowed, then maybe I can find a way for Carter to learn it for real.

"Most of it has been lost to the ages. As I said before, magic is not often the topic of conversation anymore."

"But what if someone wanted to learn it? How would they begin?"

Her smile vanishes and is replaced by a stern look. For a brief moment, I can see the hag that hides underneath the beautiful face the world sees. Just as quickly, it is gone.

"How would they begin?" she echoes. "With a quest."

CHAPTER NINE

Carter wears a cowl that hangs low over his face. An attempt to obscure his bright orange eyes until we are able to make it out of town.

"Just keep your head low and let me do the talking," I say. Not that talking has ever been my strong suit, but I'll hopefully cut to the chase and get us through the gate.

Getting past the guards will be the hardest part. After all the rumors going around, they will be very skeptical of someone hiding their face in broad daylight. We have no other options, though. Priscilla gave us a crude map of where to go. It's a long journey on foot, but if we make it, she says that is where Carter can learn magic.

Once she gave me the map, it appeared as a translucent icon in the lower corner of my vision. It only becomes readable when I focus on it. Another one of the AI's improvements. This world is beginning to feel a lot more like a game as time passes.

Still, I question what the AI's intentions are. Benjamin wanted the most realistic user experience of all time. For there to be almost no discernible difference between game and reality, but with the AI in complete control now, what are its end goals? Is it possible for an artificial intelligence to be completely benevolent, or is it now subject to the same mood swings as the men and women who created it? Right now, it feels like it is putting me on course for something. But what?

The guards focus on us as we approach. They stand sentry before the gate, spears crossed over one another, blocking our passage.

"What's your business?" asks one.

"We are heading home after selling our goods." The guards don't move, intent on keeping us inside.

"Did you sell your wagon as well? I remember you brought your friend in here bleeding yesterday. Is that him?" He uncrosses his spear and points it at Carter. "He was looking pretty rough yesterday. Seems to be walking fine today. That's awfully strange if you ask me. Remove the hood."

Shit.

"I don't think that is such a good idea. He's not feeling very well. It's best if he keeps his eyes shaded," I argue. If Carter removes his hood, then the game is up. Every soldier in Carolton will be here to lock us away. Or worse.

"I said remove the hood." He raises his voice and a few townspeople turn to look.

The other soldier reaches for the blowhorn hanging from his neck, intent on setting the alarm. It's inches from his lips and I'm about to turn and run when both men go slack. Their heads go limp, falling forward like they went to sleep, and they drop their spears.

"Don't just stand there. Get a move on," says Kindra. She stands behind Carter, a pack slung over her shoulder and one hand extended towards the two guards. "There's not as much going on in this town as people like to think. I'm ready for some real adventure."

She guides the stumbling bodies of both men to the side of the gate, propping their spears in the corner. We sneak through, closing the gate behind us. We're lucky she showed up when she did. If not, I'd probably be in the dungeon right now.

"Thanks for your help," I say.

"Let's get a move on," she replies, ignoring what I said. Kindra has a pack of supplies over her shoulder. She is dressed for a journey and wears a gray tunic with khaki pants and has her long brown hair pulled up into a messy bun. A long knife is strapped to her belt, but she carries no other weapons. Now that I think about it, we didn't pack any weapons either. Not that Kindra needs them with her mind magic. I wonder how often she can use it? If there are things like mana caps or energy limits that effect how much someone can use magic? I would ask, but her face is set in a permanent scowl and she's not the most approach-able human I have ever met.

She reminds me a lot of Grayson, actually. Distant and cold. I bet she's stubborn as hell too. Which reminds me, it's been a while since I've checked in on Grayson. I need to see how he is doing next time I log out. We've only spoken a handful of times since the tournament ended. Buzz fills me in on the details whenever we hang out, since they both still work in the mines together. It makes me feel bad knowing that I'm testing out this groundbreaking technology and they are still spending eight hours a day working in a digital mineshaft. Life is unfair in so many ways.

Have I become so distant that I no longer remember what life was like in The Boxes? With as much money as

Pangea makes, there has to be better ways to help the poor than hiding them away in the slums. Deep down, I know it is all for their public image. They don't really care about the lives of those in The Boxes. With no real source of income other than what Pangea provides, no one has ever had the chance to better their lives. Not until I came along and got lucky. Luck, it seems, is even harder to come by when you're poor.

"Hey, snap out of it," says Kindra. "Are we going or not?"

I push my thoughts of The Boxes away and focus on the task at hand.

"Yeah, let's go." I look at the map Priscilla drew for us. There is a circle where the town is. A river runs across the map a little ways out, and far against the edge is a mountain with an X on it. There is a forest and a field, with a small mark indicated in the center of the field. She was very secretive about it, but insisted we should stop by on our journey. It's not the most detailed map, but it looks like it is drawn to scale so it shouldn't be too difficult finding our way if we stick to the markers. "It looks like we should head that way." I point to a distant mountain.

"How are you feeling?" I ask Carter. The yellow portion of his health bar has grown smaller. I can only assume that it is the amount of whatever magical energy he still has in his body from Priscilla.

"I feel fine. The energy within me is fading. Not terribly fast, but I can feel a difference." He sits his pack on the ground and opens the drawstring at the top. "Can you two keep a secret?" he asks.

We both nod and he reaches in his pack, pulling out the Crawling Woundwort from Priscilla's. The creature's root-like legs move swiftly along the ground and its purple flowers sway in the breeze.

"I brought us a traveling companion." Carter smiles like a child on Christmas as the small plant, no more than a foot tall, scuttles along the dirt road. It zooms back and forth before coming to a stop behind Carter's legs.

"You shouldn't have done that," says Kindra, stone-faced.

"He wanted to come. Besides, look how cute he is." Carter bends down to one knee and the woundwort crawls into his arms.

"Does he have a name?" I ask.

"Florian. It means flower. I think it suits him just fine."

"Well, Florian, are you ready for an adventure?" I ask.

In response, the tiny plant creature leaps from Carter's arms and flutters like a leaf to the earth. Several purple flower petals detach and soar through the air behind him. A fragrant aroma fills the air. When he touches down, Florian takes the lead, turning his flower petal head back every so often to make sure we are keeping up.

We walk in silence along the dirt road for what feels like hours. Kindra keeps to her boorish ways, and I can tell Carter is deep inside his own head. The only real company I have at the moment is a walking plant with more personality than the both of them combined.

As if sensing my internal monologue, Kindra falls in step with me.

"Do you worry about being pulled back to your world before your quest is over?"

I hadn't thought about that. I have no idea how long Benjamin plans to leave me in here. Certainly not longer than would be safe. Aleesia wouldn't consent to that. They said their initial timeframes were cautious. That the body could handle way more than they had planned in the alpha testing. I remember looking at the schedule, and the goal we were planning to work up to was six hours of immersion. Would they leave me in here for six hours? That's almost eighteen hours of game time with time compression. I really wish we had discussed the details before sending me in, but Benjamin was in such haste to test out what the AI had created. It was either log in or miss out entirely.

I hope you are liking what you see, Benjamin.

"It's a possibility," I say honestly.

"What's it like where you are from? Is there magic there too?" For once, her annoyed features are replaced by something else. Curiosity.

I'm not sure how much I should tell her. Would any of it come back into play with the AI?

"It's different. We are more advanced in a way. In other ways...not so much. And yeah, we have magic, but it's a different kind of magic. Magic created by men."

"I've always known there was more than this small town. More than this kingdom, even. But now to know that there are other worlds, I'd very much like to see one someday."

Too bad you'll never have the chance is what I want to tell her, but instead I say, "Maybe you will."

A smile flits across her lips and she seems to have a little more pep in her step than normal. She outpaces me, joining Florian on the road ahead as he leads the way.

"She's a nice girl," says Carter. "Tough, yes, but nice."

"I don't doubt," I say with a laugh. "You never told me, do you have family at your farm? Is there anyone waiting on you?"

"Not anymore. My parents passed several years ago and

as much as they tried, I was the only child. Only my animals wait for me. I have a donkey, a cow, chickens, and several sheep. There's an old farm dog to help scare away the foxes, too. No one will miss me. The crops might overgrow and the weeds may come in, but they can fend for themselves for a while. It's not everyday someone like me gets offered a quest to learn magic."

"I'm awfully sorry, Carter. If not for me, then you never would have gotten hurt in the first place. You'd be nice and safe working in your field."

"Don't apologize." His face is serious. "This is possibly the greatest thing to ever happen to me. I feel like for once, I might be important."

We stop for lunch in a clearing and fill our bellies with biscuits and smoked ham. The buttery glaze on the biscuits sticks to my lips and the succulent, smoky ham actually makes me feel full. It's better than anything I ever ate in The Boxes. I can even feel the cool water from the canteen as it flows down my throat. Once this technology is approved, I can imagine a whole group of people who only log in to taste different foods without gaining weight.

Florian rests on Carter's shoulder, basking in the warm daylight of the afternoon sun. After we have all eaten, we load up our packs and hit the road again. When I focus on the map in my vision and it opens, our location shows that we have covered about half the distance to the forest Priscilla marked. Based on our current walking speed, it will take more than a day to reach the mountain. What that means for my immersion, I can't begin to guess.

"Have you been to the mountain we are going to, Kindra?" I ask.

She nods. "Once, but I was very young."

"What awaits us when we arrive?" asks Carter.

"Honestly, I'm not sure. They say it is different for everyone."

"And what about when you went, do you remember what it was like?"

"Like I said, I was very young."

Kindra speeds up, leaving Carter and I to take the rear. I'm certain that she wasn't too young to remember, but what happened that she doesn't want to talk about?

A wagon approaches from ahead and we all step off the road to let it pass. Three men wearing black tunics and hoods that cover all but their eyes sit inside. Something is not right. The only people who cover their faces in the mid-day heat are those with something to hide. Carter pulls his own hood up at their approach, concealing his eyes.

The wagon slows as it passes, and I make eye contact with one of the men. Recognition dawns on his face and he whispers to the man driving the wagon. It comes to a halt and all three jump to the ground.

Health bars flash over each of the men with the word 'Bandit' in red letters. Red must mean they are enemies, not that I couldn't have figured that out by myself.

"Stand behind me," I tell Carter and Kindra. I realize how stupid that sounds considering I am the only one with no magic or weapons, but nevertheless, they fall in behind me.

The three bandits step forward with confidence. They are used to taking what they want. The bandit who recognized me was part of the group we fought yesterday. These must be his reinforcements, because they are better equipped than the bandits yesterday.

"I remember you," says the one. "You and your stupid friend tried to take us unaware yesterday. Got several of my men hurt. Well, let's see how well you handle us face to face. No one stands against the Brotherhood." He unsheathes his sword and his two partners do the same.

"Ha! Took you unaware? Is that what you tell everyone? Or is it just too embarrassing to admit that you and your men were overtaken by a guy with a frying pan?"

He's mad, which is what I wanted. Anger makes people less focused, and I hope to use that to my advantage. The first bandit lunges at me, his sword aiming for my shoulder. I lean to the side, dodging the attack, and he slashes at air.

Increased Dodge Chance.

"Not much has changed it seems," I continue to taunt him and he slashes again, this time more wildly. The blade cuts through the air, missing my nose by inches. My dodge chance increases again.

I don't really have a plan other than to hope for an opening to disarm him.

He lunges again, this time swiping back and forth. I dodge the first swing but the second grazes my arm. I let out a yell as white-hot pain surges through the spot where he cut me. Blood seeps from the wound. I've never felt something so painful inside of a game. The cut continues to throb as blood flows down my arm, doing a great job of distracting me from the problem at hand.

"Enough of this," says the second bandit. He is the biggest of the three and the one who was driving. He must be the leader. He holds two swords and when he crosses them together, the cling of metal cuts through the air. Pushing the first bandit to the side, he takes the lead. "You decided to fight the Brotherhood. For that, we are going to kill you, and then we are going to take everything you own. Surrender now and I'll make your death clean."

"I think you have it backwards," says Carter. He removes his hood, letting his eyes shine in all their glory. The audible gasp from the three bandits doesn't go unnoticed. "There might have been a time when I would have backed down and let you have your way, but no longer. I'll give you the chance to leave your weapons, take your wagon, and go. Do so and no one has to get hurt."

"You think you can intimidate the Brotherhood?" the leader asks, pointing one of his swords at Carter, but his voice isn't as authoritative as before. "Kill them."

The other two bandits rush forward, swords raised in attack. I'm no longer standing in front but have fallen back between Kindra and Carter.

Kindra, who has not spoken a word since the wagon stopped, raises her hand and one of the bandits freezes in place. His eyes continue to move furiously, though his body remains motionless.

Carter grunts beside me, then a fireball explodes from his palms. He launches it at the other bandit. The fireball flies forward, its heat distorting the air around it, and collides with the man's chest. Flames engulf him, and he falls to the ground screaming in agony.

The leader watches, awestruck. His eyes so wide that it's almost comical.

Tears flow from the eyes of the first bandit as his arms move against his will, turning his blade in on his body. He wants to scream and beg for his life, I can see it in his eyes, but he has no control. The blade slowly inches closer and closer until it cuts through the fabric of his tunic. When it pierces his skin, there is no shout of pain, only the sickening rip of flesh parting and the trickle of blood down his stomach. His eyes tell the story his mouth cannot. Once the sword is buried to the hilt and pokes through his back, the spell is done and the bandit falls to the ground.

"What is this sorcery?" shouts the leader. "B—black magic, I tell you!" He turns to run.

"Enough!" commands Kindra, silencing the man. A flick of her wrist and the man goes limp. "Here is what happened: Your wagon broke down on the journey and you were attacked by a bear. Two of your men perished in the fight and you were lucky to make it out alive. That is all."

A stupid smile replaces the terror on the man's face. "That is all," he repeats.

"Now drop your weapon and walk to Carolton," Kindra orders.

"Why say the wagon broke down?" I ask.

"Because if we are to make it to the mountain before you return to your homeland, we will need a faster way to get there. Now take their weapons, hide the bodies, and let's get on with it. Carter, I'm assuming you can drive?"

He nods while pulling one of the bodies behind a bush. We strip them of their armor and weapons. I take a short-sword and pants from the bandit who stabbed himself and the tunic from the burn victim. They fit better than my tattered clothes from the scarecrow. Once I am dressed, I notice a new icon has appeared in my vision.

Inventory. *Max capacity, 150 pounds. Current capacity, 25 lbs.*

I focus on it and my new items are visible in tiny squares. There appears to be no limit on the number of items I can carry aside from my own strength.

Item: Singed Black Tunic.

Item: Black pants.

Item: Bronze shortsword.

I also have the satchel and all of its contents visible as well.

Once the bodies are hidden, we all climb in the wagon. Three shields along with rations and a large jug of water sit inside. I take the wooden shield and add it to my inventory as well. Unlike most games, where the items in the inventory disappear when not in use, it looks like I will have to carry everything on my person if I want to have access to it. If I want to equip a two-hundred-pound shield, then I'll need to be able to hold two hundred pounds to use it. The wooden shield weighs in at twenty pounds, bringing my total item weight up to forty-five pounds.

Kindra and I settle in the back while Carter and Florian drive the carriage. The wooden frame is bumpy and uncomfortable, but at least we are making better time.

She stares into the distance, her mind elsewhere. I look forward, toward the far-off mountain where magic and who knows what else awaits.

CHAPTER TEN

"I've never killed anyone before." Carter lifts his hood and runs his hands through his shaggy brown hair. The wagon bumps along the dirt road, jostling Kindra and I in the back.

"Well, you have now," Kindra says matter-of-factly. Several strands of brown hair escape her messy bun and blow in the wind. She's sullen. I wonder if she has ever killed before. The way she took her time, slowly inserting the sword through the bandit's stomach, makes me think she has.

"It's not like we had a choice," I say. "They would have gladly killed us if we hadn't fought back. People like that, you have to stand and fight or they will never leave you alone."

He just nods and goes back to driving the wagon. Whatever he is going through, my words aren't going to change that. I just hope he can see it for what it is. Florian sits in his lap like a newborn child. Those two have developed quite the connection in such a short time.

"In your world, are there people like the Brotherhood?"

Kindra picks at the frays of her gray tunic while waiting for me to respond.

I think about it before answering. Before I started working for Pangea Online Entertainment, I thought the developers were the bad guys. A greedy corporation that kept those in The Boxes locked away, content that meeting their basic needs for survival and offering the most crude level of entertainment Pangea Online had to offer was enough so that they didn't have to think about them.

Have I become the very thing I always rebelled against? My closest friends still live in The Boxes and what have I done to help them? Sure, I won the tournament that helped save Buzz's mom's life, but I had a lot of help. What have I done since then? I've tucked myself away in a fancy apartment eating the best foods and barely think about them. Why did it take another game for me to realize all of this? I'm ashamed of my selfishness.

"There are," I say. I make a promise to myself to talk to Benjamin about my friends once I log out. "But we don't fight them with swords and magic."

"What do you fight them with then?" she asks.

"Words." The modern-day weapon of champions. But that is something I will deal with when I'm back. For now, I must focus on the task at hand—helping Carter find magic. If I'm to do that, I need to know a lot more about the world we're in. Less than two hours out and we've already been attacked by bandits. What other obstacles await us? "Exactly how big is the Brotherhood?"

"It's hard to say," Kindra replies, her eyes full of rage. "They've plagued the kingdom for as long as I can remember. From what I've heard, they aren't as big of a problem near the castle, but every town on the outskirts has dealt with them at some point."

"Why doesn't the king send his army to root them out?" I ask.

"Ha!" laughs Carter. "The king has better things to do than worry about the safety of the commoners. What matters to him are the lords who finance the armies and keep the realm protected. A little thievery here and there probably never makes it to his ears. There are even rumors that the Brotherhood works for the king. That he pays them to keep our eyes focused away from the throne. If that's the truth of it, it's been working."

"You think there's any truth to that?" I ask Kindra.

She rolls her eyes and looks outward. "People like that, they always have something up their sleeves. They don't get in that position by playing nice."

"What about Carolton? Is there a lord you report to or anything?"

"Lord Regis, but we only ever hear from him around tax time. Jacob is the one who looks after the town, though. He's a governor of sorts. I'm not the biggest fan, but Priscilla likes him, and he does the best he can with what he has."

"And the Brotherhood just come and go freely as they like? No one ever stands up to them?"

"Not until you," says Carter, his lips in a half-smile. "No, not until us."

Something in me thinks that Carter has bigger plans for his magic than simply tending crops.

"Let's hope they stay far away until this quest is over," I say.

For the next couple of hours, I let my mind wander as I lie down in the bed of the wagon. Birds chirp in nearby trees and a gentle breeze cools my skin. Clouds float by overhead and I imagine them as various creatures from Pangea. A minotaur. A gnome. A wolf.

During the tournament, Pangea was a game of life and death. Every choice I made had the fate of Buzz's mom entwined with it. Afterward, it was just a game, but this, this feels like the stakes are real again. Just like Carter could never go back to a normal life after learning magic, how can I go back to where games are just entertainment?

We hit a bump and my arm scrapes against the side of the wagon, reigniting the pain in my cut. I hiss at the sting, and both Kindra and Carter stare in my direction. The cut isn't deep, but it burns like the fires of hell.

Carter asks for Kindra to take the reins and crawls into the back with Florian.

"Let me take a look at that. I've had my fair share of injuries on the farm, so I've gotten pretty good at patching myself up."

Florian steps in front of Carter, leaning down and inspecting my arm. Using his leafy hands, he removes a petal from his head and places it in my cut. I cry out as it burns, but then just as fast, the pain is gone.

"Woundwort," says Carter. "Great for pain and it helps stop bleeding." He gently rubs the back of Florian's stem and the small creature leans into his fingertips in ecstasy the same way Fenrir does when I scratch behind his ears. "You know, it was pretty bold what you did back there. Taking the frontline against those bandits without a weapon. I hope some of your bravery rubs off on me."

"Considering my arm, it probably wasn't the smartest move. I'll need to be more careful going forward. We're a team now. I need to remember that and we can play to everyone's strengths."

"I can see the forest!" shouts Kindra.

The road before us disappears into a forest of trees so dark they are almost black. I've played enough games to know that something bad is bound to be waiting inside.

"Stop the wagon," I say.

Kindra pulls hard on the reins and the wagon comes to an abrupt halt. The horses neigh in frustration and dust fills the air like a low hanging cloud.

She eyes me warily. "What the hell was that about?"

"I think it would be smart if we came up with a game-plan before going into the forest. You know, in case something bad happens."

"I guess that's not the worst idea I've ever heard," she says.

"It wouldn't be a quest if we weren't tested. We're searching for magic, for crying out loud. Something that could very well change society as you know it. There's no way they are going to give it up for free."

"Who?" asks Carter.

The AI is what pops into my mind, but I keep that to myself. "I don't know, gods, the earth, magic itself. Whatever makes this world go around."

"Perhaps you are right. So what is your plan?" She crosses her arms in waiting.

"We should all play to our strengths. Are there limits on your mind magic, Kindra? How often you can use it? How many can you attack at once?" I ask.

"I've never pushed my magic to its limits. Minor spells, like the ones that disorient or put someone to sleep, I've used on two people at a time. They don't last long, though. Complete body control, like what happened earlier, one person is my limit. But my powers grow the more I use them. Who knows how strong they could be in the future?"

"What happens if you push yourself too hard?"

"I grow weak. Once, I passed out."

The last thing we need is one of our group passing out in the middle of a fight. It could be devastating.

"And what about you, Carter? I know your power is fading, but do you have a gauge for how much you can use?"

Carter closes his eyes. As if searching inside himself for answers.

"I believe my magic will last me for another day, perhaps more depending on how much I use. My power does not come from within, so it does not replenish in the same way as Kindra's. Once it is gone, it will be gone forever."

Which is why we need to get to that mountain before I am pulled from the game.

"Then we should conserve your power if trouble happens. Either me or Kindra will take the initiative. You only come in if we are overwhelmed. I don't know what we might encounter in this forest, but Priscilla wanted us to go through it, so there must be a reason."

Kindra shuffles uncomfortably. "I think I might know. There have always been rumors about this forest. That monsters live within its depths. No one has ever found them, so I've always thought it a story to frighten unruly children. But maybe..."

"Maybe they are real," finishes Carter.

I've seen a lot of monsters and magical creatures during my time exploring Pangea. They've always felt realistic. Here, I can only imagine what they'll be like.

Carter retakes the reins and we set off toward the

forest. The trees that make it up become even darker the closer we come, until we are right at its edge and I can see that each of the leaves that make up the canopy are black. Each leaf looks like the footprint of some reptilian monster, with three prongs extending from the stem. The leaves aren't dead, just black. I've never seen anything like them. Using my analyze skill, I focus on the tree.

Cursed Oak. Tree. *The oak was once considered the greatest of all trees. Its hard wood was used for everything from furniture to housing to barrels for wine and whiskey. That is until the dryad Hermia fell in love with one of the most powerful mages, Lorence. Lorence spurned her advances, and Hermia, knowing his love for fine, aged wines, cursed the oak with wood so soft it would always leak. Or so the legend goes...*

Talk about a history lesson. I wonder if there is any truth to the story.

"Do either of you believe in dryads?" I ask.

The wagon enters the forest and it's like we're suddenly traveling at twilight. Only scant amounts of light break through the trees in ribbons. The undergrowth smells of must and decaying leaves, and the air feels thick against my skin.

"I've never seen one or heard of anyone seeing one," says Carter. "Still, it doesn't mean they don't exist. I didn't believe in magic before yesterday."

His response makes me think. I remember learning about mythology in school. It was pretty commonly accepted that it was all made up, but what if the stories were real? What if the gods and monsters were real, but disappeared just like magic had here?

Kindra disrupts my wild thoughts. "Perhaps some-where in the world, they exist. If you can come here from another world, why not things like that?"

It's not quite the same. I wish I could be open with them. I've never been the type to keep secrets, but I know for a fact that this isn't real. It's all numbers and commands in a computer, and I was sent here to see how it all works. To what end, I'm not sure.

We travel through the dark forest and it is eerily quiet. No insects, no bird calls, just the mush of the wagon wheels through the soft earth and the occasional crunch in the depths of the woods.

There's not much to see, so I close my eyes and listen like Benji taught me in the mountain. The sounds amplify. I can hear the soil give way to the wheels and compact. Kindra's slow and steady breaths. The rustle of Florian's leaves. A twig crunching.

I open my eyes and a prompt flashes across my vision.

Increased Hearing.

Closing my eyes again, I expand my hearing farther. Leaves rustle against the wind overhead. A bird lands on a branch and just as quickly flies away. Dead leaves crunch in the depths underneath someone's foot.

We're being followed.

I open my eyes in a panic and scan our surroundings, but it's too dark to make out anything in the depths. I tap Carter and Kindra both on the shoulder.

"We're being followed," I whisper.

"How do you know?" asks Kindra, her eyes searching the twilight.

"I heard footsteps."

"I'll use my mind magic to scan the area. If anyone is out there, I'll be able to feel the presence of their mind."

She goes still, placing both hands on her temples as we continue to make our way through the forest. After a minute, her hands fall to her sides.

"No one is there. Your ears must have been playing tricks on you."

"Uhm," says Carter. "I wouldn't be so sure about that."

About fifty yards ahead, a green-skinned woman blocks our path. Vines wrap down her arms and several branches protrude from her shoulders and back. Moss covers her chest and drapes down her legs like a dress. Her long emerald hair is dotted with crimson flowers and the black leaves of the cursed oak.

Dryad. Ancient Being. *Keepers of the forest. These primordial beings are averse to fire, taking double damage. Immune to psychic abilities and take half-damage from psionic attacks.*

"It doesn't make any sense," says Kindra. "How did I not find her?"

"She's a dryad. Your mind powers won't work on her."

"How do you know?" she asks.

"Just trust me." It makes sense to me that a magical creature could be immune to such attacks.

A brown stag appears behind the dryad, its long antlers pointed forward menacingly. It paws at the ground before charging at us.

Without thinking, I grab my shortsword and shield and leap from the wagon. The soft earth cushions my landing and I plant my feet in the ground, taking a defensive stance. With my shield pressed forward and my sword pointed down behind me, I brace for the impact of the deer barreling in my direction.

The stag lowers his antlers as it collides with my wooden shield, splintering it down the middle and tossing me to the side like I'm nothing more than a ragdoll. I smash into a tree and the impact knocks the breath out of me. Stars dot my vision. My entire body screams at me to get up, but I'm unable to move. I can hear Kindra and Carter yelling, but all I can do is lie against the cold ground. The moist earth does little to cool the burning my body feels.

I gasp for air, each breath more painful than the last. Never in my life have I felt such pain. My shoulder that held the shield throbs, telling me how stupid I was to try and block a stag that weighs probably three times as much as me. I attempt to stand so that I can help my friends, but my legs buckle and I slump back against the tree trunk that robbed me of my breath only moments before.

Kindra and Carter both stand in the wagon bed as the stag turns and charges again. This time, it collides with the wagon with a sickening thud. The wagon holds, but wood splinters off and rains down. The stag doesn't give up, though. It lodges it antlers underneath the wagon and begins to jostle it back and forth. Kindra and Carter both drop to their knees and hold on the edge.

My legs finally stop shaking and I am able to stand. My sword is buried in the ground nearby so I grab it and do my best to sneak around behind the stag. My legs are still wobbly, but if I can approach without being seen, I can stab the creature in the neck before anyone else is hurt.

The stag continues to rattle the wagon, its antlers grating against the wood. Kindra makes eye contact with me and shakes her head, telling me to back off. I'm so close that I elect to continue.

Planting its hooves in the ground, the stag pushes, lifting one side of the wagon in the air, and I make my move. Just as I am feet away from plunging my sword into its neck, roots spring from the ground and halt my movement. The roots squeeze tight around my legs, cutting off my circulation. I try to chop at them with my sword, but for every root I cut, two more replace it.

The stag releases the wagon and turns on me. Its eyes glow green. The same green as the dryad. She is controlling it with her mind. It paws at the ground and charges. This time, I have no shield to protect me. I lift my sword, knowing full well I'm about to be in a lot of pain. The stag stops mid-run and falls to the ground.

Atop the wagon, Kindra has her hands pressed to her temples just before she falls down with a gasp. I don't know how she did it, but she stopped the stag.

A scream lashes out from down the path. The dryad waves her arms furiously in our direction. Florian stands on Carter's shoulders and waves his leafy arms back at her in response.

"Fire!" I yell to Carter while continuing to cut through the roots strangling my feet, remembering the notes on the dryad when I analyzed her. "Fire deals double damage to dryads!"

He takes the reins in his hands and snaps them hard. The horses bolt toward the dryad and just as quickly come to a stop, throwing Carter and Florian from the wagon. Vines crawl out from the woods, intertwining with the wooden spokes of the wheels and bringing the wagon to a halt. Carter lands on the ground with a groan. The dryad motions with her hands and the vines clench harder, cracking the spokes of the wooden wheels. If we make it through this, the wagon is finished.

Vines circle around Carter, but keep their distance. It's then that I notice a fireball cupped in each hand.

"You picked the wrong day," I hear him say.

The dryad snarls.

"Long before the mages, humans rooted us out. It is

now our turn to retake what is ours," says the dryad. Her voice is charming, full of life, but also bitterness.

"And what is that?" he asks.

"Everything."

Suddenly, a tree sprouts up through the wagon, splitting it in half. The tree rises through the air, its trunk widening as limbs and branches shoot off into the canopy. Kindra's body is tossed to the ground, quickly covered by vines.

"No!" screams Carter. The flames in his hands grow and the dryad steps back, her eyes wide.

Carter walks toward her with purpose, his flames growing with each step. The vines retreat at his march, and even the trees seem to lean away. The air shimmers around him, heat distorting the world.

"Go back to wherever it is you came from!" he yells, tossing a fireball at the dryad. It ignites her like kindling. Her anguished cries sound above the crackle of the fire and the roots that hold me in place instantly wither.

The dryad stumbles back and forth for a moment, screams of agony echoing off the trees before she falls to the ground.

I rush to Kindra's side, who is just opening her eyes, and check her over. The vines don't seem to have broken skin.

"What the hell just happened?" she asks, looking around at the mayhem.

"We just battled a magical creature." It looks like the AI isn't wasting any time on shaking things up. "And I think we won."

When Carter joins us, the yellow part of his health bar is almost completely gone. Florian walks along the ground next to him. Carter picks up one of the swords that were tossed from the wagon when the tree sprouted.

"How are you feeling, girl?" Kindra gives him a weak smile. He feels the weight of the sword in his hand. "Guess it's time I get better with this thing."

CHAPTER ELEVEN

W e continue the rest of our journey through the forest on foot. Shadows move in the twilight, but whatever hides in them, they leave us be. For now, at least. No doubt they witnessed our battle with the dryad and are wary to test us. I prefer to keep it that way. Carter played the part of the seasoned mage well, but his magic is nearly gone.

This is espccially troublesome considering how much farther we still have to go.

"No one has ever talked about seeing magical creatures?" I ask.

"Aside from the town crazies, no one believes they exist. They are the things of myths and legends."

"Well, it sure as hell looks like they exist now." The AI isn't wasting any time. If it has put dryads in the forest, then I'm certain there will be more creatures popping up around the world. The programming evolves based on every decision I make, and I chose to engage with magical creatures.

"Could be they were hiding out of sight the last thousand years. It's kind of strange, don't you think, that they show up right around the same time you do?" Kindra arches a brow at me, but she doesn't press the subject.

"Strange, indeed," I say.

Sunlight breaks through in the distance, showcasing the edge of the forest. I'm glad we made it through in one piece. Too bad the wagon wasn't so lucky. My shoulder still aches and I feel tired, but aside from that, I'm good. I can feel my wounds healing and Stamina regenerate at a far greater rate than in the real world. However, Kindra's energy has returned much faster than my own. We've made it through two battles so far. Kindra and Carter have pulled most of the weight, but I don't let that deter me. At some point, I'm sure my skills from the other games I've played will come into effect here. So far, though, it's been the lack of pain in other games that has led to me charging in head-first into battles when I should have been more hesitant.

For someone who has spent most of his life with nothing, patience is not my virtue.

After spending the last few hours in the dense twilight of the forest, my eyes are blinded by the sun once we exit. After my eyes adjust and the blinding whiteness recedes, I'm surprised that there is still plenty of daylight left.

Florian, who was looking a little wilty in the darkness, immediately perks up. His leafy appendages and flower petals fill with life once again.

"How much farther?" asks Carter.

I pull up the map Priscilla drew and find our location. A large field stretches between us and the base of the mountain. There is a dot marked in the middle of the field, but I have no clue what it means and Priscilla was content on keeping her thoughts to herself.

"We're about halfway there, but considering our wagon was destroyed, it's going to take a lot longer for us to get there." I honestly doubt we'll make it to the mountain before I'm pulled out.

"Then we'll just have to walk faster," says Carter. A wide smile stretches across his face as he increases his pace.

A near-death experience with a magical creature not mentioned seriously for a thousand years and he seems to be more upbeat than ever. Is it the prospect of magic that has his spirits lifted, the newly-changed world, or could it be something else entirely?

"You heard the man," says Kindra. She slaps me on the backside with the flat edge of a sword and joins Carter.

I have no choice but to push through my stiff muscles and join them.

The trail takes us through a beautiful field with sunflowers and wheat that stretches for miles. Birds tweet and bugs rattle. We pass long stretches of wildflowers so fragrant that I could lay down beside them and take a nap. The flat plains turn to rolling hills and the mountain in the distance grows taller.

Then I hear a loud buzzing.

The buzzing continues to grow as we approach the nearest hill. When we reach the crest, the source of the noise becomes clear. Several dozen small, humanoid, winged creatures with pale blue skin fly through the air, attacking a group of travelers. The creatures aren't bigger than the size of a kitten, but they fly with great speed, biting and pinching the man, woman, and young child that are huddled underneath their wagon.

The woman struggles against two of the creatures as they try to rip a bag from her hands. The man huddles over the child, using his back as a shield. Some of the creatures toss rocks at him.

"We need to help them," I say. I'm already off and running before Kindra or Carter have a chance to respond.

I analyze the creatures while I run.

Fairy. Considered by many to be the most annoying of all magical creatures. These flighty, angry, self-righteous buggers will use whatever trickery they can to accomplish their goals. i.e. thievery. **Bonus effect: Fairy dust.** *This magical substance can have many uses, depending on the fairy, but the most common lures foes to sleep, often resulting in waking up with empty pockets.*

"They're fairies!" I shout over my shoulder. "Don't breathe any of their fairy dust and we should be okay."

My legs burn as I hustle down the hillside. Aches and pains shoot through my body, reminding me that this world is unlike any game I've ever played. Hours later and I'm still sore from our fight with the dryad. I take my sword in one hand and use the other to hold a piece of cloth over my mouth and nose, since I broke my shield fighting the stag.

"Ha!" laughs Carter. "Fairies! This keeps getting better and better. What do we do?"

At the bottom of the hill, some of the fairies notice us. Their eyes slant with suspicion and their long, bony fingers point in our direction. They mumble amongst themselves and then dart towards us.

"You swat them!" I say as the first one attacks. His tiny claws reach for me, but I use the flat side of my sword and swing for its head. Splat! It lands with a soft thud, sits up for a moment, dazed, and then passes out in the grass. I hit another with a quick twist of my wrist, stopping it right before it sinks its razor-sharp teeth into my nose. It stumbles around like a drunk for a moment before puking into a patch of wildflowers.

Another zigs and zags in front of me. It tosses a shiny powder in my direction, but I hold the piece of cloth closer to my face. I swing and miss, then feel a sharp pain in my calf. When I turn, the little devil is biting into my leg like it's a piece of meat. I kick my leg out and the tiny fairy falls off, my blood still staining its teeth.

Beside me, Carter has caught on to my style and uses the flat side of his sword like a swatter as well. Kindra uses her mind magic, causing several to fall right out of the sky. Their small size must mean she can use her abilities on more than one of them at a time.

A fairy tosses his dust from high overhead and it rains down like pink snow. Carter has his cowl wrapped over his nose, but Kindra has nothing to cover her face with. She focuses on the fairy and it falls from the sky, but it's too late. She breathes in its fairy dust and her eyes glaze over. I'm unable to help as her knees buckle and she joins the fairy in slumber on the grass.

There's no time to try and wake her, so Carter and I push on.

We make our way towards the wagon, where the travelers are still engaged in their own battle with the fairies.

One fairy pulls the woman's red hair while two others try to wrestle the bag from her hands. Whatever is inside, she is fighting tooth and nail to keep it. I can hear her cursing the closer we approach.

"Bloody buggers! Let go of me purse or I'll give you something you won't soon forget!"

She swings her head back hard, smashing the fairy pulling her hair against the wagon's underside. It lets go and tumbles to the ground and she presses her knee against its tiny body.

Her red hair matches her fiery personality. I'm admiring the grit it must take to fight off a creature they thought were only imaginary when I suddenly realize where I know the woman from. I woke up in her barn and she hit me with a frying pan. Why the hell is she all the way out here?

Only a dozen or so fairies remain once we are at the wagon. Carter rushes at the fairy throwing rocks and punts it like a ball high into the air. It's unconscious before it even hits the ground. He has ditched the flat-side approach I'm using and is now slicing at the fairies, separating limbs and leaving a bloody trail in his wake. His eyes glow far less than they did this morning, but there is a hint of a smile on his face. He might have been born for a life of adventure. Florian sits atop his shoulder, cheering him on. For such a cute flower, he certainly has a demented side.

I take position beside the woman and knock out both fairies trying to rob her with a single blow. It only takes a few more minutes to finish off the rest of the bunch as they try and confuse us to no avail.

My arm throbs when I finally put the sword to rest.

The woman holds her bag close to her chest when she emerges and rushes to the man and child. The child is fast asleep in the man's arms.

"Is she okay?" asks the woman. She presses her ear against the little girl's chest.

"I don't know. Those creatures, they put something on her and she fell right asleep," says the man.

"Oh no, my poor baby. My poor, poor baby." Desperation coats her voice.

"She'll be fine. It's just a little bit of fairy dust," I say. "It should wear off soon." Behind me, Carter helps Kindra to her feet. "She was hit with the same thing. I suspect it had more of an effect on the child because she is smaller."

"Fairies. I wouldn't believe it if I hadn't seen them with my own eyes," says the man. He wears the same type of straw farmer's hat Carter wore the first day we met. A long, straggly blond beard falls to his chest. His voice is dry and husky like he's parched for water.

"Wait." The woman's eyes widen. "I know you. You were sleeping in my barn!" I don't know if it's excitement or accusation in her voice.

"Yes, I'm terribly sorry about that. It was a bit out of my control."

"Be that as it may, you saved our lives here. I don't know how we could repay you."

"No repayment necessary. We're on a bit of adventure and we couldn't let those fairies rob you. Say, what was it they were after anyways?"

"We were just on our way back from selling crops. This bag has all of our coin. I've heard bad things about Carolton. Figured it was safer to sell in Bloomingdale, but it seems whatever is happening is happening everywhere."

"What do you mean?" asks Kindra. The glaze has faded from her eyes and she looks alert once again.

"Sightings of strange creatures all across the land."

Kindra, Carter, and I exchange glances.

"We've had our run-in with one already," I say. "I'd be careful going forward. If what I believe is true, then this isn't the last you've seen of strange creatures."

"We appreciate your help, but if there is nothing we can help you with then we must get going. I'd like to make it home before sunset. I don't want to be caught out here in the dark," says the man.

"Safe travels. And stay out of the forest."

The little girl begins to stir in his arms.

"Pretty flower," she says, pointing at Florian.

"Only the brave or foolish travel through the forest, we'll be taking the outskirts. Farewell, and good luck on your adventure."

They load up their wagon with items the fairies tossed aside and set off back towards Carolton. What they said about strange creatures worries me. It's only been a day and now they are showing up all across the map.

The sun reflects off something in the grass, catching my eye near where the wagon had been parked.

Upon closer inspection, I realize there are several glass vials, each filled with what looks like colored sand.

Fairy Dust. Item. *A small amount helps with a good night's sleep. More can knock a foe unconscious for hours.*

"What is that?" asks Kindra, leaning over my shoulder.

"Fairy dust. The same stuff that put you to sleep."

"Ooh, I bet Priscilla would love that for her potions." She picks up the bottle and examines it. "How do you know so much about all of these weird creatures anyhow? It's like you know what we're dealing with just by looking at it."

How do I explain that I have an ability that allows me to analyze anything I come into contact with? We're on this journey together, so I feel like I owe them at least some sort of explanation.

"Uhm, it's kind of like you said. When I look at something, I can see things about it. Things you might not normally be able to see just by staring at it."

"Oh, so it's like true sight? Priscilla has told me about it, but apparently, it's very rare."

"Yeah, kind of like true sight." There's no point in going into detail about something she can't understand.

All in all, we find thirteen vials of fairy dust. Carter and I take two each and the rest go to Kindra. If the AI is giving out loot now, I can only imagine how that might affect the world. Will new economies spring up? Will NPCs quit their jobs and take on a lives as adventurers or will that be left to those like me who log in?

It's a strange feeling, not knowing the rules. Like I'm playing a game with someone who can change them at any time.

CHAPTER TWELVE

The sun creeps ever slower to the horizon when I pull up my map.

"We're near the spot Priscilla marked. Judging by the sun, we either have enough time to check it out or make it to the mountain base by nightfall, but I doubt we can do both."

Carter and Kindra both look to the sky as if the sun might tell them something to contradict me.

"He's right. I say we go straight to the mountain. We don't even know what it is she marked. I vote we stop by on the way back. After I have magic."

"That's assuming you even get the magic," says Kindra. I can tell Carter is wounded by the comment, but he doesn't respond. "Don't you think if Priscilla marked it on the map that she did so for a reason? There is something she wants us to find there. Something that will likely help you achieve your goal." She adds a bit of kindness on the last sentence and Carter perks up.

"You're right. She's the only reason we are doing this to begin with. Let's go."

The location is off from the main road we are following, so we have to make our own path through the field and flowers. It's tough work that requires a sort of march not to get our legs caught, but the fragrant aroma of so many flowers makes it worth it. It's amazing that this game can give me glimpses of things I've never had in real life.

We walk along in silence when I hear a ding and a translucent scroll pops up in the left of my vision. I focus on it and the scroll unrolls. It's a message.

Esil,

We're pulling you out in thirty minutes. That gives you almost two hours of game time. Get to the location and tell your friends to camp there for the night. I'll explain more later.

-Aleesia

I almost forgot that they could contact me if needed. There's no way for me to respond, though. What if I was in the middle of a battle and couldn't leave? Would they just pull me out anyway?

I focus back on the world to find Kindra and Carter staring at me.

"Sometimes, I swear it's like you are looking at things that only you can see," says Kindra.

I can only imagine how I must look, eyes focused on something no one else can see, almost in a trance.

"We have about two hours before I'm pulled from the g—uhm, to my world," I correct myself. "Once we make it to the location, you should camp for the night until I return."

We all walk a little faster, not knowing exactly how

long it will take to get there. I still don't know if there is a way for me to bind anywhere or if my body respawns randomly when I log back in.

A herd of bison passes through the field up ahead. We hide in the high grass and let them pass. Not long after, a centaur wielding a bow traces their tracks.

"This is too much," says Carter as he stares after the centaur. He sports a grin that says just the opposite.

For miles, we don't pass any semblance of civilization. The vastness of this world is astounding. I wonder if, in time, it will evolve like the real world, with settlements spreading, the advent of technology growing and multiplying the population, or will it stay much like the Mortican Mountains of Pangea, grounded in its own era?

"Is that it?" asks Carter. He points at a brown speck in the distance.

We are almost at the spot on the map, so it must be. I squint and a tiny shack comes into view.

Increased Eyesight.

The walls look like they might fall down with a stiff breeze. It's not much to look at. Three windows stained with age, a rickety door with cracked wood around the doorknob, and a roof that looks like it might cave in at any moment, but there is something endearing about a dilapidated building in the midst of such beautiful nature.

A rusty lock hangs from a latch on the door, blocking our entry.

"Anyone know how to pick a lock?" I ask.

They both shake their heads, so I take my sword and place it between the latch and the lock and pry with all my might. The wood creaks in opposition, but the lock eventually gives and falls to the ground.

"You know, I probably could have just melted it off

with magic," says Carter. "It's funny, all this power and I still think to do things the old-fashioned way."

"Probably for the best considering how much you have left in you," I say.

Inside, the room is empty except for two clay pots and a worn leather trunk.

"So this is what Priscilla had us come all the way out here for?" I ask no one in particular.

Standing over the trunk, it takes me back to the mines. Back to when I found the legendary Developer's Chest that changed my life forever. It's easy to forget the past, considering how good the present is, but it's the past that made me who I am. It allows me to be thankful for the position I'm in and never take anything for granted. It also reminds me that what you have and where you live aren't the most important things in life. The most important things are people and friendships.

"Who wants to do the honors?"

"You go ahead," says Kindra. "I feel like you're the reason we are here in the first place."

I unhook the latch and flip the lid.

There's no burst of light. No chimes or mystical music. Just the click of the lid as it falls to rest behind the trunk.

Whatever is inside has been here for a long time. Spiderwebs form a thick layer and I shiver as I wipe them to the side and several hairy spiders scuttle into the far corners of the shack.

My hand rests on something slick and wooden. I lift it up and examine it.

Wooden bow. Weapon. *A well-made and sturdy weapon for ranged attack.*

"There's more," I say.

Reaching into the depths of the trunk, I find arrows

for the bow, a trident, and a lightweight, but durable metal shield.

The trident is silver with hints of green in the metal. It's very light to the touch. The middle prong is twice as long as the other two and hooks out on each side of the tip. Tridents were designed as a multi-headed spear for catching fish, but work just as well on enemies. The shield is bronze in color, but unlike any bronze weapon I have held before. It's lighter than I would have thought possible,

"Oooh, ooh, ooh! I want the trident!" Carter's orange eyes glow bright with excitement. "I mean, if neither of you want it. Reminds me of the pitchforks I use on the farm. I've scared off a coyote or two with my trusty pitchfork back home."

"Be my guest," says Kindra. "What about you, Esil? You want the shield or the bow?"

I weigh the pros and cons of each. While the bow is nice and would give me the ability to fight from a distance, that has never been my style. I run into things without thinking nine times out of ten, trusting my gut to carry me through.

I lift the shield and run my arm through the straps on the back. There is even a wooden handle to wrap my fist around so that the shield can be used as a blunt force weapon. Yeah, this definitely suits me.

"I'll take the shield."

Kindra takes the bow and I hand her the arrows from the floor.

"I was hoping you would say that." A wicked grin dances across her face.

"Want to practice for a bit since we have nothing else to do until you disappear?" she asks.

"Sounds good to me. A little practice never hurt anyone."

Inside of the two clay pots, I find several burlap bags filled with sand. Each bag is about the size of my head and they are the perfect size for target practice. I set a few of them up outside for Kindra to shoot at.

Carter holds his trident like a pro, twisting and stabbing at the air. At his side, Florian uses a twig as his weapon and mimics his movements.

My new shield is lighter than I would have imagined. I don't know what it is made of, but I can swing it almost as fast as my sword. In the heat of battle, a quick defense could be the difference between life and death.

After taking a few practice swings and defensive maneuvers, Carter and I settle in to watch Kindra with her bow. She sets three of the sandbags on top of a nearby tree stump and takes her aim.

"You ever shot a bow?" I ask.

"Once or twice as a child," she answers. If she doesn't know how to use it, then why did she want it so bad?

She nocks the arrow and releases. The first shot goes low and sticks into the stump with a thud.

The second misses completely.

She shoots another and another, faring no better until she has emptied her quiver and has not hit a single target. In spite of all her misses, she doesn't seem angered. I applaud her persistence.

"You know, we could switch if you wanted," I offer. Not that I think I could do much better, but I could hardly do much worse.

"It's okay," she says with a smile. "I think I'm just too close."

"I don't think that is how it works," mumbles Carter, too low for Kindra to hear.

She steps back until she is so far away that I doubt she will come within ten feet of the targets. If nothing else, she'll have all night to practice while I'm gone. I wonder, do NPCs actually need to sleep?

Kindra nocks the arrow, pointing it high into the sky, and fires. The arrow soars amongst the clouds before it arcs and dives back toward the earth. It pierces the ground, but misses the target completely.

Kindra just gives us a shrug and nocks another arrow. This time she points it straight at the target. With that trajectory, it won't even make it halfway.

She releases and the arrow flies perfectly straight. It soars like a bullet, never dipping, and pierces the sandbag. Tiny grains of sand pour out of the bag like a water spout.

Nocking another arrow, she lines it up the same way. The arrow soars across the field in perfect line with the sandbag. Just as it is about to hit, the arrow comes to an abrupt halt and hovers in the air. It vibrates menacingly before flipping one hundred and eighty degrees and soaring right back into Kindra's hand.

Taking another arrow from her quiver, she nocks two arrows and fires them both into the air. They soar, arc, and fall towards the earth. As they are about to hit, they change direction and run parallel to the ground, weaving in and out of the wildflowers like snakes. They break off and go in opposite directions, each arrow in perfect symmetry with the other.

"Holy—" starts Carter.

"I never would have thought..." She's controlling the arrows with her mind. I can't begin to comprehend all the ways to use such a skill, but it's evident that even with poor marksmanship, her ability to change the course of the arrows means she will never miss a target as long as she remains focused.

The arrows cut through the air, zigging and zagging, looping and twirling, demonstrating their own deadly dance. When they come to rest in Kindra's palms, she is visibly drained. Her face is pale and sweat beads around her temples. It must have taken a ton of mental energy for her to control those arrows.

"Did you know you could do that?" I ask

"I thought it might be possible. When I first began learning my magic, I used to push pebbles across a table. When I learned I could interact with other people's minds and influence their thoughts, I put all of the physical stuff on hold. It takes a lot out of me. Correcting an arrow to aim on target is easy. That last part though, I feel like I need a rest." She stumbles forward, and Carter is quick to catch her.

He takes Kindra by the arm and leads her to a spot in the grass where she can lie down.

"Take it easy." He gently squeezes her hand and she gives him a genuine smile. "We'll have all night to rest while Esil is gone. It's good you pushed yourself. It means next time, you will be stronger."

The sun has started to flirt with the horizon. Soon, it will be night and I can go back to the real world.

I help Carter and Kindra carry their packs into the cabin. They place their rolled-up blankets on the floor and I offer them mine as well since I won't be using it.

I'm putting the rest of my belongings in the corner when I see a glowing pink orb in the center of the room, right above Carter's head. It definitely wasn't there when we first came in. Clearly, I am the only one who notices it because they carry on like nothing is happening.

When I focus on the orb, a prompt appears in my vision.

Would you like to bind your body to this location? Y/N? Selecting a bind spot will return you to that spot upon reentering the world. Refuse to bind and your body will be randomly assigned throughout the kingdom.

I select yes and feel a little better knowing that I'll be reunited with my group once I return. It also explains how I ended up in the alley earlier today.

Carter pats me on the shoulder. "Oh, Esil, I was meaning to ask you—"

His words are cut off and everything goes black.

CHAPTER THIRTEEN

I'm pulled from the immersion capsule and my legs buckle as soon as they touch the floor. My body feels like it weighs a thousand pounds. My head spins. I've never felt so tired in my life.

"Easy there," says Marty. "Let's get you down from here and in a comfortable seat."

Everything blurs for the next few moments and stars swing through my vision like a pendulum. Seconds or minutes pass, I'm not really sure. Someone wraps me in a towel and muffled voices surround me. Two firm hands guide me along until I come to rest on a soft surface.

I can't really think so I accept the feeling and let my heavy eyelids close.

I wake up in a pristine white room. It smells clean, but not like freshly-washed clothes. More sterile than anything. The kind of smell that is nothing more than the absence of other smells. Lights flare overhead. A monitor beeps by my bedside and several receptors are attached to my chest and head.

"Oh, thank heavens you're awake!" Aleesia wraps me in a tight hug and kisses my cheek. Her black hair falls around me, sending tiny tingles through my body. Her smell reminds me of the wildflower fields. "How are you feeling?"

"Much better." The cloudiness that fogged my brain and weighed me down has left. Pressing my elbows into the mattress, I try and sit up. My body feels rejuvenated as well. "What happened?"

"The doctors just stepped out. They said your brain was processing so much that it needed a rest. It's nothing to worry about, kind of like when you work on a math problem too long and you start to feel tired. Like that, only amplified by all the stimulation this new world has to offer." She takes her finger and draws it down the side of my face, her big, brown, almond eyes radiate interest. "What was it like?"

"Amazing. It felt so real, like you and me right now. Everything. Sights, sounds, smells. It's like I was really there. I got a cut on my arm and it hurt like hell." I look down to make sure that it isn't still there. "And then game stuff started happening. I got prompts, skills, item details. I could literally feel the AI changing as I progressed. It felt like the real world suddenly became a game, not like a game that was realistic." Talking about it has me excited to return already.

"That sounds wonderful. I followed you every step of the way. I didn't even get up to pee," she says, and we both laugh.

"The craziest part was the NPCs. They behaved like

real people. I swear they had their own thoughts, not just generated lines."

There's a knock on the door and Benjamin enters. His black suit is as crisp as ever and not a hair is out of place on his head.

"Well done, Esil. Congrats on finding your first quest. It seems the AI has taken a liking to you and started adding some of your input into the game's visualization. Very well done, indeed." His blue eyes stare at me intently. "I know you are probably ready to dive right back in, but we're going to keep you out for a day or two."

"What do you mean a day or two? Carter and Kindra are waiting on me to proceed with the quest. I told them I'd be back in the morning." My heart races. I made them a promise.

"Easy, now. I know that full-immersion takes a lot out of you. I wanted you in there right away to see how the AI would change its interactions with you after becoming self-aware, but it seems that everything is progressing the same way in that regard. If we're going to keep sending you in for extended periods of time, you need your rest. Your body will adapt and your mind will become stronger the more you play, but let's just take it easy."

"But, I prom—"

"Esil, it's a game. I know the realism is like nothing you have ever experienced. It may become hard to identify distinctions between the game and reality. Everyone you met today, they aren't real. They'll be fine without you."

He doesn't understand. He didn't talk to them or look them in the eye and see that they were more than just commands in a computer. There was life behind their eyes.

"Go and stretch your legs. Eat a nice meal. Hang out

with your girlfriend. Log in and explore Pangea. You can literally do anything else but this for a day or two.”

With that, he exits the room.

“What a jerk!” I say, ripping the receptors off my chest and head. Aleesia takes me by the hand.

“It’s for the best, you know that, right? You were logged in for a long time today. I think it’s made you a little grumpy.”

She pinches me playfully on the elbow and some of my anger disappears. Maybe she’s right. Maybe I’m not thinking straight.

“Yeah, you’re probably right. Am I good to leave yet?”

Aleesia checks with the doctors and they give the okay for me to go home. They prescribe me some medicine to help me sleep. I doubt I’ll have trouble falling asleep, but they say it’s a precaution to make sure I’m well rested for my next session.

We walk home in silence. I’ve been so caught up in my experiences in the game that I didn’t even think to ask Aleesia how she is. We stop in front of my apartment and I place my hands on her cheeks. How did I not notice how tired she looks? Bags hang underneath her bloodshot eyes. She must be putting in more work than I realized.

“You sure you don’t need these more than me?” I shake the pill bottle in front of her.

“No, I’m fine.” She gives me a halfhearted smile and her eyes look to the side.

“Are you still enjoying yourself?” It feels like there is something she’s not telling me.

“Yes.” She pauses. “It’s just... I feel like there is more going on than I know about. I don’t know what, but I get the feeling that this world is more than just an add-on to Pangea. The way they monitor your brain, it’s like they are looking for something. Why else would they force you back in before knowing all they could about this new AI development? That's not safe. That's not how development teams handle themselves. I don't know. Maybe I'm just being paranoid."

"Have you said anything about it?" I ask.

"Are you kidding me? If I say something like that, I'm off the project tomorrow. I'm lucky to even be in the room. If not for my dad, I never would be. Pangea doesn't just let college kids in on their advanced research because they're good students." She wraps her hands around mine. "I'm sorry to drop all this on you after your day. Try and get some sleep. I'll see you tomorrow."

The sleeping pills knock me out the second my head touches the pillow and the next thing I know, I'm being awoken by a loud buzz.

Someone is calling me.

"Hello?" I say groggily and my in-room intercom connects the call.

"Are you just now waking up?" Amusement coats Aleesia's voice.

"What time is it?" My blinds are drawn, and the apartment is in total darkness.

"Two in the afternoon."

Wow, I must have been even more tired than I thought. I know mental stimulation is exhausting, but it might take more out of a person than physical exercise if used correctly.

"You there?" she asks.

"Yeah."

"My dad wants you to come over for dinner." There is a certain hesitation in her voice when she says it. I've been living at Pangea Headquarters for a while now and have yet to meet Aleesia's father. He's always busy with meetings and work. The first time I meet her father will be at dinner.

Shit.

With so much going on, the last thing I can think about is how to impress her father. Actually, maybe I can talk to him about doing something better for those who live in The Boxes. If he's on board, then Benjamin will have no choice but to take me seriously when I bring it up.

"Esil?"

"Uhm, yeah, sounds good. What time is dinner?"

"Six. Don't be late."

A pod comes to pick me up at five forty-five. The Pangea Headquarters Campus is sprawling. Many of the technicians, developers, and others who work for the company live here. Many of them raise their families here. I always thought it was strange that Aleesia and her family didn't.

I climb in the pod and the door slides shut behind me. A holographic map details the route to Aleesia's.

"Would you like to listen to music or any other entertainment on your journey?" a digitized voice asks me.

"Uhm, no, thanks."

The pod lifts into the air and the campus grows smaller as we fly away. It flies farther north, through mountainous terrain and acres of forests. It seems the farther we get away from The Boxes, the more beautiful the world becomes. I can't believe I spent so much of my life living locked away while this was out here. Even at the orphanage, we had no freedom, no beauty. It's so messed up that it is only available to the rich.

We begin our descent and several monstrous houses come into view. They are all so far apart. Privacy. Another luxury of the elite.

Aleesia's home is solid white except for the mirrored windows, which reflect the beauty of nature back to whoever looks upon them. A large swimming pool in the shape of a bean glistens like a diamond in the afternoon sun. There's freshly-manicured grass that surrounds the property, flower gardens and even a fountain that depicts an elf holding a bow with water squirting out of its arrow.

Most people spend their money on things like this in Pangea. I guess Aleesia's parents aren't most people.

"You have arrived."

We come to a stop in a landing spot out front of the house. Aleesia is already coming down to see me as the door to the pod unlocks and slides open.

"How was your trip?" she asks, in much better spirits than we parted the previous night.

"Wow, you look amazing." She wears a red dress that clings tightly to her body. A pearl necklace dangles from her neck. It's the first time I have ever seen her dress up. At the headquarters, she is always wearing either a button-up or a labcoat. This is a side of Aleesia I have never seen.

She blushes at my compliment.

"You're not so bad yourself." She winks.

I'm wearing a green button-up shirt and a pair of khakis, the modern-day version of my character in Pangea.

"You nervous?" she asks.

"A little. I didn't know you were so..."

"Well off?"

"Yeah." We really are from different worlds.

"Esil, this is all for show. It's my father. It's not who I am. I grew up in Pangea just like everyone else." She takes my hand. "Now, let's get this over with."

The inside is even more resplendent than the outside. Paintings larger than my body adorn the walls. Sculptures sit on tables and marbles floors reflect my face when I look down. Do people even live here?

Aleesia must know I'm overwhelmed by the grandeur of it all, because she squeezes my hand firmly. We walk down a hallway, past a dining room with a table of the finest wood I have ever seen, and into a kitchen.

A blonde woman pulls a pan from an oven. The dish steams when she places it on the counter. Her eyes are a brilliant blue.

"Mom, this is Esil. Esil, this is my mom." The two have very little in common physically. Is it possible Aleesia was adopted?

"Oh, dear, how nice to finally meet you!" She practically runs over to embrace me. A red apron hangs from her neck over a black dress. It's covered in flour and who knows what else. "I hope you like casserole," she says enthusiastically. "Cooking has become a hobby of mine. Sometimes I cook just for the fun of it and then dump the food in the waste bin."

Another squeeze from Aleesia. Throwing food away is something unheard of where I come from. People spend an entire day working to buy food and here, she can cook for fun. Is this the world I've been missing?

"Esil's had a crazy couple of days. I think we're going to go sit down at the table. Where's Dad?"

"Oh, you know. He's upstairs in his office. It was a miracle he had tonight free. He promised he'd be down for dinner."

We take a seat at the table. The water goblets are made of crystal, and the silverware is real silver. I can't help but think about how far the money spent on these items could go to help those less fortunate.

"Hey..." Aleesia looks me in the eye. "I know it's a lot. I always thought so too. I mean..." She picks up a crystal goblet. "Who needs this shit, really?"

I'm glad we're on the same page.

"Daughter." The voice is deep and resonant. When I look up, I finally see where Aleesia gets all of her looks. Her father stands behind her, dark hair, dark almond-shaped eyes. He wears a black suit, immaculate in the same way as Benjamin. Is it a requirement to wear suits once you reach a certain level at the company?

"And you must be Esil." He extends his hand and we shake. "I'm Curtis. Glad to have you join us for dinner."

"It's nice to finally meet you," I say. For whatever reason, I can't take my eyes off the man. His very presence commands respect. He's definitely not how I would picture any programmer looking.

"Likewise. I followed along with your journey through the Developer's Tournament. I didn't know if anyone would beat my son, but you did it. His pride and arrogance have cost him a great deal in life. But that is neither here nor there."

Aleesia's mother comes in carrying a casserole and places it on the table. Behind her, two women follow carrying the rest of the meal. Greens, beans, potatoes, tomatoes, and lamb are on the menu.

"Servants," I mumble under my breath and Aleesia pinches my leg. Of course she has servants.

We serve ourselves and dig in. The food is delicious, but I wouldn't have expected anything less. I've been eating very well since moving out of The Boxes and there's not a day that goes by that I'm not thankful to be eating something that doesn't come out of foil packets.

Silverware clashes with plates and there is the occasional slurp of water.

"How was your flight in? That's the newest model of pod they have. Smoothest and fastest ride around," asks Curtis.

"It was fine." I'm not sure if I'm supposed to be impressed or not. It got me from point A to point B the same as the pod I rented back in The Boxes. So what if it has a smoother ride?

"I knew your father, you know," Curtis says between bites. "He was a good man, and a very talented programmer. I was heartbroken when I heard the news."

"I've heard a lot of good stories about him." I never know what to say when people comment on my father. It has happened several times since I moved to Pangea Headquarters. I never knew the man. I've read articles on him, I've watched interviews he gave, and I have the letter he sent me on my eighteenth birthday, but aside from that, I only have a handful of memories because he died when I was so young. He sounds like a great man and I'm sure he was, but I'll never know. "How come we never see you at headquarters? Most of the programmers live there."

"Aleesia didn't tell you? I'm not a programmer anymore. I haven't been one for many years now. Of course, we all still get labeled as developers by the public, that just goes with the territory. I'm the head of the business side of things. I was a good programmer, turns out I'm a hell of a businessman."

"He's modest too," says Aleesia's mother.

"Don't you think it is more than just a business? You

have more power and more influence than any other company in the world. You could use that to do a lot of good."

"We do a lot of good. You of all people should know that. You've seen life outside The Boxes. What happens to those who don't take up our offer of working in the mines. If not for what we do, then the majority of those people would not be safe, they wouldn't be fed, and they'd probably be dying."

"Keeping someone alive isn't the same as letting them live," I argue. It's so frustrating trying to talk to people who will never understand because they haven't lived it. "They get by on nothing, while you...you drink from crystal glasses. How is that fair?" I push my seat back from the table, my appetite gone. "Thanks for dinner, but I feel it's time to go."

No one says anything, but Aleesia follows me as I walk outside.

"Well, I think that went well," she says dryly. "I especially like the part where you played it cool."

I can tell she's joking, but I'm not in the mood.

"You don't get it. You just don't, and I doubt you ever could unless you lived like I have. It's just not the same living up here in your ivory tower when people are working their lives away for nothing more than scraps."

"Ivory tower? Really?" Tears well up at the edge of her eyes. "You're being incredibly unfair. I can't help how I grew up. I didn't ask for any of this. I was born into it. And if your parents hadn't had that crash, you would have grown up the same way. So think about that for a minute before you start throwing stones."

Damn. She's right.

CHAPTER FOURTEEN

"Where do you want to go?" asks Buzz. We're hanging out in my home portal while we wait for Grayson. Buzz throws a ball across the room, sending Fenrir bolting after it, knocking over the sofa and rattling the floor with his massive stomps. Despite his size, he still behaves like a puppy at times.

Buzz has upgraded some of his armor since the last time I saw him. His dented battle helm has been replaced with a full-face helm in the shape of a wolf. The muzzle lifts up when not in battle so that his face is visible. A black cape hangs over his shoulders, covering his black tunic and red pants. With his large shield engraved with a wolf, soon people will be calling him 'Buzz the Wolf.'

"Doesn't matter to me. You're still spending a lot of time in Asgard, I see." I don't care where we go. None of these worlds hold the same luster they did before. Not after experiencing full-immersion.

"Oh yeah, I've gained a bit of reputation there. The locals seem to really like me." Fenrir brings back the ball and Buzz tosses it again. "What about you? Everything okay? You look a little worse for the wear."

"Eh, this new project I'm working on has me questioning a lot of things I believe in. Not to mention I met Aleesia's father for the first time last night. I kind of blew that."

Fenrir returns with the ball and this time, Buzz keeps it.

"What do you mean, 'blew it'?"

"Well, the short version is that I told him he was a prick for being rich." The more I've thought about it, the more I realize I was an ass. Regardless of my own personal beliefs on wealth, I was a guest in their home and practically attacked the man.

"Smooth. And how did Aleesia respond to all of this?" Buzz fakes throwing the ball, but Fenrir doesn't fall for it and pounces on Buzz instead, licking his face with laps of his massive tongue. Buzz squirms and moans until Fenrir rips the ball from his hands and takes it with him to the couch.

"She was actually very understanding in spite of it all." We talked this morning and I apologized. She said she knew I was under a lot of stress with testing and was much kinder to me than I probably deserved. Her dad knows all about the alpha testing as well, so it seems he wasn't too upset with me either.

Buzz stands up and flings drool from his arm. It droops to the floor in a long globby string.

"I still don't get how you managed to find someone like that. You're a lucky bastard, you know that?"

"Yeah, I know. How's your mom?" If not for her, then I never would have entered the Developer's Tournament and my life would definitely not be what it is today.

"She's doing great. She's started back working in the mines a little. For whatever reason, she says it's good to be doing some actual work. Personally, I'd rather not be mining my life away. Doctors are saying she will make a full recovery, though."

That's great to hear. I'm glad Buzz has finally gotten to the point where he doesn't thank me every time we talk about his mom. I know if the roles had been reversed, he would have done the same for me. Still, I plan on talking to Benjamin about how they treat those in The Boxes. I might not have Curtis's seal of approval, but I can't let it go. There has to be something that can be done.

Ding!

A notification pops up in my vision, letting me know I have a visitor. Grayson. I grant him permission to enter my home portal and he materializes in the middle of the room wearing his sexy pirate garb. A white vest hangs unbuttoned, exposing a roaring bear head tattooed on his chest. Several necklaces and amulets dangle from his neck. A belt with a revolver sits on his hip. Two golden battle gauntlets cover his hands. His mustache curls up around the edges, forming two semicircles above a full gray beard. Just like I remember.

"What took you so long?" asks Buzz. "I had to sit here and listen to Esil talk about how he can't get along with rich people."

There's nothing like old friends to put everything in perspective. They look happy enough. But then again, when I was poor, I wasn't unhappy. I just didn't know how different things could be. There were days I hated working in the mines. Days I loathed my position in life. But having a friend like Buzz always made things fun.

"Life on the other side not everything you thought it

would be? It's a different world, that's for sure." Grayson curls his mustache between his fingers. "Still, you're better off. Nothing will ever be perfect. That's part of life, you've got to take the good with the bad. Now, where are we going? Some of us have work in the morning."

"If you guys want to, I've got a quest I could use some help with," says Buzz. "But we might need a few more people."

You are now entering Asgard, one of the nine worlds of Norse mythology. This is a non-technological world. All electronics have been disabled upon entering Asgard.

Our group materializes at the entrance to Asgard. A long bridge is the only thing standing between us and the famed city of gods. The city is a massive maze of stone towers that reach into the heavens. Clouds cling close to the castle as if hiding its secrets.

"You have got to be kidding me," says Talia. "A non-technology world. I mean, you have looked at me, right? I'm wearing flubbing space armor. How did you think this would be a good idea?" She wears white battle armor made out of some futurist plastic and a white helmet that covers the entirety of her face. By the look of it, you could never tell she was a woman. A black visor on the helmet reflects the world around her. Her weapon of choice, a plasma rifle.

"Hey, you agreed to come," says Buzz, arms flailing. "You knew this is where my quest was."

"Oh, put a sock in it. I'm just giving you a hard time. Give me a second while I equip something more...primitive." She goes still for a moment as she sorts through her items.

I remember the first time I came to Asgard. It was the day I teamed up with Buzz, Grayson, Aleesia, and several of her dwarven followers. We battled our way to Tyr, the Norse God of War, and released Fenrir from his chains. It had been the first time I felt like a part of a team.

Now, I'm part of a new team. Talia and Benji join Buzz, Grayson, and I. When I asked Benji to team up with us, he was ecstatic. He didn't even ask what the quest entailed. Buzz has been very secretive about it, so none of us know what we're going up against.

"Ah, that should do it," Talia says. Her space armor disappears and is replaced with gray pants, a yellow tunic, and intricately engraved leather bracers. Her hair hangs in long dreadlocks tied together with a ribbon down her back. She carries a longbow that's as tall as she is. A small gold dagger hangs from her waist. "Judging by the looks of you all, we're gonna need some ranged attacks."

With Talia playing an archer, we've got a pretty good team composition. She is level fifty-two. Buzz is our tank with his thick shield and defensive spells. He's managed to raise his level to eighteen. Grayson, level forty-nine, is our brawler. His dual gauntlets pack a heavy punch and he moves with the speed of a boxer. Benji, level fifty-seven, has his healing spell, but also uses ranged battle magic. He probably has a few more tricks up his sleeve as well. And then there's me, at level twenty-four, jack of all trades, master of none. I have a mixture of spells and physical attacks, though I use most of my spells to set up my attacks. Does that make me a spell-sword? I don't know, but it works for me.

I call Fenrir to my side and heads turn in our direction.

It's not every day you see a wolf as tall as a human. I glance around and notice the dawn of recognition on people's faces as they realize where they know me from. Several of them talk to each other in hushed voices. A few point in our direction. That's part of the reason I quit exploring Pangea after the tournament. People recognized me everywhere I went. In Carolton, though, I was nobody again, and it felt kind of nice.

Today, I'm not going to let it bother me. I'm here to spend time with my friends and hopefully clear my mind of everything else that's been going on. For the next few hours, I'm going to enjoy myself.

"Alright, Buzz. Time's up. What's the quest?" I ask.

He smirks at me and a notification flashes across my vision.

You have been offered to help with the quest "Protect the Farm." Do you accept? Y/N

I accept, and a wall of text appears in my vision.

Your farm is under attack. Vermin and other creatures have discovered your eggs and descend upon your farm from the city sewers and surrounding areas. Stand fast, defeat them, and be rewarded. Reward: Increased structure building tree and healthy crops for one season.

A tiny green dot appears on the map in the bottom right corner of my vision. That must be where Buzz's farm is located.

Wait, what? "You have a farm?" I ask.

"Well, sorta. I was going to surprise you when it was finally upgraded better. Long story short is that I came upon some land. I'd rather not say how. The point is, I have upgraded it from just a piece of earth to a shack and now I have a coop with some chickens. In time, I hope to breed chickens big enough to mount. There's surprisingly little supply in that department. I've built my farm up twice already and it has been attacked. There's just too many vermin. I think with your help, maybe this time, I can save the farm."

"Buzz the farmer," scoffs Talia. "No wonder your kill-death ratio is so bad in other game modes."

"Talia, dear, you have wounded me." Buzz places his hand over his heart and she rolls her eyes. If I didn't know any better, I'd say they are hardcore flirting.

"What are we looking at here?" asks Grayson, cutting right to the point. He's never one to beat around the bush.

"Basically, waves of no-good vagrant sewer dwellers come and steal my hard-earned eggs. Each wave is harder than the last."

"And how many waves are there?"

"Not sure. Never made it past wave two."

"This is going to be fun!" says Benji. He bares his teeth in a wide smile.

"Thanks again for doing this," I say to Benji.

"Anything for you, my friend. If not for you, I would not have the Pearl of Monteluna."

We cross the bridge that leads to Asgard and instead of following everyone else into the city, we take a dirt trail that leads down into a valley. We don't pass many people along the way. The city is where all of the action and entertainment happens.

It doesn't take long for us to make it to Buzz's farm, if that's what it can be called. It's more like a shed with a single chicken coop. Several chickens run through the yard, clucking and pecking at the grass. I focus on the building and its stats flash before me.

Buzz's Chicken Farm.

Level 2.

HP: 2000/2000

"This is your farm?" asks Talia. She waves her hand as if putting it all on display.

"Hey, I never said it was glamorous. I used all of my money on the chickens and the coop. That's where the money is if I ever make it through this quest."

The surrounding countryside is empty of any other farms or settlements. Asgard looms over everything from the distance. Prairieland stretches out for miles and ends against a wall of forest and mountain.

"Is there a reason you're the only farm for miles?" I ask.

"I think most people give up after the first couple of times their farm is destroyed. But not me, I'm as stubborn as they come and before it's all said and done, the city won't be the only attraction in Asgard!" He pulls the muzzle of the wolf down over his face and it closes with a clank. "Now, let's get ready. It's about time for these turd-bags to show up."

"All hail the chicken king!" shouts Talia and we all laugh, even Buzz.

We all take our positions in front of the small farm. Talia and Benji take the rear, Buzz takes point, and Grayson and I flank him on each side.

I equip my elvish spear in one hand and my staff in the other. If we're fighting off a massive number of invaders, I want all the firepower I can muster.

While we wait for the first wave, I take the time to talk to Buzz about his farm. Town building has never really interested me, so I haven't looked much into it.

"How do you know when you can upgrade or what kind of upgrade paths your farm can take?" I ask.

"It's pretty simple, really. You have to learn the skill for building. Turns out there are skills for everything from crafting to cooking to fishing. Once my farm is upgraded enough, I want to specialize in breeding. I never knew there were so many ways to level up aside from killing monsters. Once you have certain skills, you're able to spot material when you're out in the wild. Wood, metal, and other resources. There are different building paths that you can choose to upgrade your property once you pick a base model. After that, you just gather and build. Sometimes there is a level cap for building, or in this case, a challenge you have to defeat. Different lands have different rules and requirements for building too. Like I said, it's simple, but it can be super complicated if you let it."

"Here we go," says Talia.

Wave 1 flashes across my vision. For the first few moments, nothing happens, but then something begins moving in the distance. Tiny little dots scatter through the grass.

"The goal is to keep them from the farmhouse. If they destroy it, the quest is over," says Buzz.

When I look at the small farmhouse, it now has an HP bar hovering over it. Alright, at least we know what we have to do.

Buzz pulls his sword, ready for battle. It's a short-sword with an engraved pommel, which makes perfect sense considering the size of his shield. He will mostly block and then attack only if he needs to. With his wolf helm and giant shield, he looks like a force to be reckoned with.

Grayson taps his gauntlets together and they begin to glow, an orange aura surrounding them. He dances from foot to foot like a boxer ready for the big fight.

Behind me, Talia has an arrow knocked and pointed in

the distance. Yellow tendrils of light wrap around the arrow like vines, continuously coiling.

Benji is the only one without a weapon drawn. A small dagger rests on his hip, but his power comes from his hands. From what I saw on our journey through the mountain, that's all he will need.

The black dots cross the path we followed here and I can finally make out what they are.

Rat. *Level 25. Rats are the plague of humanity.*

Why is it always rats? A dozen of the creatures chitter and chirp as they approach.

"What the hell?!" screams Buzz. "They aren't normally this high of a level. They must know I've got backup. Usually, the first wave is only five or six rats and they are the same level as me."

"We'll be fine. Three of us are around level fifty," says Talia. "Everyone do your job and we'll make it through this."

That's the thing I like about Talia. When the action gets going, she takes charge, boosts morale, and holds it down. She never points fingers unless it's done playfully. It will be good to have her for this.

"You heard the woman," says Grayson. He clinks his gauntlets together and charges the rats. "Hold the line!"

We all hold our positions and wait for Grayson's clash with the first wave. His fists glow orange just as he launches himself into the air. It's as if his gauntlet is pulling him forward when he collides with the first rat, killing it instantly.

The rest of the rats swarm in on him, but Grayson is already on the offensive, landing jabs and uppercuts as quickly as they appear, knocking the rats back and dropping their health in droves.

An arrow whizzes by overhead. Bright yellow tendrils snake out as it soars towards the battle ahead. The arrow lands in the earth next to Grayson. For a moment, I think Talia missed her shot, then the yellow tendrils reach out and wrap around four rats. The tendrils squeeze tightly before suddenly retracting and slamming the rats to the ground.

"You've got two seconds before they release," she yells to Grayson.

He charges his gauntlets and attacks with the same move he started the battle with, and all four rats crumble to the ground. Not wasting any time, Grayson turns to face the remaining vermin. The rats stare him down with demonic red eyes. They hiss at him, their long pointy teeth bared in anger, and they attack. Seven on one, the odds don't look favorable, so I take a few steps forward, ready to rush into battle if needed.

The rats have closed half the distance to Grayson when he raises his arms by his sides as if telling them to bring it on. In a matter of seconds, the rats will be on him. What is Grayson up to?

He brings his hands together with a vicious clap and a sonic boom echoes throughout the land. A beam of energy explodes from his gauntlets, smashing into the rats and leveling every one of them.

Wave 1 complete

Prepare for Wave 2

That was easy enough. We made it through the first wave with only Grayson and Talia getting their hands dirty.

"That was awesome!" cheers Buzz. He jumps up and down, clapping his hands. "You're so awesome and you don't even know it!"

I swear I see the edge of Grayson's lips twitch when he returns to us.

"Thanks for the arrow," he says to Talia.

"Don't mention it. Nice awareness for the follow-up. The spell is called Arrow of Truth. It binds the four closest enemies and pulls them toward its center for two seconds."

Grayson takes a mana potion and settles in beside Buzz once again.

Wave 2

Buzz lifts his shield and walks past us to the other side of the farm facing the woods.

"This time, they come from the woods. If we make it through this, I have no idea what comes next."

It doesn't take long before I see several orange, furry animals trotting in our direction.

Fox. *Level 27. Sly and fast, these creatures can match wits with the best of them.*

The rats weren't that difficult, but I have a feeling these foxes will be. Foxes are quick and agile. If they are able to sneak past us, they could destroy the farmhouse without us even knowing.

The closer they get, the more their swift movements becomes apparent. Grayson charges out, using his gauntlet launch, but the fox evades his punch. The critters scatter to both sides of us.

Talia hits one with a speeding arrow and it tumbles through the grass. Grayson follows up with a hard uppercut leaving one less to deal with.

"No matter what, keep them away from the farm-house," I say. It doesn't matter how many we kill if some of them make it past us.

A fox rushes at Buzz and when he tries to slash it with

his sword, the creature leaps on to his shield and pounces over his head.

"Not so fast!" I say as I cast Lunging Strike. I land on the fox at the same time it touches the ground, stunning it in place. I stab my spear into its chest and Buzz follows up with a slash of his sword. Two down.

Benji has fallen back to the farmhouse and is using his battle magic to blast away foxes as they attempt to swipe at the structure.

"We need to fall back," yells Talia. "They made it past us, now we have to defend the farm!"

The critters are fast, darting in and out of range. Hitting the farmhouse and retreating.

I focus on the building and its stats display at the side of my vision while I continue to fight.

Buzz's Chicken Farm.

Level 2.

HP: 1957/2000

It has a hefty amount of health, but that doesn't mean we can slack off when we don't know how many waves there are.

If only there was a way to slow them down.

Of course!

"Get ready to kill as many as you can!" I tell the group as I cast Mud Pits.

Mud Pits. *Cost 100 mana. Creates a field of mud pits, slowing your enemies attack, and movement speed by 50% for 20 seconds. Cooldown: 60 seconds.*

Giant pools of mud appear around the farmhouse. It's so small that they actually cover all four sides, slowing the foxes no matter where they try to attack. With half their speed gone, they are finally catchable.

Benji uses Cloud Burst to propel him from one fox to

another, punching and kicking them to defeat. Talia uses another Arrow of Truth and Grayson follows up with a gauntlet launch, killing four foxes instantly. In the twenty seconds it takes the mud to disappear, we defeat them all.

Wave 2 complete

Prepare for Wave 3

"Good job, team!" Buzz congratulates us. "Take mana potions if you've got them. I've got a feeling things are about to get hairy."

When I focus on the farmhouse, I notice it has gained a few health points, currently at 1963. It must passively regenerate over time.

"Is there any way to repair the farm?" I ask.

"I can repair it with material I have if we beat the quest, but the repair function is locked until the quest is over."

A low rumble comes from the tree line and I feel a dull quake in the earth. We all take our positions right as a stampede of horned creatures bursts from the treeline.

CHAPTER FIFTEEN

Wave 3

The ground continues to quake as a herd of golden creatures stampedes towards us.

Peryton. *Level 28. This hybrid creature combines the head and body of a stag with the wings and hindquarters of a bird.*

They charge us with fury, black antlers pointed forward for attack. Beautiful golden plumage sprouts from the peryton's back, displaying wide, powerful golden wings.

"Deer birds! Just great, we're fighting deer birds," says Buzz. He plants his shield in the earth and stretches his arms overhead.

"Don't get scared now, Buzz. The fun is just getting started," says Talia.

"I'm just limbering up!" he counters.

Several of the herd flap their wings and leap into the air.

"Talia, you're on air patrol. The rest of you, focus on the ground attack," I order.

The herd is so closely packed together that it's hard to tell how many we are up against, but there are definitely more than the last round. Everyone begins casting their buffs and charging their attacks. The fight is on.

Grayson is the first to attack. He runs out and launches into the first peryton at the same time as it attacks with a swing of its antlers. There is a violent clash and Grayson is bucked to the side, taking a hard fall and losing a good chunk of health. The peryton, on the other hand, is down by half.

Talia fires arrow after arrow at the creatures soaring overhead. Their health ticks down with each shot.

Buzz has planted his foot in the ground just as the herd reaches our location. He casts a spell and a blue aura surrounds him. Two perytons lower their antlers and collide with his shield, coming to an abrupt halt. They shake their heads in anger, but they move in slow motion. While the creatures are slowed, Buzz repeatedly stabs them in the neck with his shortsword. In the two seconds it takes for the spell to wear off, both creatures fall covered in blood.

Alright, Buzz!

The rest of the herd bypass Buzz and come charging for Benji and I. Several energy beams zoom past me and explode against different perytons. I cast Mud Pits, Haunted Earth, and Waterfall in quick succession. The mud pits slow the herd, allowing Grayson and Benji to follow up with several attacks. Roots spring up from the ground, catching one unlucky peryton mid-stride and rooting him in place. Right as the roots release, a torrent of water floods down from the sky, wiping out half of its health.

I don't waste any time jumping into the fray. Antlers clash against metal all around me and the grunts of man and animal fighting for survival fill the air. I cast Resilience on myself, increasing my attack speed, and use Lunging Strike on the closest peryton. While it's stunned, I activate Ring of Power, doubling my attack for the next thirty seconds. I kill the creature with a few strikes and move on to the next.

Alert: Buzz's Chicken Farm is under attack. Current health 1846/2000.

Two perytons have made it through and are ramming their antlers against the farmhouse.

Talia fires Arrow of Truth and both creatures are pulled back from the building and slammed against the ground, unable to move.

Benji carves a symbol into the air, his hands glowing a vibrant crimson. He uses Cloud Burst, propelling him rapidly towards the creatures. When he impacts with them, he disappears in an explosion of smoke.

When the smoke clears, both perytons are dead.

The remaining perytons, six in total, take flight.

They soar through the air, out of reach for all but Talia. She continues to pelt them with arrows, but they have grown wise and spread out their attack. Once she shoots at one, the remaining five dive for the farmhouse and attack. The farm won't last much longer if we can't stop it.

Buzz's Chicken Farm.

Level 2.

HP: 1432/2000

Benji fires his energy blasts at the creatures, but his attacks move too slow and are easily evaded. Grayson removes his gauntlets and equips his revolver, firing shots into the sky. They are accurate, but do very little damage on the whole. I equip Grappler before realizing that its beams don't work in this world.

"We need to do something fast or it's all over," I say.

Buzz stands helpless, looking at the perytons circling overhead. He has no abilities that can reach the creatures destroying his property. Forlorn, he simply shakes his head. Just like everyone else in The Boxes, he's forced to stand by, unable to fight back.

No longer.

"Talia, can you use another Arrow of Truth?" I ask.

"Yes, but it'll pull them to the arrow's location. They won't be able to move, but they'll still be in the air."

"That's all I need. Grayson, put your gauntlets back on. We're not losing the farm today."

Talia nocks the arrow and fires it toward the perytons. It' comes to a halt in the sky and yellow ropes of light reach out and grab the four closest, pulling them to its center and hovering in the air for the next two seconds.

I use Grappler's grappling ability and aim my hook at the floating mass of bird-deer. It catches one by the antlers and locks into place. I retract it and they all come barreling towards me. Dropping my weapon to the ground, I stand back and cast Haunted Earth, rooting the area where they fall, and follow up with Waterfall. In the two seconds it takes for Waterfall to take effect, Grayson pummels the creatures with his fists. I go to cast Resilience on him, but nothing happens. I'm out of mana!

Grayson is able to finish them off without my help, but that leaves two perytons left and Buzz's farm is at 1207/2000 HP.

"I'm out of mana," I say.

"Me too," says Talia.

The final two perytons are both at a quarter health, but without Talia's magical arrows, there's no stopping their attack. We can only hope to kill them before they destroy the farm.

Talia and Grayson fire their weapons at the winged creatures, sometimes hitting them, sometimes not. The lasers from Grappler don't work in this world so I am forced to sit back and watch. It takes me a moment before I realize Benji isn't attacking. I look over and see him casting a spell and then a round translucent shield surrounds him. The perytons aren't attacking him, so what in the hell is he using a shield for?

"Benji!" I shout, but he ignores me.

His hands move in front of his face as he carves his spell into the air. Clouds form beneath his feet, building in pressure. He holds the spell until his knees are hidden behind a wall of white clouds. He holds it longer and the clouds begin to turn gray, almost as if they are growing angry. Longer still and they are a dark charcoal. Small bolts of lightning crack in and out of the cloud. And then he releases.

A thunderous crack echoes around us, causing everyone to stop attacking. Even the perytons are awestruck for a moment. The Cloud Burst sends Benji soaring through the air like a bullet. His shield crashes with one of the perytons with such force that the creature's health drops instantly and it tumbles out of the sky.

The force of the impact sends Benji even higher, like a Menehune pinball ricocheting off the peryton. Clouds are already forming around his feet as he descends towards the ground once more. He doesn't hold the charge as long this time before he releases, but he doesn't have to. The Cloud Burst explodes him into the last peryton at a closer range and this time, Benji cancels his shield right after impact and carves a spell into the air. An orange blast from his hands smashes into the creature and its body goes limp.

Wave 3 complete

Prepare for Wave 4

"Dude! That was awesome!" Buzz's eyes are still wide with surprise. He runs up and gives Benji a giant bear hug, smothering the tiny man in his embrace.

"I agree. Smart thinking. Using a defensive spell as an attack." Talia pats Benji on the shoulder. "And you too, Esil. Using your grappling hook like that was a brilliant maneuver. Everyone potion up. Wave four will be here before we know it."

I use up the last of my mana potions as we wait for the next wave. The farm slowly regenerates, but currently only has 1250/2000 HP.

"Guys, whatever happens, thanks for doing this. It's been a lot of fun," says Buzz.

Buzz gave up hope in the last round. If not for smart thinking on Benji's part, then we might have lost. But that's why we have a team, to lean on each other when the going gets tough. I understand Buzz's reasoning for setting his expectations low for this next wave. It'll make it hurt less if we don't succeed, but that's not the man I know. The man who built a chicken farm in the land of gods.

"Whatever happens?" I ask. "We didn't come here to tuck our tails between our legs. We came to protect your farm! We came to make you the chicken king of Asgard!" The rest of the group echoes my sentiment with chants of "chicken king, chicken king!" and I don't know if I have ever seen Buzz smile so wide.

Buzz waves his hands through the air like a mock king addressing his people when the air suddenly grows chill.

Wave 4—Final Wave

Ice spreads along the tree line and across the grass.

"What the..." says Talia, but Buzz, Grayson, and I just look at each other. We've dealt with this before.

Three frost giants step from the woods and the trees go icy as they pass. Blue skin and icy white hair make way between the green pasture. They carry stone clubs and wear leather armor. They look far different from the ones we met in the castle. They are each level forty, so not as bad as the ones we faced last time we were in Asgard, but this time, they have companions.

Frozen Direwolf. *Level 35. Forged in an icy hell, the only thing colder than these creatures is the icy rage that dwells inside them.*

The two wolves flank the giants. Their black-blue fur is frozen in patches and frigid air blows from their nostrils. They make their approach, slow and deliberate. In a fight, we could probably take them in time. The problem is that we aren't here to fight them, we are here to defend a base. A base that is already over a third destroyed.

This is going to take everything we have.

"Everyone but Talia, move out. The giants are slow. We need to meet them in the open so we have longer to take them out," I order. "And don't forget, they are immune to slows."

Once again, Grayson leads the charge. He launches himself at the nearest giant and his fist cracks against its bearded jaw. Grayson has nine levels on the giant. It's doesn't make much of a difference, though. The attack only takes out a tenth of its health. He follows up with a quick jab, but the giant blows frigid air at Grayson, slowing his movement. The second giant counters with a hard swing of its wooden club, dropping Grayson by a tenth as well. One of the wolves sinks its fangs into Grayson's leg and drags him to the side as his health continues to drop.

I want to help Grayson, but I know he can hold his own. We need to halt the giants.

Talia and Benji are barraging the giants with ranged attacks. I wish we had Aleesia here for this. She has a far superior set of archery abilities than Talia. What we need is fire. The giants take double damage from fire.

Firestorm crosses my mind. It's the spell my father created for me before he died. It's powerful, but it will drain my mana in one use. I can only use it if the perfect opportunity presents itself.

Buzz moves into position and braces himself for the giants. Knowing that they will attack him, I use the opportunity to cast Haunted Earth right in front of Buzz's shield. It roots two of the giants in place and I cast Resilience on myself and stab as much as possible with my spear. Buzz slashes with his sword, while arrows rain down around us. Grayson is still fighting the wolf, but he's got it down to a quarter-health while he still has sixty percent of his own.

The snare wears off and a giant club smashes into Buzz, knocking him several feet away. Due to his tanky items, he only takes fifteen percent damage. I'm not so lucky.

I try to dodge the giant's swing, but it catches me in the shoulder and my vision goes red. I lose a third of my health and the frost giants stride past us.

Benji uses his new Cloud Burst/shield combo and pinballs himself against one of the giants. The giant stumbles back, losing a third of its health from the powerful attack, but the other two and the ice wolf keep moving.

I hear a loud yelp from behind me and I turn to find Grayson, covered in blood, scratches, and teeth marks, but standing over the dead direwolf. He looks terrible, but for once, he is smiling. I don't know if anyone loves the thrill of battle as much as him.

"We have to stop them!" I say.

Buzz and I crawl to our feet and Grayson joins up behind us. Benji launches himself again, this time, knocking the frost giant to the ground. I run up and use Lunging Strike on a frost giant, but it knocks me to the side with its club before I land the attack, bringing me down to just above half-health.

They are fifty yards away from the farmhouse when the direwolf takes off at a sprint, leaving the giants behind. It pounces on Talia, knocking her to the ground. It doesn't attack, though. Instead, it goes for the farm and begins pawing and biting at the structure. The HP of the farm depletes rapidly.

1143/2000

1047/2000

997/2000

Dammit! There has to be something we can do.

Fenrir! I can use his special ability. I spot him in the same place I left him, in the field to the left of the farm. His ability flashes through my mind.

Ability: Fight for my master. Fenrir is able to attack and fight alongside his owner for one minute. Cooldown: 24 hours.

Most mounts aren't allowed to fight, but his special ability limits it to once per twenty-four hours. I'm hoping it gives us the edge we need.

I focus on the ability and Fenrir jumps to his feet. He sinks his massive paws into the earth, tossing it into the air as he bolts toward the direwolf.

The direwolf continues to attack the farm. It's down to five hundred and fifty-six HP when Fenrir smashes into the direwolf's side. The icy wolf emits a loud yelp and the sound of growls and gnashing teeth surround us. Fur and dirt fly until Fenrir sinks his teeth into the beast's neck and slings it to the ground. He positions himself on top of the direwolf and doesn't release. The poor creature's health drains second by second.

Buzz, Grayson, and I are already moving in on the giants. Benji has been battling them ever since he landed and is down to a quarter-health.

"Benji, back out and heal. Let us take them on for a bit," I say.

Fenrir has killed the direwolf, so these three are all that remain. With the farmhouse being so low on health, a few hits from this group will be enough to destroy it. We can't let that happen.

"Try and split them up," says Talia.

Buzz and Grayson flank both sides and I approach from the rear. At the same time, we each attack, hoping to draw each of the giants in a different direction. I'm the only one to land a blow. Buzz and Grayson are both parried, but the giant I hit doesn't turn. Instead, it continues marching towards the farm.

"Dammit, it's not going to work. We have to stop them then. Get ready for Arrow of Truth," she says.

A moment later, the arrow pierces the chest of the center giant. The other two are pulled toward him and for two seconds, they don't move. We stab and punch and slash as much as we can, but when the time is up, the giants flail out with their clubs, knocking us all aside.

They continue their march, only twenty or so yards from the farm.

"I'm going to sacrifice myself," says Buzz. "It's the only way we stop them. My shield has an ability to stun whoever attacks it, but the cost is that I take full damage from the attack. If it's a killing blow, I will survive with one HP. If we're lucky and they attack me at the same time, it will stun them all. Then you can finish them."

He doesn't wait for us to argue, not that I would. I don't see any other way.

Buzz runs past the giants, careful to stay out of their reach, and plants himself ten yards from the farm. If this doesn't work, there won't be time to stop the frost giants before they destroy it.

The giants raise their stone clubs and swing with great power. The three clubs smash into Buzz's shield and his health drops so low I can't even see the one health point he has left. His shield does its job and freezes them all in place. It's time to go all-in. I cast Firestorm and a tiny flame ignites at the feet of the giants. It begins to grow and swirl until it becomes a raging tornado of flame. The stun releases and the giants scream in agony. One of them lifts its club and swings for Buzz.

Benji uses Cloud Burst and shoots himself into the fray, the Pearl of Monteluna glowing in his hands. He collides with Buzz seconds before the club hits and Buzz's HP bar fills completely. The club smashes into Buzz, dropping his health by half. When the fire clears, one giant remains. It's fitting that Buzz delivers the final blow.

Wave 4 complete

Congratulations! You have completed the quest "Protect the Farm!" Reward: Increased structure building and healthy crops for one season.

My experience bar goes up and a gold twenty-five flashes across my vision.

We all take a moment to catch our breath and I sort

my new stat point into Intellect. My mana pool could use a boost anyways.

Level 25:
Strength - 14
Agility - 4
Vitality - 5
Intellect - 7
Dexterity - 5
Stamina - 0

"We did it! So begins the tale of the mighty chicken king!" Buzz boasts loudly. "First round is on me."

"As much as I would love to do that, I need to get going. There's something I need to do."

"Way to be a party pooper, Esil. The rest of you are in though, right?" They all nod in agreement.

I grip each of them around the forearm in turn and thank them for the adventure. It was nice to have a moment to just get away from everything, but now, it's time I talk to Benjamin.

CHAPTER SIXTEEN

I t's a gorgeous day out. This far away from the cities, the birds actually sound louder than the drones that fly by delivering packages. That is one thing I never get tired of. To actually experience weather, even on the days when it rains and nobody wants to go outside. For me, it's a blessing. There were so many days, either at the orphanage or in my box, when all I longed for was fresh air or sun on my skin. Anything to break up the monotony of life.

A strong breeze comes through and a pile of leaves crinkle past me. There is a path that flows through Pangea Headquarters. It winds around the perimeter and through several buildings. There are enough offshoots that I could find my way anywhere just by following it. I don't have a destination in mind, so I walk aimlessly, trying to clear my head before I talk to Benjamin.

There is so much of the headquarters I haven't explored. So many buildings that I don't know what is inside.

I pass a few people along my walk. They nod or say

hello and carry on with their day. Have they ever experienced life where they had to wear a mask just to go outside? Do they know how good they have it here?

A creaking sound catches my attention and I look up to see a young girl in a swing. Her father pushes her and her pink dress flaps in the wind. Her hair soars behind her when she goes up and then clings tight to her body on the downswing. Tiny, childish giggles stop me in my tracks. One of the few memories I have as a child is of my father pushing me in a swing.

I think about my father a lot. It's hard not to when his imprint is on everything here. My mother, I think about her less. I see her face in my dreams sometimes, she has a kind face, but my father is the one they always talk about. I know it doesn't do to dwell on what might have been, but I think we would have had a great life together.

We can never go back. I know that. There's no way to tell them not to get in that car, that it's going to malfunction and crash, not only killing you both, but leaving your child an orphan to grow up without an identity in the poorest slums in the country. But honestly, even if I could, would I want to? I would never have met Buzz or Grayson or experienced The Boxes. I might not have even met Aleesia. Part of me is thankful for my past. It allows me to appreciate what I have more than most.

I'm pulled from my thoughts by loud crying and look up to see the little girl on the ground. Her father bends over her bloody knee, intensely inspecting it. She must have fallen from the swing. He lifts her in his arms and pulls her head against his shoulder, and the crying softens before they disappear down the path.

The situations drives home the fact that people get

hurt no matter what you do. That's just the way life works. The only thing I have control over is my own choices.

As I follow the trail, I come across a small bridge that crosses over a stream. The water gurgles and ripples around the smooth gray rocks underneath. Somewhere in its depths, a frog croaks. A turtle sunbathes on a log. I make a note to come here if I ever need some peace and quiet.

I lean over the bridge and stare down at my distorted reflection in the bubbling brook. I look a bit haggard, almost trollish. The water's movement gives my face lumps in strange places and it's been several days since I last shaved, not to mention I haven't even combed my hair today.

When I make my way down to the laboratory, Benjamin is in the lab working. Just as I expected. Does he spend all of his time focused on full-immersion or does he actually monitor what's happening in the rest of Pangea as well?

He sits in a chair that hovers above the ground and propels himself around the room with his feet, eyes glued to a tablet and intently focused. The whoosh of the door closing draws his attention to me.

Men wearing hard hats and blue coveralls work on both sides of the immersion capsule. They are quiet except for the occasional zip of a drill screwing something in place. Several large slabs of metal and two large clear canisters are being moved around on dollies. Are they constructing more full-immersion units?

"Esil, good to see you." He sets the tablet in his lap. "I hope your time away has been good for you. You look good, but just to be safe, we're keeping you out until tomorrow. I'm sure you'll be glad to know that the world is moving along just fine without you. Carter is very close to unlocking magic."

What?! I was supposed to be there for that. He and Kindra need my help! I want to argue for Benjamin to let me log in, but there's a reason why I'm here. I promised I would talk to him about The Boxes.

"What's with the construction?" I ask. I'm not sure how to segue into the topic, so I make idle chat first.

He stands and walks towards me.

"We're preparing to add more players to the game." He grins.

"How soon?" It seems like a rush when they've only sent me in twice. Something doesn't add up.

"Nothing is set in stone, but when the time is right, I want to have the units already in place. It'll be interesting to see how the AI reacts to more stimuli, don't you think?"

I wonder who he has in mind for the next phase of testing.

"So what brings you down here, Esil? I know it isn't my scintillating conversation and it can't be to see Aleesia because otherwise you would have already went to the viewing deck." He pauses and places his thumb and index finger on his chin. "What's up?"

My eyes wander around the lab. Past the workers and the immersion capsule and up to the viewing deck. Aleesia sits behind a screen, buried in her work. I don't know why I'm staring off. I need to just come right out and say it.

"I think—I think that what you're doing to those who live in The Boxes is wrong." Benjamin's eyes widen ever-so-slightly and I know that I have his attention. He was probably expecting me to talk about the game. Anything but this. "You treat them like animals, locking them away in units where the only interaction they have with each other is via a digital mineshaft. It's not right. They can't even explore the rest of Pangea. I mean, how screwed up is that? Not only do they not have anything in real life, they don't have anything in the game either. Would it be so hard to give them a Worldpass or do you think that that would just make things harder? But really, though, why in the hell would you build their homes in the center of a radioactive wasteland? Why not just move them somewhere safe?" I don't wait for his answer. I know that if I stop talking, I won't be able to finish, so I push through. "It seems to me like you treat them as nothing more than a PR scheme and forget the fact that they are real people. But I don't. I might have moved out, I might have found out I'm the son of a famous developer, but the truth is that I'm still a miner and I always will be."

Benjamin just stares at me for a moment. I don't know if he's shocked, speechless, or angry.

"It's a lot more complicated than just putting people in boxes, Esil. You have to know that. The part about the Worldpass, I can get behind that if you think it's a good idea. I don't know if the board will approve it, but we can try. The Boxes were built before I became president of the company. They were already in place and seemed to be working well, so I let them run their course. If not for you, I probably never would have thought about them again." He lets out a deep sigh. "I wish we could move everyone out of The Boxes, I do, but it would never pass the board. You've got to understand that when the nukes hit and major city after major city was blown apart, the world was in panic. People were dying from radiation left and right. People who couldn't afford to move or protect their homes. So we went in and built them places to live, safe places, and gave them jobs. Sure, we might have dropped the ball a bit, but if not for us, they would all be dead."

"Maybe they'd be better off," I say. I don't mean it, but I want to see his reaction.

"You can't possibly mean that. You know those people. They might not explore everything Pangea has to offer, but they live their lives in boxes just like the rest of us. They meet one another through the mines, they fall in love, they move in together and build lives. You can't possibly tell me that death is better than that. There have always been the haves and the have-nots, and that's never going to change. But it doesn't mean they can't live full lives."

The door opens from the viewing deck with a whoosh and Aleesia steps through.

"Hey, what's going on? I didn't think you were scheduled to log in today," she says. She looks so cute in her lab coat that's just a bit too big for her that it calms some of the ire I feel towards Benjamin.

"I'm not. I was talking to Benjamin."

"We were actually just finishing up," says Benjamin. "You can take a break if you want to walk Esil out." There's no room for objection in his voice. Regardless of whether or not we agree, he's still the one in charge.

Aleesia nods and joins my side. We're about to walk out into the hallway when Benjamin calls after me.

"Esil, I'll see what can be done about giving miners access to the rest of Pangea, but I can't make any promises."

"What the hell was that about?" Aleesia asks.

"I told Benjamin I didn't think it was right how they treated those in The Boxes."

Her mouth drops open.

"Are you serious? My god, Esil." She stops in her tracks. "He's the president of the company, you can't just go around telling him what to do or saying whatever pops into your mind. That's not how things work here."

I can't believe she's taking his side. "What do you want me to do? Sit down and be quiet? If not for me, nobody would know about miners. Buzz's mom would be dead. Now, I'm finally in a position where I can maybe do some good and you want me to just do my job. How is that right?"

"It's not right, but that's how it is. You can't save them all, Esil. You just can't. You're one man. Help those that you can, but you can't go around picking fights with people higher up than you."

Maybe she's right. I am just one person. An outsider in a world I never grew up in. How can I hope to change anything when I don't even know the rules these people play by? Maybe Benjamin will get them access to other parts of Pangea. That's better than nothing.

"Okay, I'm going to start by moving Buzz and his mom out of The Boxes. Grayson too if he isn't stubborn." Hopefully, I have enough power to at least do that.

"I think that's a good start. You can't change the world overnight, but you can help your friends. And I'll do anything I can to help too," she says, taking my hand and giving it a kiss. When she looks up at me, tears well up and threaten to brim over. "I wish the world was a better place."

"Me too."

CHAPTER SEVENTEEN

Two more full-immersion capsules have been constructed by the time I return to the lab the next day. They aren't filled with the gel-like nanoreceptors yet, but I don't imagine it will be long. The fact that they were constructed so fast must mean that the workers were up all night. Benjamin certainly isn't wasting any time.

"Good morning, Esil. Ready for an exciting day?" Benjamin asks me. For once, his tie is slightly askew and his eyes seem a little groggy. He's normally so put together. I wonder if the project is taking its toll on him. Whatever secrets he's keeping about the real reason behind full-immersion. I want to ask him what's going on, but after my talk with Aleesia yesterday, I think it might be best for me to keep my comments to myself for the time being.

I nod and go find Marty, who is waiting for me atop the immersion capsule. He attaches the sensors to the normal places around my chest and head, but this time, he has something new. He holds a giant needle attached to a thin tube that's filled with a pinkish liquid.

"What's that?" I ask. That's a big needle and I hope it isn't going in my body.

"It's an IV. We're testing something out today. The idea is to feed your body nutrients while you are logged in so that you don't pass out when we pull you out like last time."

Marty takes my arm in his hand. I close my eyes and a sharp pain shoots up my arm. When I open them, I try to look anywhere other than the source of the pain. My eyes find Aleesia in the viewing deck. She gives me a thumbs-up and then disappears back to her work.

My eyes open inside of the small cabin. Sunlight peeks in around the door frame and through the slats in the wall. My belongings are all placed neatly in the corner. My shield, sword, pack. Inside of my pack, I find my canteen, some vials of fairy dust, and a few pieces of sausage and bread.

Carter and Kindra are both gone, not that I expected anything less. Benjamin told me himself that Carter was close to learning magic. I wonder if he has unlocked it in the time since then.

I focus on the map that Priscilla drew for me and it pops up in my vision. I'm still a good ways off from the mountain, but I can now see two dots moving along it, one red and one green. The dots are close together and when I focus harder, the map zooms in on the location until I can see Kindra and Carter's names hovering above the dots. Beside each name it says, 'party member.' Good to know we don't disband just because I log out. Too bad we don't have party chat. Considering the state of this world, I don't think it is something that will be implemented unless there are other real-world players.

After gathering my belongings, I step out into the world. The sun momentarily blinds me and I'm greeted with the fresh scent of wildflowers. Insects buzz all around. I'm taking in the beauty of the countryside when a large shadow looms across the field. At first, I think it is a cloud. That is, until I hear the flap of large wings. They swish like billowing sails caught in a storm.

I look up and see the most fearsome creature I have ever come in contact with. It hovers in the air, the size of a house, its blue wings thrashing and sending the wildflowers rolling in tumultuous waves. Metallic scales cover the creature's neck and back. Spikes run along its spine from tail to head, where two long horns curl around its skull like a ram. Hundreds of sharp teeth hide a serpent's tongue and bright yellow eyes take in the world, but there is no fear, no hesitation.

Cerulean Dragon. *A fearsome predator of valleys and meadows, the Cerulean Dragon is one of the few dragons that dwell in nests instead of caves and make their homes high in the mountains.*

It's a mother-loving Dragon!

A family of deer bolt across the field, sensing the apex predator, but it is too late. The dragon tucks its wings and dives. Once in range, it lets out a monstrous flame that torches the deer and the flora around them. An unending stream of red and orange ignites everything in its path, and the deer fall to the ground in agony. The smell of cooked venison and burnt vegetation drifts in my direction and I find myself salivating.

The dragon lands with a thud and sinks its teeth into its freshly cooked meal. Not eager to stay for dinner, I sneak around the cabin and take off towards the mountains.

As I'm running for my life, a prompt flashes across my vision.

System alert: Greetings, Adventurer! The world has changed since you've been gone. Magic has returned to the world and magical fountains have spread across the land. Only the brave, virtuous, or cunning can unlock their potential, but beware, with great magic comes great consequences. As the arcane returns to prominence once again, so have the creatures of myth and legend. Will you fight for good or evil? For love or power? Every choice you make will lead you down a path to greatness or ruin...

What does that mean? No time to decipher it now. I don't stop running until I can no longer see the dragon in the distance. My lungs ache and a stitch forms in my side, forcing me to stop and take a breather.

Increased Stamina.

Ah, the benefits of not being eaten alive.

I wish there was a way for me to contact Carter and Kindra, but it looks like we are stuck doing things the old-fashioned way for now. I find their point on the map and plot my route in their direction. Traveling alone, I might be able to make it to the base of the mountain by nightfall if I'm lucky.

Every time I catch my breath, I take off running for as long as I can and each time, I am rewarded with increased stamina. I still don't know what it equates to, but it feels like I am able to run a little bit farther each time.

I continue this for what feels like an hour when I notice there is a new icon in the top right corner of my vision. It looks like a cutout of my body, with each part segmented. The entire thing is green at the moment, which I assume means I'm in good health. As I run farther, the legs on the icon begin to turn yellow. Once I have rested, they turn green once again.

It must be a notification system for letting me know what's been injured and my stamina, not that I couldn't tell by the realistic pain and burning in my muscles. There has to be more to it than that, so I focus on the icon and a translucent window pops across my vision.

Finally, a stat page! I can still see everything that is happening in the world behind it, so that if trouble goes down, I'll be able to spot it.

Name: Esil Allen
    Title: None
    Race: Human
    Gender: Male
    Class: N/A
    Alignment: Neutral Good
    Health: 200/200 hp
    Health Regen: 10hp/min
    Base Damage: 15
    Armor: 0
    Stamina: 87/100 (+15)
    Stamina Regen: 20/min
    Max Capacity: 150 pounds
    Current Capacity: 20 pounds
    Dodge Chance: 16%
    Hit Chance: 75%
    Mana: 0
    Mana Regen: 0/min
    Magical Affinity: N/A
    Skills: Analyze

. . .

It looks like I'm a normal human. The stats are more complex than the ones I'm used to in Pangea, but they are basically the same. It's all there—Strength, Intellect, Vitality—just in a different way. More comprehensive. Perhaps it's easier to make them more detailed when this world isn't having to play nice with a hundred others that might not have the same rules. That's one thing that has always impressed me about Pangea Online, the balance between gameworlds regardless of a player's stats. The programming they must have on the backend to make that flow so well is beyond me.

Nothing really stands out about my stats except for the fact that I have no magical affinity at the moment. Seeing as how my Stamina has a bonus, it must have been buffed from all of my running. It's good to know I can increase my stats if I grind hard enough and that it's not all based on levels.

I'm glad the AI has finally decided to give me a stat table. It'll be a lot easier to see how I stack up against opponents going forward. I focus on my items and sure enough, their stats have changed as well.

Item. Bronze short sword. *+3 damage. 1.5 lbs*

Item. Steel targe shield. *+5 armor. 9 lbs*

Food. Sausage. *Recovers 20 hp and Stamina over 60 seconds.*

Food. Bread. *Recovers 20 hp and Stamina over 60 seconds.*

Item. Fairy Dust. Effect: *Lulls opponents to sleep.*

"Shit!" I yell as a searing pain courses through my upper body. A set of blue scaly claws dig into my shoulder and lift me off the ground. It takes everything in me to keep hold of my items and not toss them away. The flap of sail-like wings jostles me as we rise higher into the air. I was so caught up in the stat page and the new item descriptions that I didn't notice a dragon the size of a small house sneaking up on me from behind.

The dragon fumes as we ascend, long rolls of steam pouring from its nostrils. The thought of stabbing the creature in the leg with my sword until it releases me crosses my mind, but the sad reality is that we are too high in the air. A fall from this height would certainly kill me. I try to ignore the pain and focus on the gravity of my situation and not the gravity that will certainly kill me if the dragon decides I'm not worth the trouble.

It's hard to focus when four-inch claws are burying themselves in your skin, but I do my best. The animals in the fields far below look like tiny insects and the trees appear as bulbous shrubs. We're so high up that it all looks like a model. The cool air mixed with sweat on my forehead sends chills down my body. Far off to the east, I can see what looks like a city, and straight ahead are the mountains. It'd be nice if the dragon would drop me at the base and take my HP it has already drained as the fare.

The pain fades the farther we fly and eventually, my HP returns to full. The dragon's talons are still gripping me with the strength of a hundred men, but it does little to disrupt my focus. I watch the map as my dot creeps closer to Kindra and Carter. I'm now close enough that if I can manage to free myself, I'll likely be able to catch up with them.

It seems the dragon has different plans.

We reach the mountains and the dragon soars even higher. It's wings flap thunderously and we rise above the clouds into the stratosphere. The air grows frosty the higher we climb until I can see the snow-capped summit above us. We begin circling the peak and the dragon lets out a roar. This high up, there is only a muted silence aside from the dragon's roar.

It roars again. Long and monstrous, its boom clamors and echoes through the wilderness.

Then, a reply.

Small, diminutive squawks answer the mother's call, and I realize I'm about to be dinner.

CHAPTER EIGHTEEN

The mother dragon descends toward the mountain and her nest comes into view. A brown dot in an otherwise winter wasteland. Two baby dragons, each about the same size as me, snap their teeth and waddle around, using their wings for extra support as we approach. Their mouths hang agape, waiting for their next meal. It's not their first time doing this. Drool runs down their jaws, hungry for sustenance. They are a much lighter blue than their mother, their scales are not made of the same impenetrable substance yet, but their bodies still radiate the fiery heat that dragons possess. The entire mountaintop is covered in snow except for the nest. Snow melts around it, running down and turning to ice, forming a dangerously slick ledge beneath the nest.

The bright, innocent eyes of newborns look up at us. They are hungry, and their ravenous teeth want nothing more than to rip me to shreds.

How in the hell am I going to get out of this?

I search my surroundings for anything I can use to my advantage. A broken tree limb peeks out of the snow overhead. What a shame I don't have Grappler with me. Aside from that, the mountain is a blanket of white. I have my sword strapped to my waist, my pack, and my shield.

I'm still contemplating my options when the tension releases from my shoulders and I plummet toward the baby dragons. Puffs of smoke pour out of their snouts as they attempt to blow flames. Sparks flutter from the nostril of one. Please, don't burn me alive!

Not knowing what else to do, I take my shield and place my feet between the arm handles, blocking my view of the creatures just as a trickle of flame erupts from one of them. The flame bounces off the shield, saving my body, but my feet grow hot. I crash into the baby dragon's head and ricochet off the nest, landing hard on the blanket of ice beneath. The ice sends me sliding uncontrollably down the mountainside.

The entire family roars in anger, the mother in frustration and the babies in hunger and disappointment. I'm just happy I didn't get eaten. Yet.

The mother comes after me, her eyes burning brighter than before. She is determined to catch me and take me back to her hungry offspring. A flame erupts and carves through the snow and ice like warm butter as she chases me. An wintry avalanche follows me and suddenly, the dragon isn't the only thing I'm trying to survive.

Snow plows into my back like a cold pillow, launching me faster and farther ahead just as the dragon unleashes another bout of flame. Her fire melts a canyon in the avalanche and changes my course.

Holding onto the shield for dear life, I have no control over steering and am left to the mercy of luck and nature. I cross beneath the layer of clouds and begin to see where the snowline ends. A moment later, the dragon breaks through the clouds and is on me again. The snow thins, and I can feel debris underneath as it scrapes against the bottom of the shield. A large rock ramps me into the air and I land with a crash. The impact tosses me from the shield and I tumble down the mountainside. My body aches as I nose-dive into the mushy snow and dirt. I come to a halt face-down in a frigid puddle. This is it. I'm about to be dragon food.

I brace for a painful death, but it never comes. Instead, I hear a roar several yards away and watch as the dragon scorches a mountain goat and carries it off. It must have seemed like less of a hassle to feed the kids goat tonight.

Thoroughly exhausted, I roll over and stare at the cloud canopy overhead. My muscles ache. My bones ache. I'm wet and covered in dirt and mud. I'm pretty sure there is a gash running down the side of my shoulder because it burns like the bowels of hell any time I move it. The dragon could come back for me right now and I doubt I would have any fight in me. My pack hangs limp from my uninjured shoulder. I fiddle with it until I find a piece of sausage.

I take a bite and let the salty goodness wash over me. Instantly, I begin to feel a little better as my HP recovers. After eating the sausage and some bread, I'm finally feeling back to myself.

"Hey! What the hell are you doing here?" I recognize Kindra's voice coming up the mountain.

A moment later, she and Carter stand over my cold, wet body. The orange glow is almost gone from Carter's eyes and his pupils are once again visible.

"Yeah, what gives?" asks Carter. "We heard a commotion up the trail and come to find you laying on your ass." Florian sits on his shoulder, his leafy arms crossed like an expectant mother waiting for her child's explanation.

"I, uh…was attacked by a dragon."

"What!?" they say simultaneously.

I sit up and recount my story of the dragon and my adventure down the mountain.

"We waited for you for half the day before leaving," says Kindra. She crosses her arms and stares blankly into my eyes.

"There were complications with my return that I couldn't overcome. How was your journey here?" I ask.

"It's been crazy since you left. As if you couldn't tell by the dragon, but more and more magical creatures keep appearing. We had to fight off a couple of lizardfolk and Carter used up nearly all of his magic. Then we ran into a group on the road who had a run-in with goblins. Who knows what else might be out there? I don't know what to make of it all."

Everything is changing so fast.

"What about magic? Have you found magic yet?" I ask Carter.

He shakes his head, but Kindra answers, "We were actually almost to the place where I learned mine when we heard you and the dragon, so I guess we're pretty lucky you didn't become dragon food."

Carter helps me to my feet and I follow them down the mountain. It turns out that my abrupt halt landed me right in the middle of a path that leads up into the snow-caps of the mountain. Though I don't know why anyone would want to hike through snow and ice.

Beneath the layer of clouds and snow, vegetation returns to the mountainside. Knobby trees curl around the mountain's edge and tiny bushes cling to soil and rock for dear life. Kindra stops in front of a voluminous pine tree and arches her eyebrows.

"Here we are," she says, sweeping her hand towards the mountain as if it has some secret entrance.

"Okay, so what do we do, press our hands against the mountain and a crack forms for us to walk through?" I ask. It seems like the most logical way to cross into a magical cave.

"Um, no. You move the tree aside and walk through," she says with a sigh.

She takes the tree by the trunk and pulls it back. Behind it, a crack runs along the mountain, no more than five feet tall. A faint green glow comes from within, but the way the mouth of the cave curves, I can't see what lies inside.

You have found the entrance to the Cave of Enlightenment. Enter at your own risk.

"Well, are you going or not?" she asks.

Not waiting for my response, Carter and Florian enter the cave. I follow them and Kindra pulls up the rear.

The glow intensifies once we turn the first corner and my jaw drops open. Hundreds of crystals adorn the cave walls, jutting out in every direction and emitting their own light. A rainbow emanates as strobes of amethyst, azure, and cerise dance along the walls and ceiling. A tiny spring sprouts beneath our feet and trickles into the depths, where glowing minnows lead us onward.

"This is beautiful," I say. Neither of them respond. I don't blame them. In all the worlds I've traveled to, I've never seen anything quite like this. It feels like there is a presence in this cave that filters into my very being.

Out of nowhere, two balls of light appear in front of us. They remind me of the light in Priscilla's parlor where her magical herbs grew. The brilliant orbs float through the air, cycling through colors every few seconds. Light projects so fuzzily around it that I'm not sure if the ball is pure light or if there is a creature inside. Whatever it is, my analyze skill doesn't work on it.

The two orbs float in and out, up and down, and bounce against each other. They swim by me and then Carter as if analyzing us. One stops in front of Florian and simply hovers. When he reaches out to touch it, it zooms away the moment his leafy finger is about to make contact.

The movement of the orbs is fascinating, mesmerizing even. I feel myself losing sight of everything else in the cave and honestly, I don't care. Something skitters in the darkness, but it doesn't distract me. The orbs are all that matter. We follow them through the cave system, left, right, left, center, on and on until I could not find my way out if I tried.

Then suddenly, we stop. The tunnel we have been following opens into a cavernous room. A dozen or so new caves open all around us.

The orbs begin circling in a rapid vortex, almost blending together as they swirl. My head begins to clear, and I realize just how out of it I was. Was that part of the plan, to get us so far into the mountain that we couldn't replicate the process if we wanted?

"Hey, where is Kindra?" I ask. She's no longer with us. I don't know where we lost her, either. She could literally be anywhere.

"I don't think she is supposed to be here for this," says Carter.

The orbs descend. One in front of each of us. This time, they are a solid, unchanging color. Carter's is green, and mine a dull violet. The brightness of them dulls and intensifies as they move slowly ahead of us like a beacon waiting for us to follow.

"I think this is how we get magic," he says.

"We? This was supposed to be your quest. I was never promised magic."

The violet orb returns and gently pushes against my chest.

"I don't think you have a choice."

I watch as Carter follows his orb into one of the tunnels. He disappears inside it and the tunnel sits in darkness once again. My orb waits patiently in front of a tunnel on the other side. Alone with no way of knowing how to exit, it looks like I have no choice but to follow.

Whatever, let's do this.

I step into the tunnel. It's much darker than the others with the only source of light coming from the violet orb leading the way. Several rocky formations protrude from the wall, so I take my time navigating each step, careful to avoid being impaled.

"Do you have a name?" I ask. The orb doesn't respond, but flickers slightly. "Hell, I don't even know if you are a sentient being."

The orb glows brighter and floats back towards me, colliding with my head in a quick, fluid motion. A sharp pain draws to my forehead.

"Okay, I'm sorry! Geez. I'm not exactly fluent with the magical creatures of this world. You're sentient, I get it. Lead the way."

What a testy little ball of light. I make note to keep comments questioning its cognitive abilities to myself in the future.

I follow the orb along the pathway, wondering what might lay in store. What kind of magic I will choose and what I will do once I have it. I've always been partial to fire spells. They look the coolest, but then again, water spells might be nice as well. Truth be told, I'll be happy with anything. I can't even begin to imagine what it will be like to learn magic in full-immersion.

The tunnel empties into a smooth, obsidian cavern. The walls are black as night and gleam with the reflection of a small pool in the middle. Glowing minnows swim in circles in the pool's shallow depths. Everything feels slick and wet, even though the rock is hard and dry.

The orb floats down near the water. It hovers above the pool for a moment and then submerges. Tiny ripples spread across its surface. I can still see the faint violet glow in its depths.

I guess I'm supposed to get inside.

I remove my clothes and dip my toes in. I expect it to be cold, considering the weather outside, but the water is warm, almost hot. It relaxes me the moment I climb in. My feet touch the silty bottom and the water reaches up to my shoulders. The minnows nibble at my toes, and I let my back rest against the pool's edge.

For a moment, I lose sight of the orb. The minnows begin to swirl rapidly in the pool's center. So fast that they almost become a blur. They contract closer together until they are the size of the orb. Their glow flares in and out, igniting the pool in a rabid display of light. And then they disappear and the cavern goes dark.

I sit in darkness. Complete darkness. I lose track of time. It could be minutes or hours. The only sounds I hear are my raging heartbeat and the splash of water as I move.

A small swash of purple light shines in the depths of the pool. It grows more vibrant as the orb rises and stops just below the surface. Slowly, deliberately, it moves close to me and I feel uneasy.

The orb presses against my body. It's cold. Much too cold to have just spent all that time in the warm water. It presses harder and dematerializes. The orb becomes one with my body and an electric madness flows through me. Power courses through me—real, true power—and then everything goes black.

CHAPTER NINETEEN

Adventurer, you have unlocked the magical secrets of The Broken Lands. Based on your actions, both inward and outward, the gods have determined you an Enchanter. Enchantment magic is both complex and ancient. You will learn just how complex in time. Your magic is forever entwined with the items which unlock it, for without items, your magic has no power.

Level 1 Enchanter: You may enchant items with your mana, giving them special characteristics or abilities. Enchantments are broken when an item is destroyed, discarded, or mana depleted. Power of enchantments are dependent on your level and mana usage. Items cannot contain more than one enchantment at a time.

Skill: Enchanting Eye. Focusing on an item will provide possible enchantment paths.

A soft glow returns to the cavern. The minnows drift aimlessly through the pool. The orb is gone. Inside of me, I suppose. Perhaps it was the embodiment of magic.

I'm an enchanter. I'm not sure of the full ramifications of that, but the system said it was based on my choices. Just like everything else in this world, apparently. If enchanting is anything like in Pangea, then it means I can use magic to make my items stronger.

I search for my pack in the dim lighting of the cavern. The metal of my shield catches the light and I spot it in the corner. I focus on the shield and a wall of text appears in my vision.

Item. Steel targe shield. *+5 armor. 9 lbs*

Possible enchantments:

Block: Shield blocks next physical attack. Cost: 50 mana per attack.

Featherweight: (Permanent) Weight of shield decreases by 90%. Initial cost: 100 mana, then 5 mana per minute while active.

Both of those are cool. The Featherweight skill in particular would make it much more maneuverable and raise the offensive potential a great deal, but that's almost half of my mana on one enchantment. If I were an assassin or a warrior who made all of my items featherweight, that would be a heck of an advantage in a fight. One hundred mana to permanently unlock that isn't bad either. The only issue is the constant mana drain while the enchantment is active. Hopefully, I can find a way to increase my mana pool. I wonder if those are the only two options, though. Are there other possible enchantments that aren't being shown to me?

I try to focus on the shield. On things I wish it could do. The dark tunnel to my left reminds me that I am going to have to find my way out of here. It would be a hell of a lot easier with a light. I push my mental energy into the shield and it starts to glow. I focus my thoughts more and the glow switches to only the front of the shield. I push harder and the glow ignites the cavern.

Congratulations! You have created Shield of Light! May it

guide you through the darkness. This is a permanent enchantment costing 100 mana. Do you accept? Y/N

I accept.

One hundred mana disappears, then it slowly begins regenerating. It replenishes at a snail's pace compared to other worlds I'm used to.

Congratulations! You have learned the skill: Innovator. You can now create unique enchantments.

Ha! That was awesome! I run my arm through the handles on the back of the shield and it lights everything in front of me. Not to mention it might come in handy blinding an opponent in a fight. I focus on the shield and the light goes away. I change my focus and it switches on and off like a lightbulb. I can even control the brightness, all the way from a dull glow to eye-scorching.

I find my clothes and dress. There is no way I'll be able to find my way out of this mountain on my own, but I have to try. Somewhere out there in this maze of rock and rubble, Carter and Kindra are trying to find their way out as well.

Before I go, I focus on my sword and two enchantments show up beneath its stats.

Item. Bronze short sword. *+3 damage. 1.5 lbs*
Possible enchantments:
Venom: Each attack deals a bonus 1% poison damage per second. Stacks up to five times. Initial cost: 100 mana, then 10 mana per attack.
Twilight Blade: (Permanent) Sword gains 5% lifesteal per attack. Initial cost: 100 mana, then 10 mana per attack.

It's not much of a choice which one to pick. With only one small piece of bread to heal me, I need the lifesteal in case I run into any creatures on my way out. My mana will be incredibly low after I make this enchantment, so I'll need to make sure I put the rest of my mana to good use.

My stat page shows that I used up two hundred of my mana enchanting the two items. Mana regenerates at twenty mana per minute. At its current rate, I could regenerate to full mana in ten minutes if I don't attack anything. That's practically unheard of in Pangea, where mana can regenerate in a tenth of that time, sometimes less. If everyone else's mana works the same way, it will mean magic works a lot differently here. There will be no spamming spells. Everything will have to be well thought out and planned.

I walk through the cavern towards where I imagine the most logical escape route is. Nothing looks familiar. Crystals catch the light of my shield and refract upon the ceiling and walls. Its stunningly beautiful, but offers me no guidance.

At each fork, I take the farthest tunnel to the right. It's a bad decision, but what else can I do? I try to look at the map Priscilla drew me, but it shows nothing inside the cave. Not even my own location. I'm going to need a miracle to get out of here.

While I walk, I continue to test out my enchantment abilities, but I make sure not to accept anything. There are spells that turn the floor to ice, the walls to mirrors, and even the option to create imaginary barriers. I'm going to be able to have a lot of fun with my magic class. With my innovator skill, there won't be anything I can't do if I have the imagination and mana.

I take the tunnel to the right and two eyes reflect my light in the depth of the cavern. They stare at me, unblinking.

Now is not the time to fight. I run back the way I came.

The thud of heavy paws racing down the stone floor carries through the tunnel. Why couldn't it just leave me alone?

By the sound of the creature's gait, I can tell I'll never outrun it. I turn to fight and right as I do, something heavy crashes into my shield. Light refracts around the cavern. Through the creature and beyond. A crystal bear stands on top of my shield, pinning me to the ground. It swats at my head and I barely dodge the blow. Shards of crystal poke out from its back like a porcupine. The light from my shield ignites the bear in a blaze of glory. Its eyes are a dark, soulless obsidian.

I try to push the bear away, but it weighs too much. My muscles burn as I push them to their limits, barely holding the shield at bay from crushing my body. Each second that passes, it becomes harder to breathe.

"Ungh." I try to roll over, to gain any sort of leverage, but it doesn't come. Not knowing what else to do, I focus on my pack that's trapped between my back and the ground. I don't care what enchantment options it has. A bottomless pack doesn't interest me right now. I need the bear off me before it rips my head off!

Pushing all but a fraction of my mana to my pack, I urge it to rocket me off the ground.

Less than a second later, an enormous pain sends the edges of my vision black and launches me and the bear into the air. We smash into the ceiling amid the sound of broken crystal. The bear lets out a loud yelp. I fall to the ground and stars dance across my vision. Panicking, I search for my sword amongst the rubble of broken crystals.

I find it buried to the hilt and dive for it just as the bear regains its senses. The bear swipes at me again, but this time, my blade slashes against its arm, deflecting the blow and replenishing a fraction of my health.

The tough, crystalline skin of the bear doesn't take much damage, but the swing keeps my head attached to my shoulders. I get in a few more hits that clink off the bear's hide, each hit replenishing my health by a small amount. The bear shakes its paws in anger and I step away.

The explosion of my pack and the attacks have depleted my mana completely. It'll be close to two minutes before I have enough for another enchantment, so I do what I can.

I run.

Bringing my sword down with all my might as I pass, I hit the bear over the head. Any normal creature would be bloody and bruised, but not this bear. The sword clamors against a lilac ear and the bear's obsidian eyes go lazy for a moment. I use the distraction to gain as much distance as possible while the bear is stunned.

Barreling down the tunnel, the light from my shield ignites the way. It doesn't take long before I hear the bear's footsteps thundering behind me.

Without enough mana to enchant more than a rock, the only option I have is to fight. Unless...

I sheath my sword as I run and pull my pack from my shoulder. Pulling out the bread and fairy dust, I uncork the vial and spread it liberally on my last sustenance. The dust glitters like sprinkles on a cupcake.

You have created a new item.

Sleeping Biscuit. *Effect: eating this item grants immediate sleep.*

The bear is right behind me when I toss the biscuit

over my shoulder and hope for the best. A moment later, I notice that the only sounds are my own footsteps clicking upon the tunnel floor.

I come to a stop and listen.

Silence.

And then a deep rattling honk drones from down the cavern. It rises and falls, repeating over and over.

It actually worked. The bear is fast asleep!

I could use the opportunity to get further away from the creature, but the experience is practically waiting for me while the bear slumbers away. This world is hard and painful enough. I need to take advantage of the situation. Now is not the time to be squeamish.

I make my way down the tunnel to find the slumbering bear face-down with a half-eaten piece of bread still hanging in its mouth. Potent stuff.

Bijou Bear. *This rare crystalline creature is found near potent magical sources. Long believed to be a source of good luck, the crystal furs of these creatures are known to fetch a high price in magical markets.*

Talk about good luck. Assuming I can carry the fur, it'll make a great bargaining chip.

I'm normally not one to take an opponent unaware, but I don't see any other way. If I leave the creature here, he could track me down later on. Considering I don't know how the hell I'm getting out of here yet, the last thing I want is to die alone in this cave.

I lean my shield against the cave wall, casting the bear in light. I lift my sword over my head with both hands and prepare to swing. There's something about the way the light travels through the bear, igniting the geometric patterns of its crystallized muscles, that makes the creature look regal. Like it's carved out of stone.

The bear snorts and moves a paw. If I'm going to do this, I have to do it now. There's no time to waste.

My sword crashes against the bear's neck with a sickening crunch. Crystal shards splinter through the cave and the bear stumbles to its feet. Its obsidian eyes are barely open and it sways back and forth. I bring the sword down again, this time forming a crack along the bear's neckline. It grunts in pain and I swing the sword again. The crack widens and the rainbow of color fades from the bear's head, turning the crystal a milky white. The bear lashes out at me, but falls to the ground. I drive the sword into the crevice forming in its neck and pry with all my might. There's a loud crack and my sword breaks in half, but not before the bear's head tumbles to the ground.

I don't know whether I should feel proud or ashamed of what I've done. It's not like I couldn't have escaped from the sleeping bear. On the other hand, considering I started from nothing, the items it drops could likely help me get started making a name for myself in this world.

Searching through the remains of the bijou bear, I find two obsidian eyes, several crystal bear claws, and a crystal bear hide. I fit them in my pack as best I can and they take up ninety pounds of my one-hundred-and-fifty-pound limit.

With my sword broken, the enchantment breaks as well. It makes me nervous not having a weapon and knowing that more than likely, there are other monsters still waiting somewhere in this cave.

My mana pool has grown by twenty-five and is now at two hundred and seventy-five. My mana is still low from all of the action with the bear, but the increase to my mana pool shows up immediately. The extra mana can go a long way with temporary enchantments.

With my new items in tow, I set off once again along the tunnels. It feels like hours pass as I travel hopelessly through the labyrinth.

My eyes begin to glaze over from the constant swirl of light bouncing around the cavern. I dull the light on my shield, but there are so many crystals that it is impossible to negate its effect.

It feels like I've been walking in circles when an idea crosses my mind. I focus on my boots to see what possible enchantments they have.

Fleetfoot: grants flight at a rate of 100 mana per minute.

Very cool, but the price is steep and I don't see any need to go flying through a cave. I'd likely impale myself on a sharp crystal.

Speed demon: grants X% increased speed at a rate of X mana per minute.

Nice! With my current mana regen, I can increase my speed by 20% and it will balance out the mana cost. I accept the enchantment and immediately my feet move faster. I walk faster. I run faster. It's amazing. And I use the same amount of Stamina that I normally would. I zoom through tunnels and finally, it feels like I am making progress. Probably in the wrong direction, but at least it feels like progress.

Wind swooshes around my hair and despite being trapped in a never-ending maze, I feel free.

I come upon an intersection of tunnels when something smashes into my side, knocking the breath out of me and sending my shield skidding along the tunnel. It comes to a stop face-down. Light barely escapes from underneath it, casting the cavern in eerie darkness.

CHAPTER TWENTY

S even hells!

My head spins and I try to suck in air to fill my lungs that have just been deflated by whatever wrecking ball took me out.

"What...the...hell?" a voice gasps next to me.

I can barely make out the shadow of a man in the dim light. Pulling my broken sword, I point it towards the man's face while I wait for my breathing to normalize.

"Don't move," I say. "I don't want any problems, but I'll hurt you if I have to." Hurt him with what, I have no idea.

There's a soft fluttering sound like a whip just before it cracks and then something tightens around my legs, cutting off the circulation. It pulls me with great strength, jerking my legs out from under me and tossing me to the ground. A sharp pain shoots up my backside.

"Florian, stop that right this instant!" Carter's voice is hoarse but still commanding.

"Carter? What are you doing here? Why the hell did you run into me?"

He walks down the tunnel with a limp, using his

trident for leverage, and retrieves my shield. The light bathes the cavern once more and I'm able to see the source of my most recent injury. Florian stands several feet away from me. Tiny vines unwind and retract into his hands. He's almost doubled in size. His arms and legs are no longer the tender leaves and roots, but have morphed into tougher, more branchlike appendages. Even his flowery head has blossomed. Where he was once a small flower, he is now a larger more bush-like creature with a few red flowers dotted throughout.

"After I learned my magic, the orb that was leading me disappeared. I've been wandering these tunnels in darkness ever since. I saw the glow of your shield from down that way and took off running. Little did I know that you would be racing through like a horse at high noon." He rubs the back of his head and I notice his eyes are their normal gray. Whatever magic he had from Priscilla is long gone.

"And what about Florian here? Did he learn magic too?" Something must have changed his appearance.

"Not quite. My branch of magic, pardon my pun, has allowed for him to evolve."

"Your branch? What is it?"

"I'm a druid. Specifically, plant magic. I can use plants to fight for me."

"That's interesting." It's funny that the game gave Carter that brand of magic since he spent his entire life as a farmer. It makes me question even more why I was chosen as an enchanter.

Carter hands me my shield and I slide my arms through the straps, once again lighting the tunnel before us.

"I'm guessing by the fact that you were blazing through

here with a light-up shield that you found your own magic as well."

"You're right." I can't help but smile. "I am an enchanter. I have no magic power on my own, but I can give normal items magical properties."

Carter's eyes light up at the news.

"Really? That's awesome!"

"Yeah, I think so too. So, Florian evolved? How's that work?"

He rubs his fingers on his chin, deep in thought.

"It's hard to explain. It's kind of like once I had this new magic, I suddenly knew stuff about how to use it. Not everything, but some things. And I feel like the better I get, the more I will know. I looked down at Florian and I had the feeling that I could make him stronger if I wanted. So I asked if he wanted me to and well, here we are. He's a lot less likely to be trampled or float away in the wind. Plus, he'll come in pretty handy in a fight."

Florian takes a fighting stance next to Carter and raises his wooden fists into the air like a boxer. I can't help but laugh at his spunk.

"How do you figure we get out of here?" I ask. "It feels like I've been walking for hours. Not to mention where the hell Kindra might be."

"Hmm, I don't really know. I've been lost myself."

Maybe this is why magic faded out. Because everyone who found their way in here died while trying to find a way out.

Not us, though. I refuse to rot away inside of this mountain while there is a wide and wild world waiting to be explored. There has to be a way to get out of this glittery prison.

"Let me think." I sit down on the cold floor and close

my eyes. Without knowing our path in here, how can I possibly get us out? The map is useless. We don't have a compass or anything to tell us which way we are even facing.

Wait! That's it!

I search the floor for a piece of stray crystal, but I don't find any. Taking my broken sword, I slash hard against a long thin crystal until a piece of it breaks off.

"I have an idea," I tell Carter, who looks at me like I've just gone mad.

Holding the pink crystal in my palm, I focus my mana into it, concentrating on making it a guidestone.

You have created Guidestone (Cave of Enlightenment) Initial cost: 250 mana, then 20 mana per minute. Do you accept? Y/N

It's a steep price, but considering its use, I didn't figure it would be cheap.

Dammit! That means that as long as I'm carrying the guidestone, I won't have enough mana to enchant anything that costs over five mana.

Why does everything have to be so difficult?

"What is it?" asks Carter, sensing my unrest.

"I've found us a way out, but the mana cost is so high that I won't be able to enchant any other items. And my sword is already broken so that will leave me little in the way of damage. I don't know what to do."

"Do what you need to do to get us out of here. Florian and I can handle any trouble that comes our way."

I accept the enchantment and the crystal hovers in the air inches from my palm, pointing forward.

"Take us out of here, please."

With the crystal hovering above my palm, we journey down the tunnel. At the first fork, the crystal changes direction and points us to the left. I let out a deep breath, relieved that my plan is actually working.

This is a good time to find out as much about Carter's new magic as possible. If trouble does go down, I'd feel more comfortable knowing what kinds of spells he has.

"How exactly does being a druid work? Can you cast spells of your own or do you have to be around plant life?"

The leaves of Florian's new form swish against each other as we walk, breaking up the otherwise eeriness of our footsteps echoing around us.

"I imagine it is similar to your own abilities in a way. You can't cast spells without an item and I need plant life in order to use mine. We haven't passed any other plant life in the tunnels. It seems this place is solid rock. Luckily, for us, I have Florian. I can raise his abilities with my own magic for a limited time. I can even give him new abilities by using some of my own energy as well."

"Do you mean mana?" I ask.

"What is mana?" His eyebrows arch in confusion.

"It's the energy that flows through me and allows me to cast enchantments. When it is low, I can't do magic anymore."

"Hmmm, then that must be it. I can sense the energy inside of me and am able to gauge how much a particular spell will cost. Some take a great deal of energy, I mean mana, and others very little. I think it depends on the effectiveness of the spell or how useful it will be."

"That sounds about right. I'm running very low on mana at the moment myself due to this guidestone. Once we are out of the cave, I can discard it and my mana will begin to replenish once again. Then I'll be more than a glorified map again."

"Lead us out of the cave and leave the fighting to us." Carter grips me on the shoulder, reaffirming his word.

We walk in silence, following the mystical compass in the hope that it will lead us out of the cave.

It doesn't take long for Carter's word to be put to the test. Around the next corner, a crystal golem blocks our path.

A smooth, pearlescent being with sharp, rocky edges around its joints and hands that threaten to rip anyone foolish enough to do battle. The guidestone points in the direction past the golem, so we have no other choice.

"Carter..."

"Don't worry, leave it to us. Florian, show this rock what you've got!"

The golem sways back and forth, oblivious to Florian running full-speed at him. He's taken by surprise when Florian reaches his vines out to the cave walls and sling-shots himself into the golem. Florian pulls himself into a bushy cannonball and collides with the golem. Leaves flutter in the air at the site of the impact. The golem tumbles to the ground, pieces of crystal breaking off and scattering along the tunnel floor.

The golem rises in anger, arms swinging wildly, but Florian has already retreated out of its reach. Carter steps up, his trident pointed forward.

"Thorn attack," he orders. The tip of the trident glows a vibrant green and Florian charges at the golem. Dozens of thorns erupt from his barky skin and detach. They swarm the golem like angry bees, bouncing off the golem's rocky skin, but not before dealing damage. It must be magical damage, otherwise I don't see how it could hurt the creature.

Before the thorns have even disappeared, Florian has

his vines wrapped around the golem, squeezing tightly. Tiny cracks form where the vines constrict.

"Poisoned lotus," shouts Carter, and Florian retracts his vines, pulling himself closer to the golem. The red flowers that run along his body blossom and glow. A glittery pollen floats through the air and falls all around. The golem thrashes and writhes in pain as the pollen covers its body. The creature's health bar ticks down rapidly until it is nearly dead. "I'm out of mana. Time to finish this." Carter joins Florian and stabs his trident against the golem repeatedly, flaking off crystals in large chunks until eventually nothing more than a rock pile remains.

Carter picks up several crystals and places them in his bag.

"See, I told you we could handle it." He smirks. Florian walks through the rubble of the once magnificent golem, kicking debris and watching it tumble down the corridor. Their relationship feels like it's more than surface level. Like they actually belong together.

"You're a pretty good team."

Carter joins Florian and rubs his fingers through the bushy part of Florian's head like a father tussling his child's hair. It reminds me of Merlin and the bond that we shared. Even in Pangea, where I knew it was a game, he and I formed a bond that still holds true. If something made up of ones and zeros can have that effect on a person, how is it ever just a game?

The guidestone leads us through the cave and though occasionally we hear movement down various tunnels we bypass, we pass no other monsters.

We turn a corner and come into the tunnel where we first entered. The glowing minnows run up and down the small stream, and far away, I can make out the light from outside. Someone stands in the entryway, the light providing only a silhouette.

"We'll take the lead," says Carter. "Until we know if they mean us harm. With the way things have been, I don't trust anyone whole-heartedly until they earn it."

I understand that sentiment completely. It could be someone who is here to discover magic in the same way as Carter did, but it could also be someone with bad intentions. Someone for who magic would be a very bad thing.

"Who goes there?" Carter asks. He has his trident at the ready and Florian at his side.

The silhouette moves closer.

"What took you two so long? I've been waiting here for hours."

I recognize the voice as Kindra's and as we get closer, I can see her slender bow and arrows draped across her back.

"How did you get back here?" I ask. "And why did you leave us?"

"Leave you? I didn't leave you. I was following along and then all of a sudden, you both disappeared. The orbs, everything, it just vanished. I imagine it was a protective spell from the cave to keep those with magical abilities from reentering. My memory fogged and the next thing I knew, I was back here. And let me tell you, there are only so many rocks you can skip to pass the time." She pauses and stares at us. "So let's hear it. What did you learn?" She places her hands on her hips expectantly.

"I'm an enchanter," I say.

"And I'm a druid," says Carter.

Kindra approaches Florian and rubs his wooden arm.

"They grow up so fast. Let's get out of here."

CHAPTER TWENTY-ONE

"You've got magic, so what now?" I ask Carter. We spent all of this time focusing on obtaining magic without thinking about what we were supposed to do once we found it. There has to be more ahead of us than just blind adventure.

"We go back to Carolton. I feel a great many things have changed since we left. The world itself has changed. We will be needed, that much I know. Priscilla sent us away for a reason. Now it is time to find out what that reason was."

Once we are out of the cave, I discard the guidestone. Without my enchantment, it is nothing more than a beautiful crystal. I toss it back inside the cave. I'm not looking to leave any clues for anyone. Anyone looking for the Cave of Enlightenment will have to search it out just like we did.

The air is cool, crisp, and refreshing as we make our way down the mountain. A wonderful change from the warm, stagnant air inside the cave. For all its beauty, the Cave of Enlightenment didn't smell like rainbows and flowers.

From this far up, I can see for miles. Carolton is but a small dot two days away, and the Cursed Forest with its black trees seems like a small patch in comparison to the sprawling countryside. Several other towns speckle across the land. One seems larger than most, and I speculate that that is where the castle lies. To the left, a lush green forest runs for as far as I can see. Many lakes are spread throughout, and to my right, there is a dark mountain range. Gray clouds hang low where lightning occasionally strikes. I wonder how many people live throughout The Broken Lands?

My map is viewable once again and there is a spot marked Cave of Enlightenment midway up the mountain. I assume that the map fills itself in the more I travel. The map is large, but it ends on both sides at the forest and mountain range. This mountain is the border to the south and far to the north, a jagged coastline battles with the sea. Does the world go on past these borders or is that the scope of the gameworld?

"Are there other kingdoms throughout The Broken Lands?" I ask.

"There are, or used to be, I'm not really sure, not that they pose much of a threat," says Kindra. She has her bow strapped to her back as we scale down a particularly rocky patch of the path. She checks to make sure each foot is securely planted, rubble scattering with each step. It'd be nice to have a dragon take us the rest of the way if there wasn't that whole problem of it eating us or feeding us to its children. "There are kingdoms on the other side of the Endless Forest and Thunder Mountain, but no one would dare bring an army across them. That's why it's called The Broken Lands, though. Not since the Age of Mages have the kingdoms been in contact. Some say the forest and mountain were put there by a great mage to keep us separated. I don't know if I believe that."

It wouldn't be surprising to me. Just like in the real world, where people in The Boxes are separated from society. Is it human nature to divide?

"Why do they call it the Endless Forest?"

She rolls her eyes before answering. "The name didn't give it away? The forest goes on for forever. Supposedly there is a way out, but I've never met anyone who has made it to the other side. Many have lost their minds and their lives trying to cross. They say that the forest has a way of playing tricks on people. And before you even ask..." She points to the dark mountain range to our right. "How do you think anyone could successfully bring an army through a mountain range that's in an eternal thunderstorm?"

"Eternal?" I ask.

"Yeah. As far as I can remember, anytime I've looked at Thunder Mountain, there have been storms. It must be hell to live there."

Our journey is long and tiresome. Even with my increased Stamina, I find myself wishing we had our wagon back. Stupid dryad.

If nothing else, it gives me time to think. About Priscilla giving us this quest, about my enchantments, about the real reason I'm here. Why is Benjamin rushing those other immersion capsules? Something is going on, but what? There's no way he could have learned enough already to log other players in, is there?

"Here, take this," says Kindra. She hands me the sword that she took from the bandits. "You need it more than I do."

"Thanks." Tossing my broken sword aside, I take the

new one from Kindra and try to think of which kind of enchantment will be best for my current situation. With the guidestone no longer draining my mana, it is slowly replenishing and soon, I will have enough for new enchantments. I don't really even need the Shield of Light anymore, but there is no point in discarding it until I find something better. Besides, we could probably use the light from it to travel at night if we wanted.

I could go with the lifesteal option I used on my last sword, but that seems too repetitive. What's the point of having this awesome magic if I can't explore its uses? Dozens of ideas cross my mind. A flaming sword that does burn damage is cool, not to mention how awesome it would look. That's more Buzz's style, though. Too flashy for my taste.

An ice sword that slows movement with each hit would be practical if we were chasing anything, but we're not. And I don't know that we ever will be.

I want something that can make me a better fighter. But do I go with a permanent enchantment or temporary? A spell Aleesia used once when we cleared our first dungeon together crosses my mind. She shot an arrow and when it hit, lightning forked out to several of the skeletons we were fighting, stunning them in place.

Sending my mana into the sword, I work out various combinations, tweaking them until the mana usage and effect match what I'm willing to give up. The result is:

Shockwave. *Every fourth attack sends out an electric shock, stunning the enemy and dealing bonus area of effect damage to three others within the shock radius. Initial cost: 100 mana, then 10 mana per attack.*

It's still a little steep compared to Pangea mana costs, but it works. I can turn the effect on and off by pushing my mana into the sword. When it is active, tiny bolts of electricity run along the blade's edge.

"Now that's a sword!" says Carter, admiring my new weapon. "Is it possible for you to enchant other people's items?"

"Hmmm, I don't see why not. I guess the real question is whether or not the mana cost comes from me or from the user."

"Why don't we try it out? No harm no foul. We're out in the middle of nowhere with no foes as far as I can see." He looks around, double-checking the area before handing me his trident.

"What kind of enchantment were you thinking?" I ask.

"Hey, you're the master, not me." He throws his hands up in the air. "Make me something useful."

I take the trident in my hands and close my eyes, taking in the feel of it. The weight. The texture. My mana reaches out to it and I try to mentally feel the item. I don't regard it as a weapon of the water, but instead, of the earth. I envision Carter using it. Casting his druid spells and invoking the power of plant life. He doesn't need damage, the plants will handle that. He needs buffs or perhaps an aura.

I've got it!

I focus my mental energy on the trident with the express intent of enchanting it for Carter when a prompt flashes across my vision.

Congratulations! You have learned the skill Designer. You now have the ability to enchant items for other people. The initial mana cost comes from your own mana pool. Any mana costs associated with the item transfer to the new owner. Effects and stats associated with each item will be dependent on the skill and power of the new user. Enchanted items cannot be resold or traded, or enchantment will be lost.

*You have created the item **Fertility Trident**. Aura: animated plant life within the aura's radius receive a 30% boost to size, HP, defense and attack for 30 seconds. 5 minute cooldown. Cost: 25% of total mana.*

It costs me one hundred mana to create the item. I hand it over to Carter and he goes silent for a moment. Will he be able to see the same prompts that I do now?

He runs his hands up and down the trident before speaking.

"Wow," he whispers. "This is going to come in handy."

"Do you know how it works?" I ask.

"Yes. It's strange, but I do. When you handed it to me, I was able to feel its power and recognize its effects. Is that how things always work for you?"

I think about it for a moment before answering. "In a way."

I'm still not sure what the effects of me telling them this is a game would be. These people are more than just NPCs to me. They feel like actual friends.

"Don't move!" shouts Kindra. "I can see someone on the road at the base of the mountain."

Sure enough, someone riding a dark horse hurries along. The way they keep looking over their shoulder makes me think they are being followed. Could be bandits, or something worse.

Once the rider takes the fork in the road that leads away from the mountain, we move again. Our goal is to make it back to Carolton as quick as possible. Hopefully, with no setbacks. Carter has an urgency to him that I can't quite explain. Kindra seems content to take precautions.

Travel speeds up when we are on flat ground again.

Judging by the sun, we have a few hours left before nightfall.

"How did you end up with Priscilla anyhow?" I ask Kindra.

Her face is stone once again and just as I am about to give up on the question, she opens up.

"She took me in when I was a teenager. My father died in an accident. He was a woodsman and went out every day cutting down lumber to sell in the city. One day, the tree fell the wrong way and he was crushed. It was several days before anyone came upon him. He clawed at the tree and eventually his own legs to try and free himself. It was a very gruesome ending."

"How do you know that?" I ask. "Were you there?"

"No, but once I learned my mind magic, I tracked down the men who found him. I wanted to know the whole story. I could hardly believe my father could be so careless, but in the end, I saw their memories and it proved that sometimes, bad things just happen."

"I'm sorry for your loss," says Carter. He places his hand on her shoulder in comfort.

"And what about your mother?" I ask.

"She died of sickness not much later. She was so dreadfully sad after Father died that I think death was a blessing for her. That is why I believe Priscilla did not save her."

She seems eerily calm about the situation, but it has me furious. Priscilla just let Kindra's mother die instead of helping her. If someone could have saved my own parents...

"Wait, what? Why didn't she save her? After what she did to Carter, she must have been able to, right?"

"I'm sure she could have. But Mother and Father loved each other like none other. It was something to aspire to, and even if Mother had been saved, she would never have been happy. I hope that wherever they are now, that they are together."

Some of my anger recedes. Who am I to judge the love of two people I never met? I'm sorry for Kindra. That she had to become an adult without parents to guide her.

"I am an orphan myself, actually. Both my parents died when I was very young. I didn't have anyone like Priscilla to look out for me, though."

"I'm sorry to hear that. I feel like death comes most often to those who deserve it least." For once, there is compassion in her voice. "Is it common for children to grow up without families where you are from?" she asks.

"Not always, but it does happen. More so in the poorer places. Life is harder there."

"It gives me hope then." She smiles. "If someone like you can travel to new worlds and learn magic, then maybe there is more to life for me as well."

"That's the spirit," says Carter.

Before night falls, we decide to stop for food. Kindra uses her bow to shoot a few game birds and we cook them over a small fire. By the time we are finished, twilight approaches.

"I still have energy if you want to travel more tonight. We can use the light of my shield for guidance," I offer.

"That's a good idea. I still have plenty of energy myself. What about you, Kindra?" says Carter.

"I can go a few more hours. We will need to be careful, for we don't know what lies ahead anymore."

Creatures of the night make their presence known across the land. Bugs rattle, birds chirp, and a myriad of other creatures fill the night with sound. It's amazing how much louder the night can be.

I dim the light of my shield so that it lights only a few feet ahead at a time. The moon hides behind a wall of clouds, so the light from the shield is the only guide we have.

The cool air sticks to my face as we walk. It feels almost wet as it clings to me. It's a heavy air that fills my lungs with refreshment.

We walk along in silence. The night is loud enough to crowd my thoughts, so I focus on putting one foot in front of the other.

"Turn your shield off," Kindra whispers in my ear.

I obey, and she pulls me and Carter into a crouching position. Florian steps up beside us.

"Do you see that? Up ahead?" It's too dark for me to see where she is pointing, but eventually, I spot a small dot of light in an otherwise dense blackness.

"A campfire?" The stupidity of my shield dawns on me and I realize just how lucky we were that we weren't attacked. If Kindra could spot a small fire so easily, then we were practically a walking target.

"Looks that way. I think we should check it out. If they are bandits, we can take them out. And if not, then we can all sleep a little easier tonight knowing we won't be killed in our sleep." Hatred coats her voice.

We creep along beside the path, careful to keep our steps in the grass to muffle our approach. The closer we get, I can begin to make out several bodies sitting around a campfire in a grove of trees. The fire rages brilliantly, a beacon in the night and much larger than I initially thought. Whoever they are, they must have no fear of being seen.

Weaseling between the thick grass of the meadow, we

come to a stop behind a thicket of bushes. Safely out of view, we watch the scene play out before us.

A half-dozen small humanoid creatures with green skin and long pointy ears grunt and cackle in conversation. Their words make no sense, sounding very barbarian.

I use my analyze skill and learn that they are all goblins. Two are goblin scouts and the other four are goblin warriors. The scouts wear dull brown cloth armor, benefiting their need for stealth and speed. The others wear studded leather armor of the same color.

The moon briefly makes an appearance from beneath the cloud cover and more of their camp becomes visible. Several tents are strung between the trees. One of the goblins holds an axe across his lap. Two others have short-swords strapped to their sides. I'm not sure what the others carry, but I would imagine the scouts have bows.

"What do we do?" asks Carter. "It's six against four."

"We don't know that they mean us harm," I say.

"You're right, but there is a way to find out," says Kindra. "If I can get close enough, I can feel their intentions with my mind."

"I'm not sure how I feel about that. It seems danger-ous," I say.

She cuts her eyes at me. "I don't need your protection, Esil. I can handle myself just fine." She moves from behind the bush when Carter calls to her.

"Wait. Take Florian with you. He can give you some cover so that you aren't seen."

Kindra nods, and she and Florian take off towards the goblin camp.

Florian takes the lead. As he walks, his bushy head expands, making him into a much larger walking bush that conceals Kindra's crouched position. In the dim light, she will be unnoticed. They creep along until she can't be more than twenty feet from their camp.

I hold my breath, nervously awaiting her return.

After a few moments, they return and Florian retracts to his normal size.

Kindra stares at us, her expression stoic.

"Well, what is it?" I ask.

Her eyes give away no hint of what she is feeling, but her voice quivers when she speaks. "An attack is coming."

CHAPTER TWENTY-TWO

"What do you mean an attack is coming? There are only six of them," says Carter.

"They come from Thunder Mountain. These are just the scouts. There is an entire tribe, and they want our land. Their lives were so much harder where they grew up. Carolton won't stand a chance." Tears brim on the edge of Kindra's eyes.

"How do you know they are attacking Carolton?" I ask. They could be going anywhere.

"Carolton is the first town between Thunder Mountain and the castle. They've already pillaged several small farms on their way here. They will take Carolton and use it as an outpost. The soldiers you saw the other day are all of the militia we have, and they aren't even from Carolton. The king could move them at any time. The townspeople don't know how to fight. Not against what's coming. We're as good as dead."

"Hey! You don't know that." I raise my voice without thinking and several of the goblins turn in our direction.

We quickly dive behind the bushes and when I venture a peek, the goblins have gone back to their bickering.

"We can help fight. We can defend the town," I say, this time more composed, careful not to attract the goblin's attention.

"He's right," says Carter. "I think this is why we were sent away. Why we needed magic. For what's coming."

The tears recede back into Kindra's eyes. The momentary fear is replaced by a grim determination. She may not have parents or many friends back in Carolton, but it's her home. I can tell she loves it and would do anything to protect it. The same way I feel about The Boxes.

"We have to take them out then. If we kill them, then that will buy us some time to prepare the town," I say.

"You're right, but we have to make sure none of them escape. If any of them do, then that means we'll have less time than if we never attacked," says Kindra. "We can't fail."

A prompt flashes across my vision.

You have been given the quest 'Save Carolton, Part 1.' Warn Carolton of an impending goblin attack. Reward: Increased standing within the town.

With the stakes set, we begin to form a plan for how to kill all six goblins without allowing any to escape.

Once we know our roles, all that is left to do is attack.

We crawl through the tall grass like a lion stalking its prey. Florian takes the lead, further disguising our approach. The goblins laugh and argue, all in the same breath, as they cook their catch of the day over the fire, burning it beyond recognition.

The goblins push and shove each other for the biggest slabs of meat and when we attack, they are taken by surprise. Startled grunts and wide eyes greet us before they have time to reach for their weapons.

We attack in unison, bringing complete chaos down upon their dinner.

Kindra freezes the two scouts in place with a mental attack and their bodies go limp. While focusing on the two goblins, she is unable to move, leaving the rest to us. Before the others even have a chance to recognize the gravity of the situation, Florian uses Vine Wrap on two warriors, immobilizing them while Carter and I each take on one of the remaining goblins. They struggle and thrash against Florian's bondage, but his vines hold strong.

I attack the closest goblin with my shortsword just as he pulls his own. Our weapons clank against each other at the last second and his blade stops mine from cleaving his face in two. He parries my next two attacks, retreating to the edge of the campsite. When our blades touch next, the electric bolts that run along Shockwave erupt with a crack, stunning the goblin in place. Only one other goblin is close enough for the area of effect ability, but it doesn't matter. With the goblin stunned, I slide my sword through his neck for a critical hit and he falls to the ground.

Next, I turn to help Carter, but his opponent is already dead as well. Blood stains the tip of his trident while the branches of a nearby tree swing furiously against the goblin's dead body.

Florian still has his goblins held tightly, so Carter and I both rush to Kindra's aid. She releases her mental grip on both goblins just as we arrive and the two goblins stumble back and forth, slowly regaining control of their bodies. One of them yells something in goblin tongue and reaches for a slingshot hanging from its side. Carter points his trident at the goblin and leaves detach from the trees, swarming at the small green creature. They collide with his body, leaving dozens of small gashes. An arrow soars into the heart of the other goblin at point-blank range, dropping it instantly. The slingshot goblin turns to run, but roots spring from the earth and trap it in place. Just like Haunted Earth, except there is no delay and Carter has complete control over the roots. They constrict and I hear the snap of bones as the goblin cries out in anguish. Carter takes pity on the creature and puts it out of its misery with his trident.

The remaining two goblins spit and curse at us as we approach. They struggle against the binding of Florian's viney appendages to no avail. Their eyes radiate hatred. For us or their situation, I'm not sure.

Kindra steps forward, her bow slung across her back, and places her fingers to her temple. A moment later, one of the goblins goes slack and all life fades from its body.

With one goblin left, it would be the perfect time to pump it for information, but without a way to communicate, there is nothing we can do. Kindra has gotten all the information we need from its mind. I'll give the goblin credit, though. Even after witnessing the death of all of his party, he still defies us in the face of certain death. Unblinking, he stares at us as my blade pierces his green skin and severs the life from his body.

We loot the bodies and take everything we can fit into our packs. The armor can be deconstructed and repurposed once we are back in Carolton and their weapons will come in handy for the inevitable battle. They are cruder than the bronze weapons most soldiers and even the bandits had, but it will be an upgrade for many of the stableboys whose only defense is a pitchfork. I take the slingshot and pebbles for myself, having an inkling of how I can put them to use.

Among their camp, we find several tents, burnt meat, and some amber liquid. I try to analyze it but learn nothing. Instead, I place it in my bag for later.

"That was some pretty good teamwork back there," says Carter as we walk on the road by the light of the moon. Our recent encounter has taught me how foolish it is to give away our location in the open. Walking in the dark with my shield as a giant beacon, we're lucky we weren't attacked. I'll save the Shield of Light for dungeons and caves from now on.

Once we are far enough from the goblin battle, we settle down for the night in a dense copse of trees using our newly acquired tents.

It's the first time I sleep in the game and I have the most vivid dreams of electrical charges traveling through my brain, each charge stopping at a memory. The memory plays like a holographic image and my brain throbs before the electrical charge moves on to another. They pass over my time in the mines, the Developer's Tournament; there are some scenes I don't remember, but I recognize myself as a child. I briefly see Merlin and try to stay in that memory, but I have no power and he is whisked away.

A gentle hand presses into my shoulder and I'm blinded by sunlight when I open my eyes.

"You were out cold," says Carter, leaning into my tent. "It's time to get a move on."

It's a bright and sunny day as we journey back towards Carolton. I use my mana to temporarily enchant our boots for one hour at a time, increasing our speed. We make good time, bypassing the Cursed Forest. Who knows what could be waiting for us in there now, and we certainly have more pressing issues. It's better to take the longer route and avoid the risk altogether.

My dreams continue to cross my mind as we walk. Was my mind actually dreaming or was whatever that energy was scanning my brain? Everything feels so real here that I often forget I am only here mentally. Could that be the real reason I'm here, to study the effect this technology has on the brain?

Those answers will have to wait. Right now, we have a town to save.

"Do you think that the king will send soldiers to defend Carolton? Or your lord? We could send a raven to the castle," I ask my group.

Carter scowls and Kindra lets out a sarcastic laugh.

"No way," she says. "The king only sends soldiers to intimidate and quell the unrest. If he has an inkling that there will be an invasion, he will pull all of his soldiers back to the castle. That's where Lord Regis will be as well. Commoners, small town... to him, those can all be replaced."

"Do you think that's true, Carter?"

"Unfortunately, I do. You saw the bandits before we left. If he wouldn't send help for them, why would he protect a town where the only information he knows is how much taxes we owe?" He says it with the luster of someone who has been let down too many times by those he has looked to for support and protection.

Aleesia's words cross my mind. 'You can't save them all, Esil. You just can't.' I can't save the kingdom, but I can do my best to help save the town.

"Then we will just have to do it on our own," I say. "How long do you think we have until the goblins realize that their scouts aren't coming back?"

"A week, maybe more, maybe less."

A week. One week to prepare a town with only a wooden wall and a handful of soldiers for an invasion of goblin warriors. I have my work cut out for me.

"It's a little surprising that all of the scouts were together last night, don't you think? Seems smarter to spread them out."

"From what I gathered from their minds, they are a more barbaric society. They thrive off of brute strength and power, not intelligence. Which is all the more reason we need to hurry."

For the rest of our journey, our enchanted boots help us make excellent time. Carter carries Florian on his shoulders. Luckily for us, we pass no other travelers on the road. Could be that all of these new magical creatures have people afraid to venture out. We don't even pass any bandits.

We encounter several new creatures and I use my analyze skill to determine what they are, but we don't stay to fight. The only time we are forced to fight is when a swarm of fairies blocks the road.

We attempt to go around, but the annoying creatures cross our path no matter which way we go. They utter high-pitched squeals and hover in the air, holding out their hands greedily as if telling us we need to pay a toll to pass.

If you want payment, here it comes.

I take the slingshot and bag of pebbles from my pack. Strapping the bag of pebbles to my belt for easy access, I load one pebble into the slingshot and focus my mana into it. The pebble grows cold in my fingers. Once the enchantment is ready, I let the pebble fly and it soars across the sky, hitting a fairy in the gut. Ice cracks out from the impact and runs along the fairy's body, freezing its wings in place. It falls to the ground, breaking off an arm and wing. The other fairies chitter in response and dive for us.

"You couldn't give us some warning?" Kindra yells. She fires an arrow and mentally guides it through the air, ripping holes in the wings of two fairies. With wounded wings, they fall to the ground and attempt to run away, squealing as Florian chases them. She then follows up with quick psionic blasts, enough to disorient but not kill.

Carter has somehow managed to summon a large flower creature the size of Florian that shoots petals like projectiles into the swarm of fairies. While the flower takes out fairies like a surface to air missile, Carter jabs his trident towards any fairy unlucky enough to come within his range.

A sharp pain courses through my neck and I reach up to find a fairy sinking its razor-sharp teeth into my skin. I pull it away and it gnashes its bloody teeth at me. In a fit of anger, I throw it to the floor and stomp down with a sickening crunch.

I load another pebble into my slingshot. This time, when it hits, a violent explosion rips the fairy apart like a hand grenade, sending pieces of it raining down on its brethren.

I lose track of Kindra and Carter in the fight, but the number of fairies continues to dwindle. They are out of reach of my sword and are now throwing projectiles at us from a distance. Several try to pour fairy dust on us, but Carter has pinwheel plants that blow the dust away any time it gets near. I stick to my slingshot, alternating between ice pebbles and explosions, and before long, we've eliminated the threat.

"Damn fairies. Most annoying creatures we've encountered by far. They're like mosquitoes, but worse," says

Kindra. She wipes a streak of purple blood from her cheek.

"I hear you on that," echoes Carter.

We gather the loot from the bodies, which include several more vials of fairy dust, and head on our way once again.

With all of the armor, weapons, and loot we've gathered over the past day, my pack is almost full and I'm nearly at my limit for what I can carry.

Checking the map, we're only a couple of hours away from Carolton. The boot enchantment has really made this trip a lot easier.

When we arrive at the gates to Carolton, they are barred shut. The guards who normally stand sentry outside have retreated inside and peer at us through a slot.

"Who goes there?" the guard asks.

"Kindra, and these are my two companions. We have grave news for the council. You must let us in at once."

The guard stares at us with suspicion.

"I have direct orders to not allow any outsiders into the town. You may enter, but your companions may not. Have them stand back and I will allow you to pass."

"That's not going to work."

"Then you shall not en—"

The guard stops mid-sentence and Kindra has her hand pressed to her temple. A moment later, the gate opens and we enter.

CHAPTER TWENTY-THREE

The streets inside Carolton are eerily quiet. We bypass the single guard at the gate and he comes to with a slight shake of his head once we are safely away. Only a few merchants have set up shop, and a fraction of the populous seems to be about.

"We need to find Priscilla and then we need to go to the town council building," says Kindra.

Heads follow us as we run through the courtyard. What few people there are gasp at the sight of Florian. It's not every day they see a bush walking through town.

We arrive at Priscilla's cottage and the black building with the white hand seems less obtrusive than I last remember. The handprint on the door is dirty and faded, making the building almost fit in with the surroundings.

Kindra knocks at the door, but there's no answer. After a few more attempts, we enter anyways. The inside is just as I remember. Dozens of vials and containers filled with various colored liquids and herbs. Papers are scattered around the room, and a cat sits idly in a leather chair.

We walk through the cottage, calling Priscilla's name to no response.

In the room where Carter first met Florian, the same glowing orb still moves through the air, bathing the plants in light. Florian extends an appendage and wraps his vines around the light source. His leaves immediately grow a brighter green and he seems stronger, healthier even. Whatever that orb is, it has power.

Priscilla isn't here.

"Where else could she be?" I ask.

"I—I don't know. She could be on a house call, but those very rarely happened. We don't have time to search her out, though. We need to warn the council of what is coming," says Kindra.

Just as we are walking out the door, an alert flashes across my vision.

System Alert: you will be logged out in one in-game hour.

"One hour?" I say to myself, but both Carter and Kindra look at me.

"What is it?" asks Carter.

"I have to go back to my world in an hour. We need to set our plan in motion before then."

Kindra takes us to a building near the town dungeon. A staircase leads up to a second story entrance. We follow her up.

This time, she doesn't knock, just barges right in. A group of people sit around a table arguing. They go silent when we enter.

An older man with a short gray beard is the first to speak. He wears nicer clothes than most of the townspeople. Whoever he is, he isn't a laborer.

"Kindra, what is the meaning of this?"

"Jacob, our town is going to be attacked by goblins."

She cuts right to the chase. "They are crossing Thunder Mountain as we speak. My companions and I came across several scouts and were able to take them out before they made it here."

The table is silent. A middle-aged brunette woman stares out the window while the other two men, one bald and the other with frizzy brown hair, whisper among themselves.

Finally, the older man speaks again. "First elves, and now goblins. What is coming of the world?"

"Elves? What do you mean?" asks Kindra.

"They have been spotted near the Endless Forest. I feel the end times are upon us."

The woman returns her gaze to the room and for the first time, notices Florian. She leaps out of her seat with a scream.

"What is that?" she asks, pointing a shaking finger at Florian.

Florian steps behind Carter's leg, concealing all but his head.

"He's mine. And he's on our side," says Carter.

"What do you mean 'our side'?" the woman spits.

"A war is coming whether you like it or not. The world has changed. You may think it's the end times, but I feel like it's a new beginning. We have the opportunity to change the world. Magic is real again. Creatures of myth roam the meadows and the forests. It is truly an amazing time to be alive, but if we are going to be around to see it, we have to stop those that want to destroy us."

"I don't believe it," says the bald man. He wears a rich robe and several gaudy rings on his fingers. "We have yet to see any of this for ourselves. All this is hearsay and conjecture. It has the town in a panic, and for what? There has been no proof."

"No proof?" asks Carter. "You want proof?" He pulls something from his pocket and tosses it on the table.

"A seed? That's your proof of magic and a new world. Of all the—"

The seed begins to shake. It bounces a little and flips over several times like a hatching egg. A crack forms and two green saplings reach out to the table. A moment later, they form into roots, more saplings shoot out and stems begin to grow into the air. It continues to grow until a large daisy stands in the middle of the table.

If that wasn't enough, Kindra presses her fingers to her temple and the table they're at rises slowly into the air. A foot off the ground, she releases the table and it falls with a smack.

"Gods help us," says the man. "We're doomed."

"Not if you let us help you," I say. "How many people do you have in Carolton?" I ask. Whatever the number, I know it's not a lot and we will need every one of them.

"Around three hundred," says Jacob. "If you take away the children and elderly, we have about two hundred who can fight. A little over half are men."

"And, Kindra, do you know how many goblins are coming?"

She shakes her head. "I can't say for sure, but from what I saw in the goblin's memories, there were at least three hundred. The difference is that they are all fighters, even the children."

You have completed the quest 'Save Carolton, Part 1.' Reward: Your standing within the town has increased.

You have been given the quest 'Save Carolton, Part 2.' Defend the town from the impending attack. Reward: High standing in the town and other benefits.

Other benefits? I wonder what that could mean. If I want to find out, we will have to defend the town first.

Over the next hour, we explain everything we know about magic, our own powers, and what we've seen in the world. Jacob, the gray-haired man, is the town governor. Being such a small town, it doesn't give him very many powers, but he convenes with the council to make all decisions at least once a week. Taking advice from others means that if nothing else, he isn't stubborn.

They all agree that the king will not send help. The reason they were meeting to begin with is to decide how to guard the town. The king had recalled his guards the day after we left on our quest. The only guards in Carolton at the moment are local militia with no experience in combat.

Regardless of whether or not the king will help, we send ravens to every town in the kingdom to warn them of other possible attacks and to request assistance. If there are elves appearing from the Endless Forest, they may mean harm as well.

"How do we prepare for a goblin invasion?" asks Jacob. "Where do we even begin?"

I don't know the first thing about actual defenses, so I stay silent. Luckily, some of the council have ideas.

Tarence, the frizzy-haired man, who is also the town blacksmith, is the first to offer help. "I can get to work on weapons immediately. I know we aren't prepared for battle. We are a farm town and a trading post. The extent of my blacksmithing has been for horseshoes and farm tools, but I still remember a thing or two from my training in the kingdom. I can make spears easy enough. Swords will take more work. As far as the town goes, it may be prudent to add turrets or some kind of defense along the perimeter."

"We also have a handful of weapons we took from the goblins," I offer.

The bald man, Clinton, is the town moneylender. Responsible for making loans to local farmers and businesses, he has a great deal to lose if the town falls and is the closest thing the town has to nobility.

"If you require money or assistance, I will do whatever I can." I don't trust the man, but I trust his self-interest, so I make a mental note of his offer.

The woman who had a panic attack over seeing Florian is named Gertle. "I can make sure the workers are well fed while they build up our town. Send me several women and we will handle the cooking en masse."

"If you don't mind, can I talk to Kindra and Carter in private for a moment?" Jacob nods and leads us into another room, where he closes the door behind us, leaving us alone.

"What's up?" Kindra asks.

"They were quick to join our cause, which is great, but I don't know the first thing about city building or preparing for war," I say.

"None of us do," says Carter. "But we will figure it out together." He seems the least worried of all of us.

"I have to go back soon. Do you think we can handle things while I am away?"

"It's not like we have a choice, is it?" Kindra smirks.

"You should call a town meeting and inform everyone of the situation. It may help ease panic if we are forthcoming with information."

"It will work itself out, Esil. I have a few ideas of my

own for defenses and it just might take a week to get them up," says Carter.

I say my good-byes and leave the council room. If I'm going to be pulled from the game, I want to bind myself somewhere so that I will be safe when I return and not dropped randomly on a street like before.

I make my way back to Priscilla's. She still hasn't returned, but once I enter, I bind myself to her cottage and wait to be pulled out.

CHAPTER TWENTY-FOUR

When I emerge from the immersion capsule, I feel tired and hungry. Not in the same debilitating way as last time, but a slight fogginess invades everything. I can stand and walk, it just feels like I've been put through the wringer.

Marty cleans me up, wiping off the nanoreceptor gel as best he can before I take a shower. I let the hot water wash over me, thoughts of war and town-building holding me hostage. I feel responsible for the lives of three hundred people. If we aren't able to fight the goblins off, those lives will be lost forever. We're up against a threat I'm not sure we can defeat. If we are going to have a chance, though, I'll need to spend my time out here wisely.

After I dry off and dress, I spend a few minutes with the doctor telling him how I feel and letting him check my vitals. Everything is normal. The IV did its job of keeping me nourished while I was in-game.

On my way out, I notice that the two new immersion capsules have been filled with the nanoreceptor gel.

Benjamin is nowhere to be seen. Is he ready to move on to phase two?

Aleesia exits the viewing dock and greets me in the lab with a firm bear hug and a kiss on the cheek. I bury my nose in her neck and let the fragrant aroma engulf me. How does she always manage to smell good, even with working so much?

"What was it like to really experience magic?" She gazes intently into my eyes, her brown eyes boring into me.

"It was crazy, like I could see the way enchanting worked in my mind and feel its power inside of me. All of the formulas, the intricacies, I can still see them in my mind. How is that even possible?"

I still remember the feeling and the formulas that ran through my head like they had always been there. It's like the information for enchanting was hardwired into my brain.

"The game feeds directly into your brain. It's the closest thing to actually being there that you can experience."

Remembering the dreams I had in-game, I decide to tell her about them.

"I had these weird dreams when I went to sleep, like I could see this energy invading my memories. It moved from one to another, replaying them. Some of the memories I didn't even know I had. Do you think it was real or just my imagination?"

Her smile disappears at the news. "That's...odd. That you had dreams. I guess it makes sense since you were still logged in."

"How long do I have to stay out before I can go back? There is a big battle we have to prepare for."

She smiles. "I know. I'm sure Benjamin will have you in as soon as he can."

"Where is he, by the way?" I ask.

"He said he had some business to attend to. I'm not really sure what he's up to. He hasn't been getting much sleep, that's for sure. I've got to get back to work, though. Do you want to grab dinner tonight when I'm done?"

"That sounds great." Maybe she will have some ideas for how I can save Carolton. We hug and then I leave.

Something doesn't feel right when I step into my apartment. My things are moved around, and I can tell someone has been here. Several pieces of clothing are tossed around and the pieces to my haptic suit are not how I left them.

I make my way around the room, checking to see if anything is missing. Everything looks like it is still here. Why would someone go through my things? What could they hope to find?

Something moves in my closet.

Is someone in there?

I search the room for any kind of weapon. Why would someone want to rob me? It's not like I have anything valuable that they couldn't find in the rest of the headquarters. I've only been here a few months and haven't bought anything really.

Not knowing what else to use, I pick up a tablet. If nothing else, I can use it as a blunt object.

With trepidation, I move towards the closet. I'm seconds away from opening the door when it slides open and someone jumps out.

"Surprise!" they shout.

It takes me a moment to recognize Buzz and his mom, Maria. I realize the source of my clothes lying around the room. Buzz is wearing some of my sponsor gear sent to me for streaming. Next to them, an old man beams at me. His hair is balding down the center, and his arms are thin and wrinkled.

"Esil," he says, and I recognize the voice.

"Grayson...holy shit. What are you all doing here?" This doesn't make any sense.

Buzz's mom hugs me while I stand there, my jaw sitting on the floor.

"You paid to move us out," she says. "Benjamin came and picked us up himself. He had nothing but nice things to say about you. Just another example of your generosity. Grayson wasn't going to come, but I threatened to make his life a living hell if he didn't."

"That she did," says Grayson, his lips in a half-smile. "I didn't think it was worth the trouble to fight her on it."

"Yeah," says Buzz. "Looks like we finally found someone who can keep the sexy pirate in check." He pats Grayson on the back.

"You look rough," says Maria. "Is everything okay?"

"I just finished up my research. I've been putting in the hours." They don't know about the alpha testing and I'm not allowed to talk about it, so I just call it research.

"Well, whatever it is, it's taking a toll on you," says Buzz. "Maybe you should lay down for a bit. We're getting settled into our new apartment, but Aleesia said you were coming home soon so we decided to surprise you. Come find us once you look like a normal human again."

I wake up feeling refreshed, able to focus and think more clearly. I know I need to go see Buzz and Grayson, but there is something I need to do first. Putting on my haptic suit, I log into Pangea. In my home portal, I have access to the world's greatest library. Fenrir spins in circles, excited to see me, but I don't have time to play. I toss him a ball while I search through the database. Bringing up everything I can on medieval warfare, I send it to my tablet so that I can view it later.

Essentially, I have one day to come up with a plan and then a week to implement it before a horde of brutal warriors descends on the town. While I'm logged in, I open a list of all the gameworlds in Pangea. There's a world I've seen several times but have never checked it out. The premise always seemed very boring to me. Now that I think of it, it might be just what I need to save Carolton.

Craftwar: Town and Tower Defense. *Set up towers to defend your town from the onrush of orcs that want to tear it to the ground.*

I couldn't have planned a better game if I tried.

Fenrir bounds across the room several more times as we play fetch. I wish I could play more, but time is of the essence.

"Once this is over, I'll have more time to play," I promise before logging out.

The secretary gives me the details of where Buzz, Maria, and Grayson are staying. It's only a few apartments down from mine. Along my walk, I briefly look through some of the medieval defenses I sent to my tablet. Several defensive obstacles catch my attention, like abatis, caltrops, and tiger pits as well as the advanced ranged weaponry of trebuchets and ballistae. These are all certainly attainable with enough wood and workers. I silently hope that Carter and Kindra have stumbled upon some of these ideas themselves.

I knock on the door a few times before it opens with a whoosh. Maria and Grayson sit at a table. Buzz greets me with a high-five.

"This place is awesome!" says Buzz. "Check this out." He tosses me an apple from the bowl of fresh fruit sitting on the table. "An apple. Who knew they were so hard? I've eaten three already."

"You might want to slow down on that," I warn. "Your body is not exactly used to fresh fruits."

"What do you mean?" he asks, but as soon as he does, Buzz's face contorts and his hand grabs his stomach. "Oh... excuse me for a moment."

"What do you think of the place?" I ask Grayson and Maria.

"It's an entirely different world," Maria says. Tears well up on the edge of her eyes. "To think we were living like that. I almost died, you know. And there are places like this. It doesn't seem fair."

I know all too well what she means. It's something that has weighed heavily on my heart, but at least I helped the three of them out of The Boxes.

"It's something else," says Grayson. "Not that I imagined anything less. I'm not sure what we are supposed to do now that we aren't in the mines."

Buzz steps back into the room, looking relieved as he wipes sweat from his forehead. "Benjamin had mentioned putting us to work. I'm not sure what he has in mind, though."

"That's great." I'm surprised that Benjamin took such an effort in moving everyone here. I had only mentioned it to Aleesia, so she must have set the wheels in motion. I wonder if he thought this would placate me for the time being so that he wouldn't have to listen to me talk about those in The Boxes or if he was simply being a decent human? "I'd love to show you around the headquarters, but there is actually something I was hoping you could help me with."

"What is it?" asks Buzz.

"We're going to need to log in to Pangea."

"We come to a place where it's actually nice enough to go outside and the first thing you want to do is log into Pangea," says Buzz. I know he's joking, but I can feel there is some truth to what he is saying. The outside world is such a magnificent place when you've never experienced it before. Still, it means more to me than he will ever know that both he and Grayson are even here at all.

"Help me with this and I can handle the rest myself. I just need a basic understanding of what it will be like so that I can make a game-plan."

"And you can't tell us anything about why you need to know how to defend a town from a horde of orcs?"

"Let it be," says Grayson, who obviously senses my stress about the situation.

We enter Craftwar: Town and Tower Defenses, and it's different from any other gameworld I've been to. We stand in the middle of a small town. It has a church, and several other buildings surrounded by a wooden wall almost iden- tical to Carolton. Ten workers stand in the middle of the town awaiting orders. They wear blue tunics with gray pants. All of the buildings have blue features as well. A timer counts down from five minutes in the top center of my vision.

To the right of my vision, there are icons for several defensive buildings and upgrade options. Underneath each, it tells me the cost in lumber, gold, and manpower. When I select one, I'm able to move a hologram of it around the map until I select the location for the workers to build it. I have no lumber or gold to start with. All of the options before us are a bit overwhelming. While I get the lay of the land, the time continues to count down.

"We should probably start by gathering materials," says Grayson. He orders half of the workers to enter the nearby forest to chop wood and the other half to mine gold. They set off muttering 'yes, sir' and 'right away, sir.'

Buildings cost lumber to build and then gold to upgrade. There are options for some of the defensive obstacles I saw in my research as well as options to upgrade the town wall, build turrets, and train advanced warriors to meet the orc forces in the field.

To create more workers and warriors, I will need to build a barracks that will spawn one new worker every thirty seconds or one warrior every minute. There is also the option for a mystical sanctum, which will spawn wizards and allow for magical upgrades to turrets.

"Here is what I'm thinking. Our primary focus will be on building defensive structures and towers. No more than three wizards at any time. Once our buildings are constructed, we can reinforce them with magic, but it's not our primary defense."

Buzz and Grayson both nod. I can see the wheels in their brains already turning.

"What about warriors?" asks Buzz.

"Basic warriors only. No knights." I want to keep this game as close to a simulation of what might happen as possible.

The workers continue to gather wood and gold. When there is enough to build a barracks, we pull two workers from the mines for construction and leave the others to farming. A long wooden building begins to form as the workers hammer away.

Once, the barracks is completed, it immediately starts churning out new workers. Each new worker heads directly to the forest or gold mine, increasing our supply. There is a limit of five miners at a time, so once the positions are filled, all workers go to the forest. After the barracks, I build a lumber mill that will allow further upgrades to buildings. Wood piles up outside of the mill and reforms as lumber on the other side.

Next, I build a blacksmith, allowing for tower upgrades, weapon upgrades, as well as caltrops, which will slow down any mobile attack the orcs might bring with them. I tell Grayson and Buzz not to upgrade our warriors with better weapons. Our fighters in Carolton will be working with whatever materials Tarence can scrape together. The mystical sanctum can wait for now as well.

We will start with constructing towers at four points around the town, protecting each side. The initial towers are for scouting only and will be equipped with projectiles once it is upgraded.

The timer hits zero before I know it and the orc forces begin to mobilize across the map. It will take them time to reach us, but we aren't nearly prepared enough.

"We need to take workers out into the field and set up obstacles to slow them down," says Grayson.

"Okay, you take care of that. Buzz, I need you to upgrade the barracks for faster warrior production and mobilize the ones we have. We have enough workers. I'm going to start on upgrades."

My first upgrade is to the towers. Twenty-five gold and lumber turns it into a ranged tower, capable of firing on anything that comes within twenty meters. All four towers get the upgrade.

Buzz forms ranks with the warriors just inside the tower's range. Grayson sets traps and obstacles along the way and is nearly back to us.

Finally, I start construction on the mystical sanctum. It produces one wizard every minute and allows for magical upgrades to weapons.

The first wizard pops out and joins up at the rear of our militia. He wears a blue hat and carries a staff topped with a glowing sapphire. While I wait for the next wizard, I check in with Grayson on the obstacles.

"I have dozens of caltrops hidden throughout. If they have any wagons or siege gear, it'll slow them down. I also set up abatis at various intervals to help funnel their forces. It won't do much but slow them down, but if we have any ranged attacks, it should help with that. My favorites are the tiger pits. You can't even see them with the brush cover. Once enough weight is on it, the orcs will fall right through and be impaled on dozens of sharp spikes. I imagine by the time they are halfway here, they'll be as focused on the ground as they are on us."

"Good job. How are the soldiers looking, Buzz?"

"We have a handful of warriors, a few archers, and one mage. We're ready to attack when you are."

"Go ahead, you and Grayson are in charge of the troops. I'm going to stay back and keep working on our defenses."

They take their place beside our small army. In this world, we are immune from attacks and damage and are also unable to interact with any of the objects, so that we can't physically influence the battles. We can set targets and movement, but the fighting is done by the warriors.

The two other wizards join Buzz and Grayson. Wizards deal magical damage, which can't be blocked by shields or armor. They also have the ability to cast a random spell every tenth attack, from a stun to increased attack speed buffs to several others.

With the magical sanctum up and running, I focus on the towers. They are the bread and butter of our defense and I want them dishing out as much power as possible. The magical upgrade increases their range to forty meters and deals bonus magical damage with each attack. I upgrade all four towers and pull all of the workers from the mines and forests.

Along with my twenty-two workers, I set off to join Buzz and Grayson on the battlefield.

I could keep farming and building, but I see no point. I want this to be a simulation of the fight to come and once the battle begins, everything will be set and there will be nothing left to do but fight.

"How's it looking up there? I'm on my way with the townsfolk."

"Esil, what the hell? Why aren't you building more towers?" asks Buzz, incredulously.

"It's the way it has to be. Now, how are things?"

"So far, it's pretty even," says Grayson. "They've pushed past a few of the obstacles I've set up. Our archers are dealing some damage, but our warriors are no match for their brute strength. The wizards are the only ones who are really making a dent."

The clamor of steel greets us as the workers join in the ranks of a massive battle. The orc warriors are nearly twice as large as their human counterparts. Two long teeth protrude over their jowls. Dark green skin, covered in black war paint, make them look all the more intimidating than the polished humans in blue tunics and chainmail. Using iron and bone weapons, they attack with great ferocity, taking down nearly two humans for every one orc lost.

Armed with only axes and pickaxes, the workers join in the chaos. Icons float on the battlefield, warning them of the tiger pits and other dangerous obstacles.

Our warriors fall back under the immense pressure of the orc ranks.

An orc shaman, black hair pulled into a ponytail and clad in an array of furs, moves in line against the workers I brought. A necklace of skulls rattles ominously as he walks. He raises a glowing bone scepter high into the air. With a flash of purple light, half of the workers keel over dead, little more than fodder. The others press on with a sense of resolve no real army would have in the face of such actions. A brute of an orc riding a bear gallops toward the helpless workers, but the bear steps on a caltrop and falls to the ground, tossing the rider off.

The orc rider crawls to his feet carrying a blade as tall as the workers themselves. With a powerful swing, he cleaves two workers in half with one blow.

I know that orcs and goblins are different creatures, but is this what awaits us in Carolton? Are the untrained townspeople no match for the goblin horde?

A wizard joins with the workers and shoots out blue streams of magic. They hit the orc rider for more damage than the entirety of the workers with each hit. After three attacks, a yellow stream erupts from the wizard's staff and the orc rider shrinks by half his size. Now the same size as a human, the orc is overwhelmed by the remaining workers.

To my left, I notice that our battle lines have fallen. Only a fraction of our army remains, even one of the wizards has died. Meanwhile, the orc army seems never-ending.

We are so screwed.

A powerful blast rips through the orc army, sending several of the peons flying.

Ha! We're in range of one of the towers. It continues to shoot a blast every few seconds, damaging the army far better than our warriors have.

"Keep them in range of the towers and fight," I order, and Buzz and Grayson reorganize our army within range of the tower. "If we can lure them a little farther to the right, they'll be in range of both towers."

I see now how I could have won the game. If I had made a funnel of towers and forced the orcs to travel down it in order to reach the town, then likely they could have been defeated much more easily, but in real life, the goblins won't be so stupid. They'll attack under cover of darkness, or from our blindside. We will have to be ready for anything.

We eventually lure the orcs into range of the second tower, but with a great loss of life on our own part. The towers continue to decimate the orc army, but their sheer numbers keep them moving. They overtake what's left of our army until all that remain are the defensive structures.

Dead orc bodies pile around the wall, but they continue to push. The health bars on the towers deplete little by little until they crumble to dust. When the towers are gone, the walls stand no chance. Even with the upgrades, the orcs tear through them easy enough.

Second by second, every building we constructed falls to our enemies. When the church crumbles down, everything goes dark and in bloody red lettering, 'DEFEAT' flashes across my vision.

"We need more towers and we need more warriors," says Grayson, crossing his arms. "More knights or mages. They are the difference-makers."

"Yeah, there are just too many orcs to defeat with what you gave us," says Buzz.

They are right, but what's the point of winning the game if it doesn't help with the reason I actually came here?

"There has to be a way. Run it again."

We run the game again. This time focusing more on warrior production and moving all four towers to the front side. We last longer, but are eventually overrun by the orcs again.

Next, we build more towers, but have less warriors. They defeat us again.

Ten more games come and go with various setups and incarnations. We never take down more than three quarters of their army.

"Dammit," Grayson yells. Even though he doesn't know the scope of the situation, the constant losses are frustrating him none the less.

"Let's call it a day." I finally resign. "Thanks for all your help." I grasp them both around the forearm in turn.

"Whatever it is you're working on, you'll figure it out," says Buzz.

I sure hope so.

CHAPTER TWENTY-FIVE

With my spirit dampened and no way of knowing if my ideas to save Carolton will be enough, I settle down on the sofa and pour through the resources I downloaded earlier.

Medieval warfare is so simple and primitive compared to modern technology. A hole in the ground with spikes or a movable partition to prevent a cavalry charge would have such little effect against a robotic soldier, chemical warfare, or a large nuclear arsenal. Back then, though, that was how kingdoms were built, on a battlefield where the price was paid with the lives of common people who simply wanted to protect their way of life.

Not much has really changed, I guess. The common people are still the ones who pay the steepest prices.

Buzz and Grayson are out exploring the Pangea headquarters. It's a lovely place and the sky lights up like a painting at sunset. I'm sure they are awestruck like I was when I first got here. I'd love to spend the evening with my friends and show them around, but I have a town that is depending on me. They'll understand one day.

Think, Esil. Think.

In Craftwar, it was the mages and the turrets that made the biggest impact on the battle. Kindra, Carter, and I will be doing our fair share of work when the time comes, but we can't let the villagers be slaughtered the same way the workers were in the game. Every villager that dies is a life lost. A life the town will have to go on without.

If only we knew where Priscilla was. She has more magical power than the three of us combined. But, of course, she disappears at the moment we need her most.

I'm looking over whether or not ballistae can be used as a defensive measure when a woman's voice greets me through my intercom.

"Esil, are you there?" asks the voice.

"Uh, yeah."

"Benjamin would like to see you in his office. Please report there as soon as possible." There is a quick click letting me know she ended the call.

What could he possibly want with me? Maybe to check in on Buzz and Grayson. If it was about the game, then he would have been there when I logged out.

I throw on a hoodie and read my tablet as I walk to Benjamin's office.

When I arrive, Benjamin has his back turned, facing out the window. The collar of his shirt is askew, showing the tie beneath it.

"You wanted to see me?"

He turns around and I can immediately see bags under his eyes. He sports a salt and pepper beard, his manicured looks all but gone. What is he dealing with that has him so out of sorts?

"Have a seat." He motions lazily to the chair in front of

his desk.

I take a seat and watch him as his icy blue eyes lose focus.

"Thank you for moving Buzz, Maria, and Grayson out of The Boxes." I say it more to break the awkward silence than anything else.

"Don't mention it. You're a good kid and your heart's in the right place. I can't move them all out...maybe one day, but not now. It's the least I could do to help bring you some happiness."

Why is he talking to me like I'm on my deathbed?

"Is everything okay, Benjamin?"

He shakes his head as if clearing his mind and looks at me like he just now realized I'm here.

"Uhm, yes, everything is fine. I called you here to talk to you about your time in-game. Sorry I wasn't there when you logged out, but I had some personal issues to deal with. I talked to the doctors earlier and looked over your report. The IV seemed to help a lot, but I was wondering, have you been feeling any different outside of the game? Just between you and I." He stares at me intently. Like he's expecting something.

"What do you mean?"

"I don't know. Do you feel more aware? Like your brain is functioning differently? Anything like that?"

What the hell is he getting at? Am I some kind of special brain experiment?

"No, everything is norm—" Then I remember what I told Aleesia earlier.

"What is it?" he looks at me with greed in his eyes. Like what I'm about to say might just be the most important thing he has ever heard.

"When I learned magic in the cave, it was like the

information was fed to my brain. Not like in Pangea, where you learn a spell and you learn the movement and the ability to cast it. Or like reading a book and then knowing what you read. No, this was different. It was a massive influx of knowledge there in an instant. It's all still in my head right now. I can remember the exact formulas for calculating how powerful a spell will be versus how long it will last."

Benjamin presses his fingers together ominously.

"Excellent. That's all I needed to know. Get a good night's sleep and be in the lab first thing in the morning. You'll be going on a deep dive."

After I leave Benjamin's office, I make plans for dinner with Aleesia, Buzz, Maria, and Grayson.

I order food from the cafeteria and have it delivered as soon as everyone shows up. For the next hour, I try to put my thoughts of Carolton aside and focus on my friends.

"So, Aleesia," says Buzz with a mouth full of potatoes, "we haven't seen you in Pangea in quite a while. What gives?"

"I've been busy with school and my internship. This is my last semester so I'm really going hard to try and be prepared for what's next."

"And what's that?" asks Grayson. He's a very meticulous eater, cutting his chicken into tiny cubes and keeping his potatoes and peas separated from each other.

"If I'm lucky, they'll let me stay on with my current project. I'm an intern, but I'm basically an unpaid developer at this point."

"What are you working on exactly?" asks Buzz.

"It's top secret." She winks.

"Dammit, I thought you might let it slip. Esil's mouth is as tight as a clam on the subject."

Aleesia reaches over and takes my hand.

"It's good to know he can be trusted," she teases.

For the rest of the meal, we talk about The Boxes, Buzz's childhood, and what everyone hopes to do now that they are here. It feels good to just sit around and talk. All too soon, the dinner is over and it's time for everyone to leave.

After Buzz, Maria, and Grayson leave, I pull Aleesia aside.

"Hey, did you mention anything to Benjamin earlier? About my dream or how I felt after learning magic?" I ask.

Aleesia looks confused for a moment.

"No, I haven't seen him since you left. What's up?"

"He was asking me how I felt. Not physically, but mentally. Like he was expecting something."

"That's very strange..." Her voice trails off.

"Yeah, and he said I'm going on a deep dive tomorrow. Do you know anything about what that might mean?"

Concern radiates from her face. "It means he's putting you in extended play. It looks like you'll get to see the battle through till the end."

Sleep comes hard. I toss and turn, echoes of our defeat in Craftwar replaying in my mind, only this time, the warriors and the workers are all people from Carolton. They are guards and townspeople I passed in the streets. The mages are Carter and Kindra. As much as we try, the goblins are too much. They attack with blunted knives and brute force, pulling the life from anything in their way.

Running into the fray, my enchantments do damage,

but it's never enough. A great goblin warrior steps in my path, brandishing a two-handed axe. I raise my sword in defense, but he knocks it aside, the icy blade ripping into my flesh.

I wake up in a cold sweat. How is it that a game is having this kind of effect on me? Raising my heartbeat even when I'm not there, controlling my thoughts, making me care...

For the rest of the night, I continue to study and run through enchantment possibilities in my mind. My mana is too low to make a difference on a grand scale. I can't enchant the entire wall with the density of steel or make every blade unbreakable, but maybe I can do just enough. That's all we need. Just enough to succeed.

When my alarm goes off, I'm already dressed. I eat a breakfast of sliced berries and oatmeal, then head to the lab for my first deep dive.

Everyone is already at work, scurrying around the lab like bees in a hive.

Sensors and monitors are set up over the two new immersion capsules.

"Let's get you ready," says Marty. He waits for me at the top of the immersion capsule I've been using. A smile stretches across his freckled face.

I strip down and let him attach the sensors. It no longer bothers me that I'm naked in front of a room full of people. They are all focused on doing their jobs. Well, maybe except for one person.

Aleesia makes eye contact with me and gives me a thumbs-up.

"I'm not going to lie," says Marty. "I can't wait to see this battle go down. It's going to be epic."

"What do you mean?" I ask.

"Just wait and see. Carter and Kindra have been busy while you were gone."

Marty must have been watching the feed while I've been resting. You would think he'd have seen enough of the game watching me run around for hours on end.

I open my eyes slouched against a chair in Priscilla's study. The cottage is empty but for a cat that crawls across the table, tail swishing back and forth. Several of the vials and potions that adorned the room are missing. As I walk through the house, I notice that most of the plants are gone as well.

Stepping out into the street, Carolton is once again booming with activity. It reminds me of the city on the day I first showed up, only everyone talks of work. There's no laughter, only hard work.

Men carry wooden planks on their shoulders. The blacksmith's forge rings throughout the streets. Boxes filled with farm tools wait outside its doors. Hammers rise and fall in a hypnotic rhythm outside the town walls.

I call to a man carrying a handful of wooden planks. "Excuse me, have you seen Carter or Kindra about?"

He nods. "Carter is outside the wall, prepping the defenses. The last I saw of Kindra, she was training with the archers."

"Thank you."

Archers? We have archers? I'll give it to them, they've made a lot of progress in the time I've been gone.

A group of villagers sits at a table eating in the town's center. Gertle and a group of women have a buffet set up for people to eat. Bread and stew waft through the streets, making my mouth water.

The gate that leads into town is open, allowing villagers to come and go as they desire. I pass an area where all of the village children are being kept together. From the looks of it, an elderly woman is teaching them about basket weaving.

Put everyone to use, I suppose.

Several men work on the construction of a guard tower at the corner of the wall. We'll need one of those at all four corners and we'll have to have someone posted at all hours once they are completed.

I freeze in place when I step through the gate.

How is this even possible?

The outside wall is covered in thorny vines. From the ground up to the top of the wall, thick, green vines blot out the wood underneath. I rub my finger against one of the thorns and it pricks me, drawing blood. No one is climbing over the wall without enduring a lot of pain. But that's not even the best of it.

Every five feet or so, large plants with brilliantly colored flowers stand sentry. Each one is three to four feet high. If I know Carter, I bet they have some sort of projectile ability. In front of them, monstrous plants that look like hungry mouths snap their jaws.

Giant Flytrap. *These carnivorous plants snatch birds from the air and decompose their flesh for nutrients.*

I bet birds aren't the only thing they will eat if it gets close enough. The villagers give the plants a wide berth as they walk past, careful to stay out of reach of their hungry mouths.

It's crazy. I was so focused on the practical defense of a town that I didn't take into account that magic might be the one thing that saves us.

Carter stands by a large tree, casting a spell on a seed

after he plants it in the ground. The seed grows faster than any plant I have ever seen, blossoming into a fully-grown flower in under a minute.

"Esil!" Carter notices me. "Boy, am I glad to see you!" He runs up to me and squeezes me firmly on the shoulder.

"I can't believe you've done all of this while I've been gone."

Carter's eyes are sunken with large bags forming underneath, but his spirits are high.

"I haven't slept in two days. It takes a lot of mana to grow this many plants, but as soon as it replenishes, I'm on to the next one."

I'm completely blown away by his dedication.

The tree that Carter stood next to suddenly moves and I notice two holes where eyes would be staring down at me. Roots rip from the ground with each step the tree takes until it bends down and offers a massive branchy hand to me.

"Is that—"

"This is Florian's final form. I'd like to see goblins try and mess with him now." Carter beams with pride at Florian's new figure.

No longer the walking bush, Florian is a fully-formed tree. He stands over twenty feet tall, moss running down the bark that makes up his skin. His body now formed of massive tree trunks. Small branches shoot off in various directions. Florian is a natural tank, capable of taking a massive beating and dishing out pain. I feel a lot better knowing he is on our side.

"Where's Kindra? And did you ever find Priscilla?" I ask.

"No one has seen or heard from Priscilla since she left."

He shakes his head in frustration. "And Kindra, she's out in the field practicing with the archers."

"Okay, I'm going to go pay her a visit. I think you should get some rest for a few hours at least."

He nods. "Now that you're here, I feel a little better about taking a breather. Tarence has been working on weapons nonstop since you left. If you need men, talk to Jacob and I'm sure he will send them your way."

Kindra stands among a group of people in a field to the side of the town. There are about a dozen people, organized in three rows of four each. They all hold longbows and have a satchel of arrows slung over their shoulders. A dozen archers is not a lot, but it's better than nothing.

Several hundred yards away, a small army of scarecrows has been assembled. A small boy runs back from the scarecrows with a bag full of arrows. He drops them at Kindra's feet when he returns, and she raises her hand.

At this signal, the archers nock their arrows and take aim at the far-off targets. I'm extremely nervous to see how accurate the aim of these untrained archers will be.

Kindra drops her hand and the bowstrings thrum as they release their arrows. The arrows shoot off in varying directions, but it's clear that none of them are going to hit their targets.

That's why we have practice. But there are only so many days left.

I'm about to call out to Kindra when I notice the trajectory of the arrows changes. They all straighten and move in towards one another in a tighter formation. Kindra has her hand pressed to her temple. The arrows move in perfect harmony and each one hits a vital location on the scarecrows.

I should have known. All the archers need to do is fire the arrows and Kindra handles the rest.

"Well done!" I applaud as I move in closer. "Brilliant work, everyone."

"Esil! It's good to see you!" Kindra rushes to me and does something completely out of character. She hugs me.

"You all have been busy. The town is far more prepared than I had imagined it would be. I think we have a good chance at holding our own."

"We may indeed. I'm hoping you have the final pieces to the puzzle." She smiles.

"I have a few ideas. Have you seen Jacob? I'm going to need workers and lots of tree branches. I also need to see Tarence so I can have him start on a few designs. I convinced Carter to lay down for a while. He looked like hell from setting up all of our defenses so far."

"He's pushing himself harder than I thought possible. Jacob should be in the council room and Tarence is at his forge. He's been working just as hard as Carter, if not more so."

First, I go to the blacksmith. The task for Tarence is simpler and won't need my supervision once I give him the details.

Tarence stands hammering at a glowing piece of metal that he has just pulled from the furnace. Sweat streams down his face and his powerful muscles contract as he works. Sparks fly and the anvil rings with each powerful hit. His frizzy hair bounces around like foam caught in a turbulent sea. A pile of farm tools lays at Tarence's feet. Next to them in another pile are the reforged weapons, where shovels and pitchforks have been hammered into spears with much sharper and deadlier tips.

"How's the progress?" I ask.

"You're back," he says in between strikes. The glowing metal shapes into a pointed edge and then Tarence cools it in a bucket of water before setting it to the side. "We will have enough spears for every man and woman who wishes to fight. Swords are another matter altogether. We have the goblin's swords you brought back, and we have the swords from the guards. Not nearly enough, but we will make do with what we must."

"Do you think you could take some time away from this to make something for me?" I ask.

"What is it?"

"They are called caltrops. Basically, it's a sharp piece of jagged metal with four pointy ends. Three of the ends are always on the ground with the fourth pointed in the air. Kind of like a jack. If we have enough of them, we can set them in the fields and take out some of their cavalry."

"Interesting. Can you show me a design?" he asks.

On a piece of parchment, I draw a caltrop. Making sure to note that three prongs should always touch the ground. Tarence looks the parchment over and nods.

"I can do this. I'll need more metal, though. I have enough to get started, but if you want to surround the town, I'll need a hell of a lot more. Tell Jacob I have need of him."

"Will do."

Jacob sits at the table in the council room, looking over a map of the countryside. He has a handful of brightly colored rocks placed in various locations on the map. He runs his fingers through his gray beard.

"How's it looking?" I ask.

He lets out a deep sigh.

"I've never had to defend against an invasion before.

I've dealt with the bandits as best I could. This... I was not prepared for this."

Jacob buries his head in his hand. I can only imagine what he must be feeling. Tasked with governing a small town for the king and then thrust into a battle with creatures that were largely thought to be myth.

"You're doing a fine job. The city is better defended with each passing hour. When the time comes to fight, we will be ready."

"Do you really think so?" His brown eyes plead with me.

"I do, but I need your help with something."

"Anything if it will help save the city."

"Gather me every man with an axe and as many wagons as we can spare."

It doesn't take long for Jacob to gather some two dozen men who are not working on other defenses. We pile into three wagons and set off for the closest forest.

We arrive at the forest and I gather all the men around me. Both fear and excitement radiate from their eyes.

"You weren't prepared for what is about to come. Hell, how could you be? The world changed right before your eyes, and now you have no choice but to change with it. My friends and I, we're going to do our best to make sure that Carolton goes into this new age as strong as she left the old one. You will all be a part of that."

They all stare at me. Men of different ages, some younger than me, and others past their prime, one looks to be older than Grayson. Perhaps not knowing what to say. Maybe afraid to speak it into existence.

"Can someone lend me an axe?" I ask.

A young man, not much younger than me, holds his axe out to me.

"My goal is to have their army hurting before they ever make it to the walls of Carolton. Maybe even convince them to turn back. That's going to start with abatis. They are one of the most simple forms of defense known to man."

The axe feels natural in my hand as I swing at a tree trunk about the size of my wrist. The tree itself is maybe fifteen feet tall, perfect for what we are about to make.

With the tree cut down, I take the axe and begin chopping the branches and shaping them into sharp points. When I'm finished, there are dozens of sharp points ready to rip into anything that tries to cross them.

"This is an abati. Cut the tree, sharpen the branches, and then set them in line together to form a barricade that cavalry cannot cross and soldiers have to divert around. If we place them strategically, with small gaps in between each row, then it will force the army to funnel their soldiers and our archers will be able to pick them off. Not to mention, it will slow their progress and if we're lucky, it might impale a few riders."

For the next several hours, some of the men chop trees and sharpen their branches while others load them into wagons and begin forming a barricade around Carolton. The town looks more formidable with each passing minute.

"Jacob, can you monitor the rest of the construction? I have a few more things I need to take care of."

"Absolutely. This is a great idea you had, Esil." He looks more relieved than when I found him in the council room.

"Don't mention it. And, Jacob, make sure you take the same route back. I don't want anyone getting hurt with what I'm about to try."

Now that the physical defenses are being taken care of,

it's time for me to work my magic. I doubt I'll be able to create a small army of plant creatures that can be left alone to fight, but maybe I can do something to help turn the tide when the moment comes.

With my enchantments removed from my sword and shield, I have the full mana pool available for today's work.

What is the most practical use of enchantments for the coming battle? I need something that will disrupt and damage the enemy. It would be a bonus if it also caused panic. Something where they must fear every step they take.

The tiger pits cross my mind again. I chose not to construct them because it seems like the time it would take to dig the holes and plant the spikes could be used more effectively elsewhere. Once the first goblin falls through the pit, then it would be unlikely the others would fall in unless we were fighting at night.

But what if I could cause that same fear without giving warning to the rest of the horde?

I find a rock and pick it up. Channeling my mana, I focus it into the rock with the intent of having it explode once stepped on.

Congratulations! You have created **Rock Land Mine**. *When pressure is applied to the rock, it will explode for 50 damage. One-time use. Cost: 100 mana per rock.*

Curious as to how well my medieval magic mine will work, I toss the rock high into the air and step back. It hits the ground with an explosion of dirt and grass and when I check the scene, a crater a foot wide and six inches deep is all that remains.

Hell yeah!

I create two more mines and place them at various locations throughout the field. Tiny red dots let me know where they are so I don't accidentally step on them. Other members of my group and the townspeople won't be so lucky. I'll need to place them far out and then add the remainder when we are no longer traveling to the woods for lumber. The last thing I would want is to inadvertently kill a villager. Once the battle is over, I can disenchant any remainders all at once.

I walk the perimeter of the town for the remainder of the afternoon, setting up landmines. Whichever direction the goblins decide to attack from, they'll pay a steep price before they ever make it to our defenses.

When the sun sets, the entire town gathers in the courtyard to eat the dinner Gertle and her helpers cooked. I talk with Kindra, Carter, and the town council on the day's progress, making sure to warn them about the mines I have placed in every direction except for the path to the forest.

Tarence informs me that he has made roughly fifty caltrops and has plans for at least a hundred more.

The only person with nothing to contribute is Clinton, the moneylender. We have made so much progress with magic and natural items, plus re-forging tools into weapons, that there has been no need for his money, not that any of the neighboring towns would likely part with their items under the circumstances.

We finish eating and I find two nearby torches. They cast enough light for us to eat under, but nothing more. I enchant them both to produce enough light to ignite the courtyard like it is day.

People gasp at the sudden influx of light and I use the opportunity to grab their attention.

"You've made great progress today, but defenses are only half of the battle. Now you must learn to fight."

CHAPTER TWENTY-SIX

Y*ou have created **Training Sword.** While active, this blade deals no damage. Cost: 50 mana*

Excellent! This is even better than a wooden training sword because it feels and moves like the real thing. It will give the townspeople a feel for what real battle is like and the fatigue of holding a weapon for hours.

"Who wants to go first?" I ask the crowd of villagers before me.

The courtyard hangs in silence until a young man steps up. I remember him from the alleyway when I first spawned back in the city after being pulled from the game. He looks sheepish, wearing tattered clothing with his shaggy red hair hanging over his eyes.

"I'll go," he mumbles.

"What's your name?"

"Neil."

"Alright, Neil, let's see what you've got."

I toss him a sword. He catches it by the hilt just before it hits the ground. Feeling the blade in his hand, he stands a little taller.

"Nice catch," I say at the same time as I slash at him. He's too slow to react and the blade hits him in the shoulder.

He falls to the ground and stands up shocked that it didn't hurt.

"Had that been a real hit, you would have lost your arm. The first thing you must always remember is to be prepared. Your enemies will not wait until you are ready. They will cheat because out there—" I point beyond the walls, "—it is life and death." I swing again and this time, he raises his sword. Our blades connect with a clink and he parries my sword to the side.

I attack again, and he blocks. Over and over, I slash as Neil practices the move that may save his life someday soon. We go until the boy's arms shake and he can barely hold the weight of the sword.

"Good job, Neil. Now take a break and give someone else a chance."

My mana pool increased over the course of the day as I kept constructing more and more mines, bringing my total mana pool up to four hundred. I'm able to create eight training swords and have the villagers pair up into groups, taking turns attacking and defending. I'm not an expert by any means, but my time in Pangea has equipped me with at least a basic sense of sword-fighting.

For the next couple of hours, I drill with as many villagers as possible, correcting their stances and offering feedback where I can. They have a lot to learn, but hopefully the next couple of days will give us the opportunity to improve.

I feel proud of the day's progress when I dismiss them for the night. Jacob approaches me, smiling.

"Not a bad training session. Some of them look like they might actually have promise."

"They do. And they will only get better. I think we should all get rest if we can. I'd put someone in the guard towers on a four hour rotation to be safe. We want to be in the habit of preparedness."

Taking our leave, Kindra, Carter, and I retire to Priscilla's for the night.

"Where do you think she is?" I ask Kindra. In the pit of my stomach, I have a feeling that Priscilla knew what was coming. That this is all some kind of test.

"No idea." She shrugs.

"Has she ever done this before? Just up and vanished?"

Kindra shakes her head as Carter steps into the room.

"Florian is sleeping outside. When he doesn't move, he looks just like a tree. Sometimes he's so still that I forget he's there. Poor guy has gotten too big to come inside." There's a slight frown when he says it.

"It's nice to have him watching over us, though," says Kindra. She takes Carter by the arm. "Get some rest."

Carter takes Priscilla's bed, and I fall asleep in a large cushioned chair.

I have the same dreams as before. My brain glows with a neon aura as tiny sparks travel across its surface, replaying memories. It's almost like I can feel the static as they travel about, making my head feel warm and fuzzy. Before I know it, the crow of a rooster sounds through the town, telling me it's time to rise.

Groggily, I sit up and attempt to gather my thoughts, mentally recounting what still needs to be done, when a loud bang on the door startles me.

The beating continues frantically until I open the door, where a wide-eyed woman screams at me.

"There are people at the gate! Naked and covered in blood. Jacob sent me for you."

Kindra and Carter stumble into the room behind me just in time to hear the woman's words.

"We best go check it out," says Carter, stretching his arms over his head.

We hustle to the gate as the sun begins to rise over the wall. What the hell could possibly be going on? My first thought is that the goblins have attacked a small farm. Could they already be so close?

A crowd gathers around the gate by the time we arrive. Guards peer through the slats and Jacob stands behind them expectantly.

"They say they know you," he says.

"What? How? You are the only people I know."

"Take a look for yourself." He motions towards the gate.

I peer through the slat in the gate. Buzz and Grayson stand on the other side, hands covering their nethers. It's not the version of them I have seen in Pangea so many times. No, they look the same as in real life. Buzz is young and lean with his hair buzzed close, a scar running down his left cheek. Grayson, old and fragile compared to his avatar and much less bearded. I don't even know how it is possible that they are here.

"Let us in. Let us in. Let us in!" chants Buzz. "There are so many painful and scary things out here."

"Open the gate. And see if we can find these two some clothes," I tell no one in particular.

Buzz and Grayson rush through the gate and it is quickly slammed shut behind them.

"Esil, it's so good to see you!" says Buzz. "I'd give you a hug, but, you know." He looks down at his hands.

"What are you two doing here? How are you two here?" I ask.

"Well, actually—"

"Hold that thought. Jacob, can we use the council room for a moment?" I don't want anything they say to be overheard by the town.

"Be my guest, but I hope to have a full explanation when you are finished."

"Kindra, Carter, I hope you'll understand, but I need to talk to them in private first."

They both nod and someone comes running, carrying clothes for both Buzz and Grayson. They turn away from us and pull the tunics and pants on quickly.

In the council room, we are finally able to speak freely.

"So..."

"This place is crazy!" says Buzz. "I didn't know it was possible to feel a game like this. Look at my feet." He lifts his foot up. They are bloodied and bruised, pieces of flesh hanging off in spots. "I can already feel them healing. Everywhere I stepped, the ground just kept exploding. It hurt like a son of a bitch. You have this place really well defended."

"We're preparing for an attack. We can talk about the game later. First, I want to know how you are here."

"Benjamin offered us a job," says Grayson. "He asked if we wanted to know where you had been spending all your time. This is truly something else."

"Yeah, we went through a physical, and next thing we know, they were hooking us up with wires and dropping us in this jelly goop. We spawned in the middle of a field completely naked with no instructions. This was the first town we saw. I'm running through the field and the next thing I know, the ground starts exploding under my feet. I mentioned your name at the gate and you have no idea how happy I was when they recognized it."

For the next little while, I fill Buzz and Grayson in on Carolton and The Broken Lands, telling them about magic, the goblins, the people, and most importantly, not to tell the NPCs this is a game.

"So let me get this straight. There is the ancient, beautiful, sometimes ugly, but always powerful lady who sends you on a quest to find magic and then she just disappears when you get back?" asks Buzz.

"Yep."

"Ha! Sounds like your typical meddling god to me."

"And you have what, three, maybe four days to prepare for this attack?" asks Grayson.

"If we're lucky."

"How can we help?"

I call in Carter and Kindra first, telling them that Buzz and Grayson are like me, adventurers from another world. They are quick to accept and grateful to have more people with knowledge of battle on our side.

Next, we meet with the council and inform them that Buzz and Grayson will be helping to train the villagers while the rest of us work on defenses.

"When do we get magic?" asks Buzz, and I can't help but laugh.

"How about once this is over?"

Jacob just shakes his head. "First magic, then goblins, now we have adventurers from other worlds. When does it end?"

We go down into the courtyard, where Jacob introduces Buzz and Grayson to the town.

Buzz immediately picks up a sword and starts swinging.

"Alright, chumps, who's up first?"

I leave them to their training, content in knowing that with the enchantment, Buzz won't be able to wound more than their spirits. Grayson will be there to make sure he doesn't get too out of hand.

Kindra meets with her archers in the field, drilling them on reload times. With her ability to guide the arrows, the faster they can nock and fire, the more damage she can do. The key is for everyone to load and fire at the same speed. Judging by what I saw yesterday, she has her work cut out for her.

I meet with Tarence to pick up the caltrops he made yesterday so that I can start placing them between the mines and other defenses.

With a small wagon loaded with caltrops, I make my way outside. I can see the top branches of Florian's head just around the other side of the wall. I pass the outer defense of the giant flytraps to a stretch of field several hundred feet between them and the mines. Jacob has already stationed several rows of abatis on this side of town, their sharpened points ready to rip goblins to shreds.

Reaching into the wagon, I pull the first caltrop out. Its heavy, solid metal feels formidable. The sharp points on the ends are even more dangerous. I toss it to the ground and it lands with three prongs facing the ground and the fourth stabbing into the air.

I pick the caltrop back up, this time focusing my mana into its sharp, jagged points. I imagine it filled with electricity, a powerful current jolting anyone or anything that steps upon it.

Congratulations! You have created **Lighting Caltrop.** *A* *powerful burst of electricity shocks anyone who touches this item. One-time use. Cost: 100 mana per item.*

In quick succession, I make three more and wait for my mana to regenerate. In the distance, Jacob and his men travel along the safe route with more abatis.

I spend hours enchanting the caltrops and spreading them around the battlefield. By the time I'm finished, my vision is filled with red dots showing me the locations of all my items. Far off in the distance, Thunder Mountain looms. The occasional crack of lightning reinforces what's coming, a reminder of the chaos where the goblin army was forged. The people of Carolton live a tough life of manual labor, but it is not brutal. It doesn't forge monsters.

I break for dinner and find Buzz and Grayson drilling with some of the townspeople, this time with spears. We don't have enough swords for everyone, so it's best to keep them in the hands of our best fighters. The rest of our ragtag army will be using spears.

Jacob finds me as I'm taking a seat at a long wooden table.

"How are the abatis coming?" I ask.

"Good. We have close to ninety percent of the town defended. The rest should be finished tomorrow."

"Good to hear. Once everything is set, I'd like to take our army out into the field and run over some formations. It would be smart to let them have an idea of how the battle might unfold."

We drill for the rest of the evening, giving all of the fighting men an opportunity with both the spear and sword. By the night's end, we have fifteen men as designated swordsmen, myself included, a dozen archers, and the rest are given spears. The children and elderly, along with the women who are unable to fight, will remain safe behind the walls during the battle, leaving us with just over a hundred and fifty fighters against three hundred goblins.

Priscilla's cottage is more crowded than ever with Buzz and Grayson staying there. Without enough beds, Buzz and I end up sleeping on the floor and Grayson takes the chair I had the previous night.

"The townspeople show a lot of promise." Grayson looks down at us from the chair. "Their hearts are in it, that's for sure. It's almost like they are real people."

"Yeah." Buzz props himself up on his elbows. "No wonder you've been so out of it. This is almost like living a second life, it really takes it out of you. I'm ready to hit the hay."

It's nice to finally have someone here who knows exactly how I feel. As much as I've tried to explain to Aleesia and Benjamin, they won't be able to truly understand unless they log in.

A hand squeezes my shoulder, forcing me awake. Buzz stares at me, eyes wide. It's still dark outside. What could he possibly want at this hour?

"Do you dream like this every night?" he asks.

"What do you mean?" I feel like I already know what he is going to say.

"It's like I could see my brain. I watched as something traveled across it, replaying my memories. Things I didn't even remember until it happened."

"Yeah, it's happened to me too. I think there are other reasons we're playing this game," I whisper. "I think they are testing something."

"What could it be?"

"I don't know."

We sit in silence until the rooster crows, bringing the town to life.

We're some of the first to arrive in the courtyard. I begin sectioning people off based on their weapons—separating the swordsmen, the archers, and those with spears. Tarence was able to smith enough weapons so that no one is using farm tools.

When the council arrives, Jacob and Clinton both carry spears. Tarence holds a massive warhammer in both hands.

They must notice my shocked expression because Jacob speaks up. "What? You didn't think we would stay behind the walls while everyone else fights to save the town, did you?"

"I had to make something special for myself. I hope you understand," says Tarence, brandishing his warhammer.

"Absolutely." I smile. It will be good to have them on the front lines. I think it will help to further inspire the townspeople, knowing that their leaders are just as invested in the battle.

"Lead the way," says Jacob. "I'm entrusting the battle to you, Esil."

"What? Are you sure?" I ask. The memories of Craftwar come back into my mind. I don't think I have it in me to lead these people. Certainly there is someone better.

"You and your friends are the only reason we even have a chance of survival. I trust you. We all do."

I don't know what to say. I felt it was my responsibility to help prepare the town. To help fight even, but to lead them, how can I do that? It's too much. I'm not qualified. This isn't just a game anymore.

"Maybe Carter or Kindra—" I start.

"No," says Kindra. "It has to be you."

Carter nods in agreement.

"We will fight together, but you will lead us," he says.

Standing in the midst of the town, I look them over. Men, women, fathers, mothers, sons, and daughters all looking to me for salvation.

I can't let them down.

The gates open and the fragrant aroma of the hundreds of giant plants that now surround Carolton wafts through the city. If this were any other time, Carolton would be an attraction of the kingdom where people would travel from far and wide to gaze upon it. Instead, we prepare for war. For survival.

I lead our small army past the garden of doom into the space between it and the abatis.

"This is where we will make our stand. The abatis that Jacob has placed around the city will serve to funnel their forces and offer us protection from a cavalry attack. Beyond them, I have placed hundreds of mines and caltrops, to hopefully weaken their army before we ever do battle. Our archers will pick them off from a distance, and the rest of you will protect the gaps as they try to push through."

Everyone watches me intently, hanging on every word I say. They're scared. I can feel it in the air.

"We will be outnumbered. If they somehow push through and overwhelm us, then we will fall back behind the plants and make them fight their way through. As a last resort, we retreat into the city and make them storm the walls."

I separate them into groups of six and spread them around the town. They don't go very far and leave too much ground uncovered. I can only hope that the goblins attack in a massive force and don't have the wherewithal to spread themselves out.

We drill them on formations, using their spears to keep the enemy at bay while they attempt to push through the spaces between the abatis. Only the swordsmen have shields, since we simply didn't have enough.

I can already tell, this battle is going to be brutal.

CHAPTER TWENTY-SEVEN

A blaring horn cuts through the night, waking me from my electric dreams.

The long, deep trumpet of the horn resonates in perpetuity through the town. A call to arms. Something is wrong.

"What's going on?" Buzz stirs, tossing his blanket to the floor.

"Are we under attack?" Carter rushes into the room, Kindra right behind him.

"How is that possible? I thought we had two more days?" I give Kindra a questioning look.

"I don't know. I thought we did too."

"To the courtyard," I order.

Villagers rush through the streets with hushed voices, mild panic saturating the air.

Jacob is atop one of the guard towers. He motions for me to join him when he sees me standing among the crowd.

I climb in earnest, nearly slipping as I move my feet rapidly through the rungs of the ladder.

My heart sinks when I make it up and finally have a view.

In the distance, hundreds of torches move like fireflies through the night sky. They'll be here by morning.

"How is this possible?" Jacob echoes my own thoughts. "We're not ready for battle. We need more time to train." His voice is filled with exasperation.

"We could use more time to train, I agree, but we are ready. All of the defenses are set. We've gone over the formations." I place both my hands on his shoulders and stare into his eyes. The torchlight below casts eerie shadows in the recesses of his face. "We can do this. They need to believe that we can do this."

Jacob sets his face. "You're right."

If he gives up hope, the battle is already lost.

Jacob calls one of the women to the tower and gives her orders to find us immediately if anything changes. Following his lead, I climb down and start our call to arms.

The entire town has joined us in the courtyard. Whispers carry across the group like snakes. They're all worried. They were expecting more time. It's my job to lead them. To inspire them.

That will come later. First, I have to arm them.

"Okay, everyone. I want you all to grab your weapons, equip whatever armor you may have, and form ranks."

It takes several minutes for our fighting men to gather their weapons and group up. The women sit around with worried looks and several children cry, their screams cutting through the night.

For myself, I take my sword, shield, and slingshot. All enchantments they once possessed are gone. I will wait until the battle is closer before I decide on what to use.

Once everyone is in formation, we open the gates and

march out into the darkness. Far away, the goblin torches continue to flicker.

Florian and Carter take the lead. Carter holds his trident at the ready and Florian's massive feet quake the earth with each step.

Myself, Buzz, Grayson, Jacob, and Tarence each command a battalion of men. When the fighting starts, it will be up to each of us to hold our ground.

Kindra takes the rear with her archers. She will move around as needed, offering support where it is most beneficial.

The gate closes behind us. Atop above the wall, in the guard towers, several women wait with rocks to throw down on any goblins who may make it that far.

I take my place at the head of my battalion and all eyes fall on me once again. I breathe in the smell of wildflower and honeysuckle, knowing good and well that in a few hours, it will be replaced by the stench of blood.

"We thought we would have more time. Isn't that how it always goes, though? We think we will have more time with our loved ones, more time to do all the things we ever wanted. More time to prepare. But time is not promised. We only have control over what we do with the time we are given. For me, I'm grateful to be here with you. I am humbled to be chosen to lead this battle in what might be your finest moment as a city. The force that you see in the distance with their glowing torches, they aim to take everything you have. They want your town, your families, your very lives. And once they have those, they'll move on and do the same thing to someone else. But we aren't going to let that happen! We've set our defenses. We've prepared for war. And when those goblin forces come marching on our turf, we're going to give them a hell that Thunder Mountain could only dream of!"

Cheers ring out and weapons clash against each other and I think that for the moment, I've raised their morale enough for what comes next. When blood starts to shed and they feel the pain of battle, I don't know what will happen.

We take our positions and for the next few hours, the sun creeps towards the horizon, turning the black night sky gray around the edges. There is nothing to do but wait. I continuously hear the shuffle of feet and spears being rearranged in the ground. They are nervous.

Most of these people have never been in a fight, let alone a battle, and now they are faced with the task of defending their town from monsters far tougher and stronger.

"They approach!" someone shouts to my right.

The first rays of sun cross the tree line, exposing the goblin army that is now only a couple of miles away.

A dull beat echoes from their direction. It pounds repeatedly, growing in intensity the closer they come.

The drums of war.

The townspeople falter at the grandness of the goblins' approach. As day breaks, I can begin to make out more details of the army. Several goblins ride large animals ranging from wolves to warthogs. Clad in fur and bone clothing, their weapons are crudely-forged iron, dull and heavy, but deadly. The majority of their forces march on foot, carrying swords or spears.

They move without order. Complete chaos. They'll fight with brute force. That is the one area where we will have the advantage, our tactics.

Taking my sword in hand, it's time to focus on my

enchantments for the battle. I try to think of what will be most beneficial to my battalion. What can I do to make their job easier?

With that in mind, I focus my mana into my sword.

*You have created **Frosted Blade**. Enemies will be slowed by 25% upon being hit. Cost: 150 mana*

Perfect! Once the goblins are slowed, my battalion can move in. It'll also keep us from being overrun and prevent any goblins from escaping.

Due to all of the caltrops I enchanted, my mana pool has now grown to five hundred, leaving me with three hundred and fifty remaining. What I really need is armor, but I don't want heavy mail or plates weighing me down. Focusing on my tunic and pants, I attempt to make them stronger.

*You have created **Hearty Pants and Tunic**. These items have the same durability as plate mail, but wear like regular clothing. Cost: 200 mana.*

With my remaining mana, I use it to enchant the pebbles for my slingshot.

The first wave of goblins is nearly in range of the mines.

I hold my breath, hoping that everything works as well as we have planned.

The goblin forces come to a halt. Drumbeats boom through the silence, their bass rumbling in our chests. They beat the drums more rapidly until the beats are nothing more than a constant hum.

There is one final beat, then silence.

It seems to hang in the air for an eternity as we all wait for what's next.

The roar of hundreds of charging goblins breaks the quiet.

Kindra's archers continue to fire volley after volley. They are by far the most dangerous part of our army right now. With their next attack, she aims all twelve arrows at the goblin mage, but they splinter against an invisible barrier inches from the goblin's skin.

Carter's trident glows a bright green as the goblins march through a patch of field. The grass shimmers and a pink, powdery substance flutters through the air. The goblins begin to sway and then one after another, they collapse to the ground. Did he just put them to sleep?

Florian rushes in, arms flailing wildly, and stomps the goblins to death with a sickening crunch.

The goblin caster pushes forward, burning the grass and everything else in his path, even his own sleeping comrades. Florian reaches for the caster just as another flame erupts from the scepter. Fire runs up Florian's arm. He tries to swat the flames, but they spread to his hand and up his other arm. Carter rushes to Florian's defense, but there is nothing he can do. He casts a spell, trying to smother out the fire with a barrage of leaves, but they only ignite the flames bigger, spreading like wildfire across his body.

Knowing there is nothing that can be done, Florian rushes into the goblin army. He stomps and punches, grabbing goblins and throwing them into the air. He smashes two together and their heads burst like tomatoes. The mage hits him with a fireball that explodes upon his chest. Goblins chop at his feet and legs. Wood splinters from his flaming figure until Florian tumbles to the ground, unable to stand. Carter's screams carry over the chaos. Florian was the child he never had. We all watch in horror as he becomes nothing more than debris on the battlefield.

It's heartbreaking, but I can't for the life of me look away.

"Everyone! Behind the plants!" I shout with all the authority I can muster. Carter's plants are scary, but they won't attack us, only our enemies.

We fall back into their temporary safety as the last of the abatis burn to ash.

The goblins push, and the plants come to life. The giant flytraps attack with vigor, severing arms and eating some of the smaller goblins whole. The only problem is that they can't keep consuming. Once their mouths are full, the flytraps are useless and the goblins can cut them down.

The goblin mage continues to pour fire on the battle-field, burning everything in his path. If we are going to have a chance, we need to stop him.

The giant flowers Carter planted shoot leafy projectiles that deal magical damage to the goblins. They are our last row of defense before we have to fall back behind the walls. In the chaos of the battle, I've lost sight of Kindra and most of the others. Tarence swings his mighty warhammer into a crowd of goblins and takes a sword to the throat. So many of our soldiers are bloodied and bruised. Far too many are dead.

Somehow, Carter finds me in the battle. "Esil." Hhis voice is strained. "We have to retreat behind the walls. It's the only way."

I know he's right. We are losing the battle.

"I'll create a distraction," he says. "When I do, gather as many men as you can and fall back."

Carter points his trident into the air and it glows a vibrant green. An aura surrounds him and spreads out around the battlefield. For a moment, the smell of blood and death is replaced by something more fragrant. Like a spring morning. The flytraps and flower cannons grow in size and attack with increased speed. Petals of every color soar across the battlefield, ripping through the armor of the goblin warriors. It's the enchantment I added to his trident.

"You've got thirty seconds!" he yells.

I run back to the gate and notice the slat is open. Some of the women have been watching the battle unfold.

"Open the gate! We have to fall back!"

A moment later, the gate opens and I usher our people through the opening. Many more are still engaged in battle.

Not everyone is going to make it inside. Jacob passes me, his eyes wide with terror. Buzz runs past, blood flowing from a cut on his head. Grayson is nowhere to be found. Carter is still fighting and when the plants shrink back to their normal size, he turns for the gate. That's when I see Kindra coming from the edge of my vision, a handful of bloodthirsty goblins chasing her.

"Close the gate!" she screams.

I step inside and hold the gate open just enough for her to be able to fit inside. She's several feet away when she turns, places both hands to her head, and the goblins that chase her go flying back as if hit by a wrecking ball.

Kindra collapses to the ground, but not before I pull her through.

Inside the wall, everyone is in a panic.

There are no archers, and we've lost more than half of our fighters.

"They are going to storm the walls any minute now. What do we do?" asks Jacob.

For the life of me, I don't know.

"Take the elderly and children and hide them in the dungeon." If we're about to fight in the streets, then we need to move them to safety.

"They're climbing the walls!" a woman shouts from the guard tower.

I can't let this city fall. I just can't. There has to be something I can do.

A bold, dangerous, and completely idiotic idea crosses my mind.

"Everyone, stand back. You—" I point to the woman in the guard tower, "—get down now."

"Esil, what are you doing?" asks Buzz.

"Whatever I can."

I discard my weapons and my mana pool returns to full. I approach the wall, where the grunts of the goblins can be heard on the other side. I know I don't have much time, so I place my hands against the wall. It vibrates beneath my touch. I'm certain Carter's thorns are ripping through goblin flesh trying to ascend on the other side.

There's a thud as the first goblin jumps from wall and lands in the courtyard behind me. Swords clash and I hear a grunt of pain. Someone falls to the ground.

Closing my eyes, I feel my mana coursing through me. Taking every ounce of it, I focus it into the front wall. Using my innovator skill, I try for something that shouldn't be possible. I channel my HP into mana. I pray that this works, because if not, I've just sentenced everyone in town to death. With one last mental push, the wall explodes around me and everything goes black.

CHAPTER TWENTY-EIGHT

Flesh rips from my bones and an unimaginable heat courses through my body just before I die.

The next thing I know, I'm in the warm gel of the immersion capsule.

"Did it work? Did I save them?" It's the first thing I ask when I emerge from the capsule.

Marty sports a wide grin as he detaches the receptors from my body.

"You saved the town. Between your blast, the crumbling wall, and the remaining soldiers on the other side, it was just enough to stop the goblin army. That was some real ingenuity, by the way. Converting your health to mana for a more powerful blast. The viewing deck went wild when it happened."

I let out a sigh of relief. I wish I could have saved them all, but at least all was not lost. It will take time to rebuild Carolton, time they might not have with other threats now looming. There's no way of knowing if there were other goblin settlements. It could have been but one of many.

The worst part is that there are so many children without mothers and fathers now. That is a feeling I know all too well.

The battle replays in my head and I almost don't notice Grayson sitting in a chair by the wall, visibly shaken.

"What happened to you?" I ask.

"Stabbed through the heart. I can remember the feel of the blade going through me." He shivers at the thought.

I can only imagine. The pain I experienced was brief, but excruciating. Feeling a blade being driven through your heart and looking at the killer as it happens, that's scarring. It's just another reason why The Broken Lands feels like more than a game.

Looking back at the immersion capsules, I notice Buzz is still inside his.

"Why isn't Buzz logged out?" I ask Marty.

Benjamin is the one who answers. The viewing deck opens with a swoosh and he steps out. He looks a lot better than the last time we talked.

"He's still alive. The system only boots players if they die in game. You did really well in there. Really stuck it to the man," he says with a smirk.

"So what now?" I ask.

"There is a mandatory lockout period for players once they die. Or, there will be. We can bypass it for the testing phases, but I think it might be best for you to get some rest. You were in there for a while."

I don't understand why Benjamin is all of a sudden so chipper. For the past week, he's seemed like he was on the verge of losing his mind, and now it's like everything is back to normal.

"Just one thing, though. Once you're cleaned up, come

to my office. There is something I would like to show you."

A holographic brain hovers in the air on top of Benjamin's desk when I walk in. It's eerily similar to the dreams I experienced during my time in the game.

"Have a seat." He motions.

Benjamin smiles and raps his fingers against one another.

The brain in front of me slowly throbs as electrical currents run along its surface.

"Do you know what that is?" he asks, nodding at the hologram.

"A brain?" I say it as a question, not sure what he is getting at.

"Not just any brain. That's your brain." He pauses.

"Okay, what's the big deal?"

"You're a smart kid, Esil. I'm sure you know there was more to this game than just full-immersion. I mean, why go through all of this trouble when Pangea is great just the way it is? Why rush you back in?" His blue eyes pierce into me.

"I suspected as much."

"Well, here's the good news. Everything I've had to keep under wraps, I can finally talk about. We weren't sure if it was working. If we had given the AI too much freedom and it had wandered off to do its own thing. We were right to let it go, though. You see these tiny sparks here?" He points to one of the curls of my brain matter. "Those weren't there when you first started playing."

"Are you saying you've been messing with my brain

without my knowledge?" I don't even know how to respond to that.

"Not at all. As you have played the game, it has unlocked areas of your brain that were cut off from one another. It has repaired broken connectors. Don't you see what this means? Dementia, Alzheimer's, neurological disorders that have plagued the aging for hundreds of years might finally be curable if this works out."

"So what now?"

His smile grows even wider. "We're constructing one hundred more immersion capsules as quickly as we can. Once we noticed the effect taking place in your brain, we needed more data. Buzz and Grayson were the perfect match. And lo and behold, they each had a new synapse form within one day of game time. There is still so much to learn and study, but it's working, Esil. Don't you see?"

That's when I notice the picture that stands on Benjamin's desk. An elderly lady with a kind smile and gray hair stares blankly at the camera. She has the same eyes as Benjamin, only they don't seem so aware.

"You did this for her?" I ask.

Tears brim around his eyes.

"If only. She passed away last week. She didn't even remember my name the last time I went to see her. Who knows what would have happened if this had been discovered several years ago? But as it is, we are on the verge of making sure no one else has to suffer through something like that again. And even for those who have gone down that path, there is a chance for recovery."

Maybe Benjamin isn't the elitist that I thought he was. We all have our own causes that we think are important. If he needs one hundred more people to continue this project, then I know exactly where to find them.

. . .

The End

ACKNOWLEDGMENTS

First and foremost, thank you for reading my book. I hope you loved it! If so, please leave a wonderful review. Reviews are as rare as Developer's Chests and the more positive reviews I have, the more likely it is that others will read my books as well.

This book was a process. It took longer to write than I had planned. Its pages are the result of happiness, heartache and most importantly, persistence. There were days where I didn't write, where I couldn't write, and there where moments where the words flowed like a waterfall.

First, I would like to thank my beta readers. Jake Goodrich, Bobby Bjurstrom, Jennifer Haviland, William Doyle and Ezben Gerardo. You read through the worst parts and made them better. Jake and Bobby, thanks for sorting out that pesky mechanics issue.

Secondly, I am so thankful for the fans. Those of you who have recommended *Pangea Online* to your friends, your family, and spread the love across facebook. Nothing helps independent authors like myself more than word of mouth. I owe a lot of the first book's success to you. I hope you have enjoyed book two and continue to share the kind words.

I would like to give a special shoutout to Lea Ann and Kiwi for reading literally everything I have ever published. To Michaela, for spreading the word like it's gospel. To

Cody, Tyler, Grace, Eden, Kevin, Ellis, Brooke, Sarah, Jessie, Jess and Brittany for the constant laughs and entertainment.

If you're looking for more books similar to my own, check out LitRPG Books.

ALSO BY S.L. ROWLAND

Tales of Aedrea

Cursed Cocktails

Sword & Thistle

Pangea Online

Pangea Online: Death and Axes

Pangea Online 2: Magic and Mayhem

Pangea Online 3: Vials and Tribulations

Sentenced to Troll

Sentenced to Troll

Sentenced to Troll 2

Sentenced to Troll 3

Sentenced to Troll 4

Sentenced to Troll 5

Path to Villainy: An NPC Kobold's Tale

Collected Editions

Pangea Online: The Complete Trilogy

Sentenced to Troll Compendium: Books 1-3

www.ingramcontent.com/pod-product-compliance
Lightning Source LLC
Chambersburg PA
CBHW061223310726
48971CB00007B/1921